The Library of Scandinavian Literature

AN INTERRUPTED PASSAGE

AN INTERRUPTED PASSAGE

Terje Stigen

TRANSLATED FROM THE NORWEGIAN BY
AMANDA LANGEMO

INTRODUCTION BY
OLE LANGSETH

LIBRARY OF SCANDINAVIAN LITERATURE

TWAYNE PUBLISHERS, INC., NEW YORK

&

THE AMERICAN-SCANDINAVIAN FOUNDATION

The Library of Scandinavian Literature
Erik J. Friis, *General Editor*

Volume 24

An Interrupted Passage, by Terje Stigen
Title of the original: *Vindstille underveis,*
published by Gyldendal Norsk Forlag, Oslo, 1956.

Contents

INTRODUCTION   1

SUDDENLY BECALMED   13

HALVOR MIKKELSEN'S JOURNEY . *Governor*   27

    The Sheep Raid   27

    The Porpoise   41

    Rough Sailing   52

    On Reaching Land   64

    Halvor and the Cowardly Curate 77

    The Squirrel Hunt   88

THE TALE OF PASTOR BARTHOLIN - *Celia*   111

FERNANDO RIAZOLA'S REPORT   - *Roy*   130

    The Shipwreck   130

    On an Island in the Sea   140

    In the Peat Bog   155

    The Escape   174

REGINE'S WORLD   - *Soph*   188

THE VOYAGE RESUMES   252

Introduction

Terje Stigen is one Norwegian writer who still keeps in mind that fictional writing used to play an important role as a source of entertainment—and he wants to make it so again. Furthermore, he writes in a way that does give fiction some chance of continuing to play such a role. He creates a plot, tells an imaginative story at a lively pace without going off on minor side excursions into psychology or politics, and expresses himself in a prose in which deep feeling and tragedy compete with comedy and burlesque, jostling each other aside in the process. A flash of humor can serve to break a heavy mood, and by means of an almost unnoticeable twist in the narrative he will open up deeply human perspectives of something which ostensibly calls for laughter or ridicule. Life's own fabulous and incalculable diversity is mirrored in Terje Stigen's writings.

This is why we have seen that some critics run into problems when they try to analyze and classify him. It is said that he lacks true seriousness, that he gets too romantic about nature, and so on. It is generally maintained that he is primarily a *storyteller,* and then the reader is left to

1

decide for himself what attitude to take toward such an incontrovertible fact.

It is indeed a fact that Terje Stigen is a storyteller, and, we may well add, a gifted one. During his nearly twenty-five years as an author he has probably told more stories than any other Norwegian writer over a similar period. Through his books flows a stream of stories dealing with human beings, their fate, and incidents in their lives; they are sometimes formulated with considerable detail, sometimes loosely drawn. Several of his novels are of the open, flexible type—accounts of travels or escapes such as *Frode budbæreren* (*Frode the Messenger*) and *Åsmund Armodsons saga* (*The Saga of Åsmund Armodson*) or milieu-portrayals such as *Stjernøy* (*Star Island*), *Elskere* (*Lovers*), and *Kjærlighet* (*Love*)—indeed, he is not one to deny himself the pleasure of telling a tale if he happens to have one at hand. In any event, his many digressions give one the comfortable feeling of a surplus of material, something which is a rare phenomenon among contemporary writers. And since in addition his digressions are as a rule accomplished with short, quick strokes, we are not at all tempted to look closely into whether the work, as seen from the solemn viewpoint of the literary critic, has been subjected to an unnecessary excrescence.

In view of what has been said here, no one will be surprised to learn that Terje Stigen has won short-story contests in competition with outstanding older writers. Besides, readers will be able to judge this aspect of his talent for themselves from the book being presented here, namely, *Vindstille underveis* (1956), his first major public success. In this work, four short tales have been made into an entity that tells us in an exciting and artful manner something not only about the people involved but also about the essential nature of man.

2

Stigen's sure grip on the short-story form has not, however, prevented him from being a storyteller who has also
mastered the novel, or from doing justice to his characters
and conflicts throughout a longer and more fully developed
work. He does so, with fine lyrical undertones and portrayals
of the natural beauty and ambience of North Norway, in
the moving romantic novel *Før solnedgang* (*Before Sunset*,
1954), with more robustness and epic elbowroom in his
historical novels such as *Frode the Messenger* (1957), *The
Saga of Åsmund Armodson* (1958), *Det flyktige hjerte* (*The
Fickle Heart*, 1967), and *De tente lys* (*The Lighted Candles*,
1968), and with an intimate knowledge of the child mind,
as well as recollections of the bittersweet experiences of the
migration into the adult world, in *Krystallstjernen* (*The
Crystal Star*, 1965).

That Terje Stigen was born in 1922 on the island of
Magerøy, Norway's northernmost outpost at the edge of
the Arctic Ocean, that he later moved to Oslo, obtained
a university degree in philology, and was a teacher for some
years are facts which perhaps do not contribute a great
deal to an understanding of his works. But neither are these
facts entirely without significance. He belongs to a generation whose formative years were spent under the stresses
of war and the German occupation, and who then had to
strike roots in a confused postwar reality marked by political
struggles, mechanization, and sweeping official organization
of everything human. Many of that generation, to put it
bluntly, came through the war better than they did the
peace. They have not found a place for themselves or their
emotional makeup within the workaday monotony of the
affluent society, and in one way or another have become
the losers in the new world, unsuited to life in our career-
oriented society and to trivial routine work as well.

Many of the leading characters in Stigen's earliest novels

3

are defeated persons of this type. In some instances—for example, the former soldier in his first published book, *To døgn* (*Two Days*, 1950)—their wartime experiences remain clearly implanted in their consciousness, whereas in others the traces of them are less evident. Stigen is not, on the whole, a writer who, step by step, laboriously gives the psychological reasons for his characters' actions. We must accept the premise that we are dealing with fugitives, persons who cannot cope with life, and especially not with love, which in this author's work is held to be the prime criterion of spiritual well-being.

But Terje Stigen does not necessarily have to resort to suicide or psychoanalysis in order to solve the emotional and spiritual disturbances of his characters. He keeps another form of therapy in reserve for his losers, fugitives, and fantasts. He sends them out into the solitude of the forests and mountains, particularly into the unspoiled reaches of North Norway, the memory of which he retains from his childhood and cherishes as an inner bulwark against the banalities of our over-civilization. "There are two odors that you will never forget," he says in one of his nature sketches, "the fragrance of sun-warmed pine barrens and the smell of the sea. The first reminds you that you belong somewhere, the other that you are on your way and can never settle down."

The deep and refreshing drafts of nature poetry with which Stigen surrounds the grim wreckage of present and past fugitive and played-out civilizations, as well as his descriptions of small, simply organized communities of unsophisticated people, afford protection against both exaggerated psychological introspection and cheap romanticism. Typical in this respect is the account in the somber and moving novel *Star Island* of a desolate locale at the outer edge of Norway. It can be hazardous for a writer to

4

cultivate his lost Edens; a cloying sentimentality is likely to lurk behind the slightest false step. But beneath the boundless vault of the heavens, and to the accompaniment of the unceasing reverberation of the sea, Stigen manages to elevate his perspective to the level of the myth. Atlantis or Utrøst cannot be measured against trivial, everyday experience. The reader accepts without protest the thesis that gods and devils are roaming about here in human form and that passions flare up, red and feverish, like flowers during the brief arctic summer.

Like many of Stigen's other narratives, *Star Island* is especially a novel having to do with longing, the anticipatory yearning to leave the young and inexperienced and the nostalgic yearning back of the weary, battered mind. But the author perceives with painful clarity that the map of Norway hardly includes a single small place, a single out-of-the-way community, that approximately resembles Star Island. In one of his latest books, *Det siste paradiset* (*The Last Paradise*, 1969), he hides his sorrow behind comic-situation sketches and obvious parodies. Since it does no good to cry, one may just as well smile—yes, now and then indulge in the luxury of sardonic laughter. It is thus that ancient Bottenfjord, "one of the many appendixes in the northern part of our country's anatomy," faces the prospect of its destruction. With construction of the new highway and the big wharf, with the arrival of the experts and the engineers, technology and turmoil take over. The people go to work in industry, in plants and factories, and the service trades, while the rowboat and the old fishing smack lie rotting on the beach. And no one can any longer find meaning in the sound of the surf lapping the beach on a summer day or the mad blasts of a winter night's gale.

There are critics, especially among the younger ones, who have accused Terje Stigen of fleeing from reality and romanticizing about the past. Most others are convinced that such criticism is based on a superficial consideration of his work. Stigen's wide circle of readers know that the fundamental problems of our time receive as full consideration in his books as they do in those of any other writer. But to a greater degree than most of the others, he has the ability to vary his themes and give poetic expression to his ideas.

Central to his work is an affection for everything that is genuinely human, as well as respect for the individual as a unique product of the Creator's hand. His deepest attachment is to those strong enough and mature enough to order their lives in accordance with their own distinctive qualities, those who do not cringe before the pressure of conventionality and the terrorism of mass sentimentality. He looks upon technology as an imminent peril, foreshadowing banality and standardization, and threatening to transform humanity into types and pale imitations.

Few Norwegian writers today manage so well to unite idea and action, perspective and entertainment value. Stigen is more than a storyteller in the simple and primitive sense of the word. Through his writing he has told us some important things about our time, about a dream that hardly any longer finds a foothold in reality, about a hidden yearning for the primitive and contact with the elements both on land and sea, about unaffected minds and emotional integrity. He is among those who have given color to postwar Norwegian literature.

An Interrupted Passage, published in 1956, may with good reason be regarded as his breakthrough as an author. With it he earned wide acclaim among the critics and the public. While his earliest novels are marked by a certain tradition-bound caution in choice of subject and stylistic formulation, in this book he plunges into some boldly imaginative writing and presents his characters and events in vivid, action-packed pages, without psychological frills or stagnant poeticism.

In its basic form the book resembles several other short-story collections of a type long familiar, especially in literature of the past, in which a group of individuals keep each other entertained by telling stories. Boccaccio's *Decameron* and Chaucer's *Canterbury Tales* are classic examples of the genre. But Stigen here weaves the framework story and the narratives of the individuals together in so intricate a fashion that the result is clearly a unified whole, and characterization of the book as a novel is fully justified.

The action takes place in the coastal traffic lane off North Norway during the course of a few bright summer days at the beginning of this century. Among the passengers on a southbound express steamer is a group of four persons who have known one another in the past, and therefore keep one another company during the voyage. One of them is Ladie Sophie Tennyson, Norwegian by birth but widow of an English lord and, at the time, a resident of England. The others are Governor Florelius, Pastor Celion, and a merchant named Berg. At the beginning of the novel the ship has come to a stop because of a mechanical breakdown, and we meet the group in an atmosphere of casual and jovial conversation, tinged perhaps with a certain amount of unexpressed tension that is faintly discernible in their remarks.

Instead of sitting in their wicker chairs and waiting until the damage to the ship is repaired, the four decide to board a fishing vessel that happens to be passing by, and to continue their voyage in it until the ship can catch up with them.

And there on the deck above the sailing vessel's cabin, released from their bourgeois identities and in contact with the sea, the wind, and all the elements of nature, it is as if they shed the outer layers of their personalities. Their pasts come alive again, and they see their lives in clear continuity. When at the suggestion of Lady Tennyson they begin to tell their stories, these become something more than merely a diversion intended to pass the time. The narratives assume the nature of confessions, become explanations of fateful but puzzling incidents, as well as of hidden relationships between cause and effect. By means of frequent interpolations that indicate the narrators' and the listeners' changing reactions, the author conveys a distinct impression of the states of mind among the four, of the charged atmosphere and the expectancy with regard to what is coming next. The mood is one of vibrant suspense, of an intenseness that is related to the wild and constantly shifting scenery before their eyes. In telling their more or less fanciful tales, the characters reveal, to those who can penetrate beyond the words and interpret what lies behind them, the crucial situations in their lives. And, interwoven as these lives have been in the past, each listener tries to detect, in the story being told, not only the narrator's but also his or her own role.

The most effective disguises are in the semi-mythical tales of the merchant and the governor. The merchant tells about his colleague from Genoa, Fernando Riazola, who during a business trip is caught in a storm in the English Channel and driven northward to the coast of North Norway. There, after a shipwreck and other dramatic events, he falls in love with the devil's daughter and fails in a bold attempt to take her home with him. The governor's *alter ego* is the fisherman Halvor Mikkelsen, who lives on an island at the mouth of a fjord and who, during a period of hunger, steals a sheep in order to save his sick child. Later he is pursued by mysterious forces and flees to the mainland to become a farmer, but is never able completely to shake off his pursuers. There are also mythical elements in the pastor's story about a clergyman, Bartholin, and his struggle with the devil over the human souls in an impoverished parish up north. Ladie Sophie's story about Regine, the daughter of a merchant, and her adolescence in a North Norwegian trading post has more the character of a realistic modern short story. In her narrative, too, many of the elements of the others' stories fall into place, the overall pattern emerges, and the reader gets the impression of a game of solitaire in which everything falls into place.

Despite the special literary form that the author employs, *An Interrupted Passage* is truly a typical Stigen book. It is a novel about man and the forces that control him, about the obscure tricks of fate that shape our lives, about longing and dreams, about defeats and the bitter desire for revenge. It makes clear that we are all island dwellers, in that when we have walked far enough in circles we will inevitably cross our own tracks. The more deeply we probe into the book, the more clearly we perceive that the fanciful stories come to grips with aspects that are common to human nature and contain ideas that concern us all.

OLE LANGSETH

AN INTERRUPTED PASSAGE

Suddenly Becalmed

One warm summer night about fifty years ago the express coastal steamer was hurriedly making its way southward when the cylinder head gasket exploded.

In and of itself this blast was no major catastrophe; it set off no reverberations beyond the confines of the engine room, the earth continued on its whirring course around the sun, and the stoker who suffered a steam burn on his upper arm was back in the boiler room within forty-eight hours.

Nor did it seem necessary to alarm the passengers. The ship would simply have to be delayed ten or twelve hours at the most. Since four of the voyagers, however, had preferred wicker chairs on the airy deck to their stuffy little cabins and the craft was obviously losing speed, the captain thought it incumbent on him to explain the reason.

"Actually it's only a minor matter." He smiled and waved his hand. "But unfortunately it may take several hours to put in the new gasket." With that he saluted them and went on.

13

This happened halfway between Svolvær and Bodø. On the western horizon the sun shone big and blood-red. The West Fjord wore a calm fine-weather luster like a glossy mantle overspreading the lazy swells rolling in toward shore. The motor was dead. All engine noises were stilled. The clanking of the metal from the open cabin door had stopped, the corner of the tarpaulin had ceased flapping against the frame of the hatchway, and the steam vents no longer whistled and whined. The swish of foam at the prow, that had drowned out all other sounds for just an instant when the engine failed, was gradually disappearing into placid water. Frustrated seagulls circled inquisitively above the motionless ship; one shrieked frantically a few times, and then they settled down, one by one, and remained motionless on the surface of the sea.

Now at last the ship was completely becalmed, and for the first moments even the crew were silent. The wake, the very last sign of movement, vanished as if wiped away with a sponge. A distrustful person might have asked whether Our Lord Himself had interrupted the voyage with the mere lifting of His hand since he had discovered a motif and was about to begin a painting.—

Sweet memories of untold tales,
Of ocean and forgotten voices,
Of blood and lust and hearts' decay—

The voice broke off and then picked up the rhythm laughingly, low and clear as a bell, like an apology.

"Why didn't you continue, Sophie?" The man at her left was serious, and the wicker chair creaked deferentially as if in applause. "Now you can be heard way out on Röst."

"If I didn't know you, Richard, I'd consider that a sarcasm. Or what do you think, Pastor Celion?"

"The governor's insults are directed only at clergymen, never at that trinity he calls 'beauty, godlessness, and nobility.' The 'godlessness' of course does not apply to Mylady."

"And what about you, Eberhardt?" The voice became somewhat good-naturedly mocking when directed to the fourth member of the group.

"Well, Mylady, or perhaps I may call you Sophie, as we have known each other since we were very young, in my line of work we don't really know what sarcasm is. It is of such a general nature that it can in no way be entered into a ledger either in the debit or in the credit column, but if your voice can be heard all the way to Röst, as the governor just said, in that event Mylady may certainly have a job as boatswain on one of my ships."

For a moment there was not a sound except for the creaking of the reed chairs. Then Mylady stretched out her arms toward the big, round, sinking sun as if trying to draw it into her embrace. "Oh, what a spot," she sighed. "If we could only stay here forever!"

"You don't know Captain Nilsen if you think we'll be dawdling here very long." The merchant straightened up in his chair. "Indeed, Mylady doesn't know him because she went off to England and got married before he was given his first commission as captain, and that was in—"

"Of course, of course," Mylady cut in, laughing nervously. "We all know, except possibly Pastor Celion, when I was married and precisely how old I was at the time. You have much too good a memory for numbers, Mr. Merchant. Don't you remember some other things, things having nothing to do with numbers?"

"Oh, yes, a great many things. I remember them all too well. But memory deceives a person about things, but not about numbers. Numbers remain, and things themselves remain, but what one ponders—words and feelings and the like—all that changes, alters somehow beyond all comprehension, grows like a fungus in one's memory."

"But your numbers also grow like a fungus, don't they?"

"Surely, but I always know what they represent: ships, docks, warehouses, nets, buildings."

"But don't you feel either a melancholy shudder or a passionate thrill when you think about your things so that, for example, you want to burst out with:

Oh ship, oh net, oh warehouse,
My one, my all, my throbbing force,
Embrace me, fill me with your sounds—"

At this point Mylady was interrupted by the governor's deep-throated laughter. "Sophie, you're still the same. You haven't changed one iota; only perhaps you've grown a little more malicious."

He stopped abruptly. A hurt expression had passed over her face, a flash of remorse perhaps, or was it only a momentary hint of despondency?

"Sophie, forgive me. I didn't mean—"

He was whispering, but the words came out aloud in the quietness, more clearly than if he had shouted them.

The four on the deck became tensely silent; then the pastor's wicker chair began to squeak steadily to cover up the tacit ill-humor. All at once two sailors appeared, struggling with a coil of rope.

"So, just the same," reflected the governor, "it is the merchant's 'things' that clear the air for us. A word would likely have made bad matters worse. Who knows when words serve best or when things have more to say? Words and things, bridges between minds. When is one correct and when the other?"

The sailors left, but the veneer of gaiety was not to be

16

recaptured. For a while no one spoke. Eventually the pastor broke the silence and addressed the governor.

"I believe I told you that among making other contacts I shall pay the Department a visit when I get to the city. It's still a matter of this blessed roof on the parsonage. Now the north half leaks like a sieve. I wrote four letters to the Department before I got an answer. And can you imagine what they said? 'The administration does not at present find itself in a position to allocate any money out of current funds to mend leaky roofs, but you ought to place basins to catch the drips.' Well, I set basins everywhere, and when it rained I lay listening to the dripping all night. I tried to find a kind of melody in it, and one night in May I actually succeeded in fitting this drip-rhythm to the composer's 'God is God though all the earth lay barren,' and that was a great consolation.

"But then came the day I ran out of basins, so I went to the church and borrowed the pewter dish that belongs in the baptismal font. It was given the most honored place in the house on the top of the living-room table. That ruined my pleasant nightly entertainment, however, because the pewter gave a ringing, silvery note to the drip; it was louder than the pot and the wash bowl and the soup tureen. I could no longer hear the tune of the mighty chorale. As a matter of fact, it made me nervous. I couldn't sleep. My mind reviewed the complete Lindemann."

The pastor stopped to catch his breath. "Oh Heavens! What weather we're having these days! This spring I had to get up twice every night to empty basins out of the garret window."

Celion sighed and smoothed his silver-gray hair over his crown. He was short and stocky. When he laid his arms on the edge of the pulpit, he looked as if he were hanging onto it. His eyes were blue and clear as a child's, and his cheeks plump and pink, without a furrow. He resembled an over-aged cherub. He wore a suit of the latest cut, brownish-gray with light green stripes.

"Those stripes will be your undoing, Celion," the governor used to say. "You will never be invited to a better call until you rid yourself of those garish stripes. But your vanity no doubt prevails over your desire for a career."

"At that I decided to climb up on the roof myself," the pastor continued, fidgeting restlessly. "I gathered some birch bark and clumps of sod, but then, so help me, there was no ladder."

The speaker finally ran out of words. He looked around at his listeners who still persisted in keeping silent. Suddenly he brightened, rose halfway up from his chair, and pointed out across the water. "Look! Isn't that a boat heading south? We ought certainly to seize it!"

Neither the governor nor the merchant responded, and the pastor leaned back again in his chair. He was about to reconcile himself to the fact that his good intentions were to no avail when Mylady quickly jumped to her feet. "Of course!" she shouted excitedly. "Now you said something, Pastor Celion. That's exactly what we'll do. For we'll be stuck here at least twelve hours. And such boats surely have enough accommodations for no more than we are; at least they did in my time."

"In Mylady's time—yes, yes," said the merchant, not without a certain sardonic delight, "and accommodations have indeed been enlarged and improved since that time, but just the same—a boat with dried fish bound for Bergen—yes, well—"

"I'm serious really." Mylady spoke as eagerly as before and looked from one to the other. "Should our steamer overtake us, that matter could be easily managed. We will simply have our cabins reserved. Oh, Richard darling," she

18

continued, turning to the governor, "a boat with dried fish and everything else out of the past and to sail down the coast in this weather! It was truly for something like this that I embarked on this voyage."

"Was it?" The governor's tone was cold. His eyes scanned the sea.

Lady Sophie glanced at him for a brief second. She made no answer, but the merchant had caught her expression. He had detected both wonder and tenderness. He stood up. "Surely," he said with a kind of careless abandon. Pastor Celion noticed and watched, amazed. "Surely that can be done, especially since it is one of my own fleet, and I know there's room. So if Mylady and my fellow voyagers are in earnest about it, there's nothing to prevent our resuming the passage shortly."

"Well, can we proceed without further ado? Are you sure the boat is seaworthy?" queried the pastor.

"My dear"—by now Mylady was also standing up—"if the worst should happen, we could float to shore with the dried fish. You heard Merchant Berg approve the plan. He never jokes, and besides he knows all about such matters. Isn't that so, Eberhardt," she shouted in his direction.

Berg stared intently at the boat steadily drawing nearer as if he had never seen his own property before. "Of course," he mumbled, "as I was just saying—"

"Great idea!" intruded the governor, getting up from his chair. "I refuse to be left here by myself."

"All right, then it's all settled. Now I'll ask the captain to hail the boat, and maybe my lords and Mylady will see to it that the baggage they want with them is brought on deck."

There was a moment's hush, a strained silence; the atmosphere was charged. Pastor Celion felt as if apart from the rest. He was aware of it: a comment, a slight gesture had

19

sparked the thought in each of them to play along in the game.

Ten minutes later the four were ready to step down into the boat. When the luggage was brought on deck, Mylady's alone was much more of a load than all the other pieces put together. "The remainder will have to stay on board until we get to Bergen." She smiled sweetly at the captain who stood at the rail. "But those two cases of wine I've lugged around with me all the way from London must go with us. I don't suppose your men think they will create any problem?"

Like magic her words effected something that had been lacking the last several minutes. They all got busy at once. In the meanwhile the boat had drawn up alongside their steamer. The gangplank was presently lowered, and the first one to embark was Merchant Eberhardt Berg, king of the headland on Eksöy, trader in flour and cod, fish-nets and boathouses, now on his way to transact business in Trondheim.

The merchant was big and rough-hewn. His very appearance suggested his means of livelihood. He moved like a heavily loaded barge. Almost everything about him was reddish. His thin hair and whiskers were reddish blond, and his rust-colored eyebrows formed tufts at the bridge of his nose. On the backs of his hands also there were wisps of three or four brownish-red hairs. His complexion was ruddy, and he had bluish blotches on his cheeks and under his eyes. The midnight sun was wasted on him, for stubbornly he wore the same hue in sunshine as in cloudy weather. He seemed to have acquired it through laborious struggle, and now it served him as his trademark.

"I'll be late," he fretted. "At least a day late coming in to Trondheim."

Lady Sophie Tennyson, née Sophie Utvik, smiled beguilingly and nodded to the captain, lifted her dress above her ankles (the soft green dress that always reminded her of the bay at Utvik) and stepped onto the gangplank as gracefully as if she were making her entry to His Majesty's garden party.

"It's twenty-seven years ago," she remembered suddenly, panic-stricken, "twenty-seven years ago since I last saw Richard and Eberhardt. How old they are! Am I that old? Forty-five, an old woman—My Heavens!"

She smoothed her hair. Yes, it lay as it ought, golden now in the evening sunlight. Her mouth was youthful and soft, her skin pink and white and delicate, her body supple and straight, hips slender, and bosom held high. Just as young? Yes, but a little bigger at the waistline perhaps.

The imperial tea merchant, the third Lord Tennyson, had dealt kindly with her figure, and when he eventually died, properly and fittingly as he had lived, he bequeathed her a cold heart and 200,000 pounds. She was therefore, in plain terms, worth her weight in gold, according to the day's market, right where she was standing on the gangplank, a recent widow, a prize example of the feminine sex.

And no children. "You have no children, Sophie," she said secretly to herself and walked slowly down to where Merchant Berg waited to meet her, his arms outstretched.

Lady Tennyson had a singular psychical makeup; everything enhanced her beauty—sorrow, joy, disappointment, abundance. She was equally receptive to all. When the occasion demanded, she immediately could refer to a sorrow, and sorrow made her eyes wistful and mysterious. Then joy burst out in her whole being like beauty spots, in her rosebud mouth, her dimpled cheeks, her dancing eyes. And sorrow was expressed in the tired upraised hand which made one long to hold it, to comfort—in any event on first acquaintance.

21

Governor Richard Florelius was thinking: "She is still beautiful—but no longer beautiful like a young charmer. Now she is beautiful in a way she never was in her youth. What has become of all the years? Where have they gone? What have they done to her? A gasket in a steamship engine explodes, and then? At any rate I shall arrive in Bergen too late for the meeting. A word is spoken, and then? A glance is exchanged, and then?"

Richard Florelius was a tall, slender man. His hair and eyes were dark, and when he was caught off guard his face wore a cloud—often a hunted expression as if he were tormented by ghosts.

When Florelius stepped onto the gangplank, Mylady's laughter met him, ringing out clearly into the night. "Richard," she called from the far end of the gangplank, pointing to the nameplate on the vessel. "Look! He has named it in honor of Sophie. Isn't that exciting! Obviously I'm not completely forgotten. Do you think I look much like a ship, Richard?"

Merchant Berg was already standing on the deck, smiling equivocally. "There are so many Sophies, Mylady."

"When we were very young," thought Florelius taking a step down, "when we were very young, you were a thoughtless enchantress, Sophie, and stirred up a storm all around you. Now you have turned into a designing siren. Have we all aged as much?"

The last to go on board was Pastor Celion, his small black portfolio in hand. "In any case I have plenty of time," he reasoned, "and this may develop into a pleasant voyage." He blinked against the sunlight; his round boyish face was glowing. "This is better than trying to save souls in winter weather. Heaven guard my lips! I wonder what kind of wine this woman has in her cases?"

Thereupon the four wicker chairs were lowered to the

22

deck. The passengers had come to an agreement with the captain that they would go along to Trondheim if necessary. As soon as they began to move, a slight breeze blew from the north. The West Fjord turned gray and ruffled like a loose pelt. The sail was hoisted and they glided slowly away from the motionless steamer.

"Oh, it's wonderful to be off that steamer!" Mylady exclaimed when they were all comfortably settled in their deck chairs. "Now we can sail wherever we want, can't we?"

"With Mylady's permission, I have contracted to get the fish to Bergen this week," replied the merchant.

They sailed on at a leisurely rate in the direction of Landego. Lady Sophie gave orders for one of her iron-bound cases to be opened. It contained fifteen bottles in addition to six crystal glasses packed in a velvet-lined box in the upper part of the case. She did not slight the crew. They got two bottles to share among them, and Merchant Berg expressed appreciation on their behalf.

The glasses were promptly filled with ruby-red Burgundy that made the night-time sun look pale in comparison. Only the odor of dried fish robbed the idyllic atmosphere of perfection, and on Mylady's far from ironic insistence that the stench came from cod heads hanging on a line nearby, the offending objects were quickly pulled down and consigned to the deep from where they had come.

"You're mocking us now," thought Florelius with a glance in her direction. "It was indeed this very smell and everything related to it you wanted to return to."

An hour passed. The islands far to the west disappeared in the haze; two little clouds, like narrow slices of gulls' wings, hung in front of the sun and divided it into semicircles.

23

After his third drink the governor stood up and announced that he had to go down to his cabin for his pipe.

"Let me join you," said Lady Tennyson. "I have forgotten my rings. This is really an opportunity, isn't it, Pastor, for me to see how they look in the light of the midnight sun, especially my ruby. Oh, you must see it, Pastor!"

Pastor Celion sipped his wine and loosened his tight collar. "The midnight sun is Mylady's noblest adornment right now." He smiled as he said it. Berg remained silent.

As Florelius was helping her climb down from the upper deck, he noticed that she cast one of her longing, melancholic glances at the helmsman, a young man from Öksnes. He was slender and fairhaired; his shirt was open at the neck.

"She assumes that solemn expression so none of us will suspect her. And just the same," reflected the governor—and hating himself for it—"and just the same I would plunge into the sea if she took a coquettish notion to toss her shoe overboard."

A little later when they were alone in the darkened cabin, he asked quietly, "Sophie, why did you come here?"

"The helmsman can see us, Richard."

"No, not in here."

"He is listening. Can't you see?"

"He can't hear us in here."

"Yes, he can. I can tell by his eyes."

Florelius touched her arm lightly. "Why, Sophie?"

She laughed in the half-darkness. "I'm looking at familiar places, Richard. But come on now. We must go back to the others."

In the meanwhile Pastor Celion had tried in vain to pursue the conversation, but the merchant was uncommunicative. The only sound from him was one last gulp as he emptied his glass. The pastor talked about the market for dried fish, but Berg stared steadily out across the West

24

Fjord. Both were trying to listen through the solid floor of the upper deck.

When the second bottle was opened, Lady Tennyson proposed a toast to the district and to her friends and said thoughtfully, "Look at that sun. It's getting smaller and soon morning will be here. Now it's nearing the dream hour. At any rate, I experienced my deepest and most lasting dreams exactly at this hour. I cannot endure silence, certainly not when I'm awake. And my dear departed Michael said I couldn't endure it in sleep either. That came from drinking his competitor's tea, he maintained, and then to tease him I would speak disparagingly of his own brand of tea. Ah, yes, our life together was a dream. And for that reason I suggest we each tell a story, or as many stories as the voyage demands. Bear in mind that we live in a part of the world where we are forced to listen the greater part of the year—listen for storms, for avalanches, for ship-wrecks. You men surely are well trained in listening. But now for a little while we're rulers of both land and sea, and if anyone feels his audience is too small, he can address himself to the ocean and the islands and the mountains and all the pebbles on the shore. I'll invite the governor to be the first."

Mylady held up her skirt like a little sail; the ruby stood out like a lump of solidified blood on her bare white hand. She ended her speech with a smile that elicited a vigorous nod of agreement from Pastor Celion. "That's a fine idea. We'll do just that, and Florelius will start."

The governor pushed back his chair so none of the others could look at him without turning around.

"Very well. I shall tell you about a man whom I should like to have had as a friend. Unfortunately he died long before I was born, but now and then when the world turns

25

against me, he is at my side. He offers no advice when I ask for it; he only sits there chuckling and baring his teeth as if he does not quite understand what I am dabbling with."

Halvor Mikkelsen's Journey

THE SHEEP RAID

"I have chosen to title the first part of my story 'The Sheep Raid' because this innocent creature whose sole distinction is usually incredible stupidity came to have a significant role in this tale.

"As you likely have read in accounts of that era, the harvest of 1696 was meager on the Nordland coast. My departed colleague on Bodögård recorded in that same year that in the one winter alone 160 people in a single parish died of starvation and diseases resulting from starvation. The racks for drying fish hung empty on into the second winter, and frost killed all the crops. From two districts in Vesterålen appeals were sent simultaneously to the king with a list of names of those who had died of hunger. One of the reports began: 'Herman Guldvigen* with his wife and two children are dead of starvation, so tragically that the younger child lay on his mother's breast, her nipple in his mouth.'"

---

* Guldvigen means "gold cove."

27

Governor Florelius cleared his throat and grinned. "Gold did not help in that cove—Heaven forgive my joking—even if they had had any, for it was not possible to go anywhere because of bad weather, and of course there was nothing to be bought in that place. No cod had showed up that year, and little did it avail those suffering people to lament their state like Peter Dass did:

Should the codfish fail us, what then would we have
What then could we carry to Bergen from here,—
The cargo ships would sail empty away.

"Well, so back to my story:

"Outside of Salten, about fifty miles from shore, lies a small island. As far as I know it bears no name. It hasn't enough individuality for that. Its topography has no resemblance to a lion or to a man on horseback, nor is there a hole through it—at least no hole large enough to be noticed. It is simply a clump of earth dropped from Our Lord's hand once upon a time and compacted into a commonplace mountain in the sea with a strip of beach the width of a stone's throw.

"It lies there without any legends surrounding it; it has been consigned to oblivion, and a passer-by on the mainland would need sharp eyes even to trace the ruby-red lump against the horizon in the midnight sun and to discover the mounting froth when the northwest wind whips around it. Only the most sensitive of voyagers would see it as a miniscule continent, solitary and defiant, and wonder at the Creator's unfathomable waste.

"During this winter of privation a fisherman by the name of Halvor Mikkelsen lived on the island. He was not much better off than the others along the coast, but at least he had managed to keep himself and his family alive past New

Year's. By now the storms had raged for weeks, and not even with the help of the Devil himself did he dare venture out with the expectation of ever reaching land again.

"On the south side of the island, however, there was an inlet where the storms didn't strike so violently. This spot was sheltered by a mountain wall, a shield against the sea, and there Halvor was lucky enough to catch a bewildered cod or a lumpfish even in the worst of times.

"Halvor Mikkelsen was a widower—quite an unusual state to be in on the Nordland coast—and, as a matter of fact, he had been virtually a widower also when his wife was alive, for there was no more spirit in her than in a dried fish. She really did put a person in mind of a dried fish when she walked among the racks. She creaked with every step. Her hips and bosom were of like pattern: one had to see which direction she was facing in order to distinguish front from back. Furthermore, she was dried out all the way into her soul as well; there wasn't a spark in her, so Halvor might as well have been married to a stack of peat. And she was so slow-witted that when he spoke to her on Sunday, she would not come forth with an answer until Wednesday, and even then making no sense.

"But now and then she would sing dark, ominous hymns, and then Halvor knew they were in for a storm from the northwest. She was therefore not completely useless. She had premonitions of raging tempests when others saw only blue skies.

"Halvor could well endure her taciturn nature because he was a man who knew how to live on an island. His own soul was an island, without his being shy of people. Consequently within him and round about him there developed a balance of tension between flood tide and ebb tide. Routine never made him despair. He moved about among his fish-drying racks with the same indifference as did the sea. And

29

his wife—the wordless one—had eventually also become for him a kind of figure in the landscape, or more rightly a kind of shifting marker in shallow water to stay clear of in order to avoid sinking.

"But one Monday morning when he overheard her talking to herself wildly and incoherently, he was so terrified that he hid behind the racks to ponder the situation. Drying racks covered with cod can serve a fisherman as his private retreat. There he is at home among his own things, the fruit of his toil; there he feels secure. He stands as if behind a fortification, a familiar smell in his nostrils, and he knows that nothing on earth can crush him completely.

"One morning not long afterwards her whole world went to pieces. She went mad. She ran into the sea, shrieking, her skirt billowing in the wind, and sank straight down like a chunk of lead.

"Halvor didn't mourn her death more than was befitting. To be sure, he dropped a drag line for her a few days but all he collected was the foot of a worn-out stocking, and that reminded him of the least beautiful part of her. He soon gave up the dragging and instead walked along the sandy shore, folded his hands, and prayed—looking out to sea. He did that one day when there was a strong breeze from the south, for he privately believed his wife had ended up north at Trollebotn, and with a strong headwind his prayer would fly on wings like a swallow over islands and the sea and perhaps reach its destination before a Lapp sorcerer could get possession of her soul.

❀   *   ❀

"Now he was alone on the sea. He managed by attaching an extra-long towline to the rocks on shore and letting his boat drift out as far as it could. Then he sat there, bobbing up and down, dawdling with his gear, until the Good Lord granted him a nibble.

"Many an odd creature got caught on Halvor's hook that winter: tiny redspotted freaks with heads on the middle of their bellies and with two tailfins, yard-long eel-like fish with four rows of teeth as sharp as awls. Once he caught a one-eyed rosefish—that one eye as red and scaly as the fish itself. Another time he pulled up a monstrosity that looked like a coalfish, except that it had little white feet with claws instead of fins.

"But until now he had not yet seen a merman.

"Halvor remembered his father's story of a man from Helgeland who caught a merman on his hook. A merman is a little mite of a fish-like man as big as your thumb, completely green, with the head of a human fetus. His eyes are almost closed like two narrow slits, and he has a sort of mouth through which he croaks in Nordland dialect.

"The fisherman had tucked him into the thumb of his mitten, tied a piece of string around the open end, and all winter the merman had guided him to choice fishing banks. When people asked why the thumb of his mitten stuck straight up, he said because he had injured a tendon he had to hold his thumb in that position. But when spring came the merman begged to be set free again, and the fisherman had emptied his mitten over the side of the boat; from then on he never had a barren day at sea.

"It was usually at dusk when Halvor sat bent over on the seat, his stomach growling with hunger, his mind hypnotized by the continuous tugging at the line, that those hybrids of the deep came into the light of day, so to speak, but he was able nonetheless to distinguish their identifying peculiarities.

"Like all other fishermen living along this jagged coast, Halvor Mikkelsen was a God-fearing man; he knew that

31

the Creator had two hands, one clenched and one open, and that a man could never know whether a lashing or a blessing was the next gift in store for him. But he was also a man living on an outpost; he believed he could well fend for himself, and he allowed himself the right to be offended and inhospitable when Fate mocked him.

"For that reason he made the sign of the Cross when one of these atrocities came up along the gunwale, and he immediately cut it loose with his sheath-knife to let it return to its source.

"Both in stature and demeanor Halvor seemed to have been created in distraction, like a by-product while the Almighty was mainly occupied with the making of a sketch for a Bach or a Christian IV. He was not especially tall; his shoulders were bony and always a little hunched, so he often blended into his natural surroundings. Only when he had pulled in his boat and stood on the beach staring wearily across the churning sea would anyone guess that Halvor was a headstrong, persistent man, all alone on a long, rugged shoreline.

"His hair and his beard had originally been black, but with the passing of time shreds of congealed sea spray had made it stiff and gray—like the grass along the coast in autumn. His lips protruded slightly, his teeth were small and sharp, his face resembled that of a codfish, and his skin was a dead gray color, like soaked-out coalfish. And his eyes—yes, his eyes were the last feature one would notice. They were tiny, grayish-brown like lichen, shaded by bristly hairs and a network of puckers, but on rare occasions when he looked up at the sky they could sparkle like mirror-clear water in the hollow of a marsh.

"Halvor Mikkelsen had two children, a boy of seven and a girl of four, and whenever he looked at them he knew God had not slighted him in what was really most important. They were both blond like their mother. Fortunately that was the only inheritance she had passed on to them, and they had not yet acquired the cadaverous color of her skin.

"When Halvor was out on the water in silent single combat against the Omnipotent and the weather, the children would sometimes run down to the beach and stand there transfixed watching their father, and whenever he pulled in something or other their arms went up like miniature windmills. When he came to land they never asked what he had done with his catch, because he had explained to them once and for all that he was forever getting a mess of seaweed on his hook, that the seaweed could so easily change itself to look like something else, and that they must pray to God to protect them from ever having to eat shells or red algae or seaweed.

"Thus the winter wore on until the latter part of February, and with the passing of each day Halvor became more and more confident that they would be able to escape a diet of red algae and shells. Daily he beat a path from the house to the boat-landing. Viewed from above, his footprints in the snow were like a row of strange symbols. Here and there his boots designed a dash, here and there a loop as if in fun, and in places there were puddles where he had stopped to pass water with the habitual straightforwardness of the fisherman when he stands alone, absorbed in thought. The path had taken on a succession of little exclamation marks during the course of the season.

"With each new day dawn came earlier and dusk lingered later on the snow-covered mountains. All in all it looked as if they would survive unharmed. But on returning home one evening he found his little girl weak and ill."

The governor stopped abruptly, grasped his empty glass, and rotated it slowly on his knee, his eyes fixed on the crimson drops circling the bottom.

"In those times," he went on, "two particular misfortunes aggravated the already miserable condition of the inhabitants in this district. First of all, the trade monopoly always kept fishermen's families from being able to provide a sufficient store-house of groceries; and, second, really a direct result of the first, in lean years the people were afflicted with spotted typhus. This dreaded poor man's disease —rightly termed hunger typhus—together with scurvy had brought more tragedy to this district than all the storms and disasters on the sea.

"When Halvor learned the nature of his child's illness, he left the house and walked down to the shore. There he stood on a rock farthest out by the landing, his eyes riveted on the water, believing that if God were going to give him a sign it must appear where they regularly held their daily rendezvous.

"What kind of sign did he expect? Well, perhaps a dark spot out there on the sea, or the back of a big fish that might look like the keel of a boat, or perhaps an oar afloat. Or that the wind might cease its buffeting so he could listen to God's own voice and not only Nature's arbitrary echo of it, which he had grown so accustomed to hearing in the incessant splashing of the waves against the rocks or in the sneering force of the undertow pulling itself out from land. The sea laughs in all kinds of weather. On calm days it hides its malice in little hollow chuckles where there are inlets; during storms it guffaws openly, boisterously, with full force. And in the undertow the sea takes back its laughter and leaves nothing of itself in return. It sucks into its depths all human life and all the works of man it can get hold of until, satiated with substance, with sluggish disdain it vomits up on land a corpse, an overturned boat, a rotted jacket.

> When Jupiter's fireworks kindle,
> Heavens and oceans quake,
> Sandbars and beaches tremble.
> Then come tidings from alternate isles
> Of shipwrecked sailors perished at sea,
> Frozen on fjords and lost in the deep.

"It was getting dark. Halvor Mikkelsen stood there, but no sign appeared. In the meanwhile the water had risen to his ankles, and when it soaked through his boots, he felt ice-cold way up to his heart and without great ado he called the Lord to task for making such a fool of him. Then he sloshed to dry ground and made his way slowly toward the house to take care of his sick child.

"The next morning in the gray of early dawn, Halvor set out westward along the coast in search of the nearest neighbor to ask for help. He knew the man had a sheep on his premises, and he realized that to cure his little girl he must get hold of fresh meat, for it was scurvy she was suffering from.

"Though it was daylight when he got there, there was no sign of life either in the yard or at the boat-landing. It was a wretched shelter, no better than a Lapp's hut, built of stones and turf with no windows and only a smoke-hole in the roof covered over with the belly-skin of a halibut. On opening the door he was met by thick smoke and a damp sealed-in stench that compelled him to wait a while at the entrance to adjust to the dark. The husband and the wife were in bed; they were the sort that believed they could stretch their food supply to last longer by lying still than by taxing their strength maneuvering boats and throwing out fishlines. For that reason they made no move as Halvor came in; they merely turned their faces toward him, and the whites of their eyes stood out like shining dots in the blackness. When he had made known his errand, they did not respond but only looked in the direction of three little starving bodies huddled together on a bench along the wall.

"As Halvor stepped outside again, he discovered that rain had begun to fall. He stood on the leeward side of the hut, his back against the stone wall, looking up at the mountain. The lone sheep was grazing in a hollow where the snow had melted; it uprooted the moss in search of something to fill its stomach.

"Suddenly Halvor Mikkelsen's whole body shook; a palsied tremor seized him. He pressed himself against the turf, his teeth chattered, and he bit hard trying to control himself— but not too hard lest the few stubs he had left would break off. Last winter's famine had damaged his teeth, and in all likelihood the Maker's mockery had a purpose in that, too, for why should he have teeth when there was nothing to bite into?

"All at once the sheep turned to stare at him. It tilted its head, gave out one thin, pleading bleat, turned its back again, and trotted a short way off.

"Halvor surveyed the murky sky. The cloud-cover hung low, heavy, and rumpled like a canopy of animal skin, and he was struck by its close resemblance to the sea—sea and sky compressing all creation between them. It was as if he were caught between the tongue and the palate of a monster, and the island where he lived was only a molar in the mouth of the world.

"The sheep had changed its stance. Now it turned once more to look at him.

36

"Halvor Mikkelsen made his way homeward, hurried and determined, his heart beating loud and fast like the impatient ticking of a clock in his breast. When he was far enough away that he could not be seen from the hut, he quickly changed his course and scrambled up the mountain. I must make a tour up to the summit, he thought, because a boat might be drifting by. Perhaps someone will come along who doesn't know where he is, someone who may need the help of one acquainted in this region.

"As Halvor neared the mossy hollow, the sheep began bleating gently and expectantly. He held out his hand toward it and cocked his head to one side. The animal promptly stopped chewing; it also cocked its head and stared with yellow eyes at the empty hand coming closer. The man was moving about on a giant molar in the mouth of the sea, and he stole shrewdly and cautiously forward so the powers under the sea and the powers in the heavens would not be alerted.

"The sheep froze in its track. Quickly it jerked its head from one side to the other to see whether the retreat was clear and then withdrew backward into the hollow, its yellow eyes all the time fixed on the empty hand. So the man and the sheep gradually drew nearer to the edge where the cliff dropped sharply a hundred yards down to the shore.

"Meanwhile the wind had calmed and it was still all around them. The clouds had ceased their drifting, and the sea its rolling. It was—" The governor kept looking down steadily into his empty glass as if it were a crystal ball from whose shining inner world he drew his story.—"It was one of those rare moments when angels hold their breath while watching a phenomenal happening on the earth below. And while they are so absorbed, for one moment Nature gambols freely. In this way came the eclipse of the sun before the Battle of Stiklestad, the moving of the star across the heavens

37

toward Bethlehem, and the darkness that occurred at the ninth hour on Golgotha. Some sign of nature surely was manifest also before the Battle of Waterloo and before the birth of Leonardo. Whether these portents really did happen or have been invented in retrospect? One need only observe that when events have later proved to be of major significance in the history of the world, men have felt constrained to introduce a miracle—like a distinct theme in the overture—to dispel any doubt of the greatness of the event. But now when Halvor Mikkelsen induced a sheep to retreat backward over the precipice, all nature became a sign. The sky lowered its brow and grayed with tension; the sea crested in order not to miss out on one single detail."

Governor Florelius suddenly straightened up in his chair, flourished his glass, then just as suddenly settled back, laughing quietly. "I am ruining everything for Halvor, poor fellow. For him poaching sheep was really serious, and I am making a joke of it."

The governor's glass was refilled. His eyes scanned the room for a moment as if he had lost the end of the story, and then presently he continued. "When the sheep felt that its hind feet no longer took hold, it bunched all four hoofs on a clump at the outermost edge of the precipice. The bulging yellow eyes stared at Halvor's work-stained hand and saw plainly there was nothing there except swellings and small open sores from repeatedly dipping into salt water.

"Halvor came closer. When he stuck out his chin, he looked more than ever like a greedy codfish.

"Suddenly the sheep let out a long quivering baa. The pitiful cry grew louder as if sounded through a megaphone on its way into the hollow. It echoed across the water, and it is rumored that fishermen rowing through the inshore channel, on hearing a blood-curdling wail from one of the

38

islands, took refuge immediately under an overhanging cliff where they waited forty-eight hours before venturing farther.

"All at once Halvor sprang forward the last few feet and shoved the animal over the brink. Have you ever seen such a sheep, he thought, frightened; have you ever seen such a dunce? I was only going to pat you."

"Now he is mocking us again," interrupted the pastor. He smiled and shook his head, looking at the others as if he wanted to share a secret with them. "Now he would have us believe that a poor hungry fisherman climbs on top of a mountain to befriend a sheep."

Florelius returned the smile, his thin face a tangle of wrinkles. Two deep lines of laughter formed at the corners of his mouth.

"We are all sheep before Our Shepherd, and the pastor ought not so underestimate one of the least of his flock as to doubt his intention of showing kindness to a brother."

All of them, Merchant Berg included, laughed heartily at the governor's flash of wit and thereupon toasted him cordially.

"What I mean," continued Florelius, "is that deep in his mind Halvor did really intend only to stroke the sheep, and all the time he was coming closer and closer to it he kept thinking, I shall only pet you a little—I shall only stroke your wool, and then, well, then he pushed the sheep over the edge.

"That's how it was. Afterwards as Halvor stood leaning out over the precipice, his face took on a terrified expression like that of one witnessing a natural disaster. Things like storms and shipwrecks he had had to accept. They were the tools God used when He was angry, at times when He meted out punishment, severe and extensive, without due concern about position and rank. But that he, Halvor, had

39

sent an innocent sheep over the ledge instantly made him feel singled out for damnation, the only condemned man on the Nordland coast.

"Finally the sheep struck the bottom. It had bounded noiselessly from one rock to another until it came at last to rest motionless in the shallows. All the while the animal kept falling, Halvor, too, felt as if he were falling, and when the woolly mass at last sank into the sand, he, too, had the sensation of having gone to the bottom. But nothing happened. The sheep just lay there, and after a while Halvor got up. He looked skyward. A strong wind was blowing again, and the clouds chased one another impatiently as if resentful at letting themselves be slowed down by a trifling incident in a faraway fishing settlement. They tumbled on, southward, high above the earth, to places where more significant events might be destined to happen.

"Halvor Mikkelsen scrambled down the mountain as fast as he could. He had become a man again, a man with nothing to rely on but himself. On the sand lay promise of fresh meat, but he would have to kill the creature so it would not suffer too long in the event it had survived the fall.

"He plunged his knife into the sheep—an act of mercy, he thought. The glazed yellow eyes followed his hand as the steel blade approached, and they did not even blink when it went all the way in to its very shaft. Gently and carefully he skinned the sheep so that not one shred of meat would be wasted. Afterwards he cut off the head, wrapped it in the skin, made the sign of the Cross over the fleecy bundle, and consigned it tenderly to the depths of the sea.

"In the very moment when the sheepskin disappeared under water Halvor caught sight of the back of a huge fish. It was the shape and size of a porpoise, but its color was a greenish shimmering blue, much like that of the ocean in

40

spring on those rare occasions when light frolics with different kinds of unusual shades."

The Porpoise

"Halvor wasted no time brooding. He knew the sea harbored many living things the like of which he had never seen—golden fish from the realms of India, and octopuses almost as big as an eight-oared boat—and they must be free to stray to a Nordland skerry without anyone's showing the whites of his eyes because of it. But he also realized it is wise to take no chances with things unfamiliar. With that, he picked up a stone the size of a man's hand, scratched a cross on it with his knife, and threw it high in an arc above the strange-looking fish. But the creature lay undisturbed except for a slight swaying of its tail-fin. There were both apathy and scorn in that sluggish motion.

"Halvor turned pale. This was an evil omen, and things were happening here that forewarned of more dire consequences than witchcraft and sorcery. It was as if a new source of vaulting breakers were being created right before his very eyes.

"He thought about his ill child at home, made a defiant motion at the thing in the sea, lifted the sheep carcass onto his back like the Good Shepherd in Scripture, and started homeward without as much as a backward glance.

"Climbing the steep slopes, bent under the weight of his prey, he looked like a strange, mysterious animal upright in the snow. The limp burden hung like a naked hump over his back. He bared his pointed teeth to draw his breath. On the mountainside above, fierce gales blew the new-fallen snow in frenzied swirls that appeared and disappeared and appeared again in the gray-white air. Halvor plodded

41

onward, a heavy-hearted groundling beneath a heaven of exultant spirits.

"On arriving home he set about to cook strong broth for the child, adding dried roots he had gathered during the summer. Every morning he prepared meat for her breakfast, and every noon-time he gave her soup made of finely ground sheep joints and cod liver. Then he left the boy to watch over her on the beach while he had to be out of their sight far out at sea with hook and line.

"Within a month the little girl had recovered, and so far at least no further misfortune had struck. The neighbor had not appeared, no one had come to demand an account, and when he saw that his child had regained her strength, he regarded his act as a deed he could justify.

"Nevertheless he didn't feel completely secure, and one night he gathered the bones that were left—by now so soft and over-cooked that had he been a sculptor he could, no doubt, have molded them into a new form—and buried them under the high-water mark somewhere on the north end of the island. He did this on a cold night under a full moon. He dug a grave two feet deep in the sand and placed the bones so they would point in separate directions; he did this to dissipate their power and deter them from uniting against him.

"In the course of time Halvor had developed his own ritual of private rites to protect himself and his children. He believed in magical words as well, a faith no longer shared by others. Now and then he went about mumbling incantations to himself."

At this point Pastor Celion began to squirm. His smooth, round, childlike face turned purple with suppressed laughter. He hid behind his glass and closed his eyes tightly as if seeking protection against forbidden pleasure. "The Devil! What a liar you are, Florelius!" he gasped. "Would that

42

our land might be spared such governors as you in the future. Moreover," he added with a chuckle, "now I understand more clearly your strict regard for truth in official matters. You unload all your deception on us, your associates, so the public may have full benefit of your unblemished integrity. Indeed you have arranged things wisely."

The governor's expression was as inflexible as that of a judge. The cane chairs made no noise. Then suddenly came the sound of the low, timeless flapping of gulls' wings streaking past. Florelius continued his story.

"The winter wore on, and it was March. Halvor went to sea daily, and while other men's drying racks in Nordland stood bare, his were covered with big pieces of cod day after day. He stayed out of sight whenever ten-oared boats drifted by; he preferred not having to admit drying such an abundance of fish. But he harbored new and dangerous thoughts; the crime had turned into a blessing, a blessing that could in due course provoke a new crime—if jealousy should enter the hearts of the passers-by.

"The children resumed their play among the rocks along the shore, and again he watched their arms moving like little windmills in the distance whenever he pulled up fish across the gunwale.

"Then something happened. It was the day after St. Gregory's Mass. Halvor Mikkelsen was in his boat as usual. The wind had stopped blowing during the day, but he had not noticed the change because it had come about as quietly and peacefully as when one's breath dies out. All was perfectly still except for an occasional gray speck moving like a shiver across the surface of the water. The wind had finished its sport with ghostly specters on the sides of mountains. An early thaw was setting in, and the rocky slopes were beginning to look gray and striped as the snow had melted little by little each day. Now and then a half-frozen clump would sigh and disappear in silence. These were the first ugly signs of spring.

"Halvor sat in his boat, toil-worn and drowsy, his arm in monotonous rhythm with the line—this persistent, unchanging, slow tugging, the fisherman's usual motion—left hand on the gunwale, right hand holding the line, and then—let out, pull in—let out, haul up—

"Halvor just sat there thinking about nothing. Off and on he wiggled a loose tooth. Everything was all right. Then all at once the boat lurched as if a huge fish brushed against the keel. Quickly he looked up, and there no more than ten yards away, lying still in the sea, was the shimmering blue back he had seen in the winter.

"Halvor watched the fish, his arm holding still, and then he cast a glance inward toward the house and up on the mountain whose summit was already black and bare of snow. He lowered his head and looked down into the bottom of the boat. The fish lay completely still like a rock jutting out of the sea.

"Well, now, well—Halvor was thinking as he watched his dripping line. Well now, in Heaven's name! But he said nothing aloud; he only wound up his line, took his gear—hook, line, and sinker—carefully on board, and fumbled around for the oars. He succeeded in putting out the one, but he was so jittery that he lost the other in the water, and at once it started to drift out of reach. Now there was only one course to take. He paddled—something a Nordland man does very clumsily—and he kept on paddling. All the while he was thinking—in Heaven's name—and he finally got hold of the floating oar and began to backwater, he felt scared and sad. This is going backward, he thought; now I'll have to watch every move and every stroke of the oar.

"The next day was no different. He fished for an hour and hauled in a good catch, but then the porpoise re-

44

appeared, rising out of the water like a mountain alongside him, and lay there as if enjoying the mute companionship.

"This went on for three consecutive days. Every morning when he rowed out the same thing happened. The formidable object lifted itself quietly out of the water a few yards from the boat. Now and then it moved its tail sluggishly as if only to remind him of its presence.

"The fourth day, however, Halvor made his countermove. He had found a small clock in his grandfather's old chest. He attached the clock to his fishline, and presently as he sat there pulling his line a thin silvery tinkle sounded across the water. With repeated ringing he managed to keep the porpoise at a fifty-yard distance. At first it swam round and round at full speed leaving a foamy green wake behind it, but soon it grew tired of that and eventually amused itself by zigzagging back and forth between the boat and the island.

"As the days progressed the music of Halvor's tiny clock was heard far out on the sea. He tinkled his way into sheltered places with little clear notes, and one could sometimes tell from the ringing whether he had cod or haddock, coalfish or lumpfish, on his hook.

"But new circumstances developed: Halvor became the victim of a whole series of minor misfortunes, one on the heels of another, trivial mishaps, and at first he thought nothing of it. One day he gashed his hand when gutting a fish—something he hadn't done since he was a small boy. He took to stumbling frequently when trying to straddle the gunwale, and once he fell into the water near his landing spot so he had to stay indoors half the day to dry his clothing. His lines tangled, he even lost his grip on the lines, and more often than not a fish got off his hook just as he was about to land it.

"Little by little things seemed to show a malicious will

45

of their own. One evening a trough crashed down from a shelf and scraped the skin off his nose. The next morning a rusty nail went right through his boot deep into his foot.

"Halvor became nervous and a sad sight. With a scab that made his nose look mangy, he was so loathsome that he could have scared his own reflection twice through the wall.

"One day he got so violently angry that the children ran away to hide in the mountains, and he had to spend half the afternoon hunting them. He called, coaxed, pleaded— but mainly he threatened them. Finally they came down to the house. The little girl cried and sobbed for her mother. It was the first time she had done that since her mother had disappeared, and that gave Halvor something new to ponder.

"Everything got into a snarl for him. He could cope with major disasters like storms and shipwrecks and famine, but to be made to look ridiculous like a want-wit—these recurring vexations and irritations paled his face and soured his disposition. He began to chew his fingernails, he heard sudden noises outside where nothing ever happened, and these imagined noises were enough to send him wheeling around and grabbing for something to hit with.

"Halvor Mikkelsen came to be the first person on the Nordland coast to suffer a nervous breakdown. He was so crazed that he sat still a whole day at the boat-landing just staring out over the water.

"Then he decided to try a new approach. Since neither Cross nor clock were to any avail, he determined to use plain common sense to defend himself against these nuisances. He made up his mind to be ultra-cautious in every undertaking, and he measured each step, lifted his feet unnecessarily high, and set them down with studied care. He made sure he had dry lines each morning, and he tied extra knots on his ropes. When he set foot on land, he did so with numerous ceremonial rites so that the spirits could not point to one single fault to hold against him. Whenever he entered or left the house, he made it a practice to hold the door open a half minute. On the whole, he conducted himself as if he were living on an island built of pieces of glass.

"But nothing helped. There was a steady commotion around him, and if he was particularly careful on rough terrain then he would trip over his own feet on level ground.

"Halvor's face turned gray as mold. His eyes twitched, and he slept little these spring nights which gradually became lighter. When his lines tangled, it was almost impossible for him to straighten them out because he had chewed his nails to the quick.

"When troubles were the worst, he sat still and bared his teeth so his face was as ugly as that of a lumpfish, and he nearly burst into tears. He found relief only by swearing loud and long, and he tried to use the most blasphemous words a Nordland man knows so that even the Omniscient wouldn't understand what he was saying. And when he had denounced his invisible enemy as a damned cheat and swindler, he regained courage momentarily, for he knew strong language is the only recourse for a solitary man on a rocky island in the sea.

"But in his heart and in the innermost recesses of his mind where pulses churn about in tumult in the subconscious, Halvor knew this was to be a lifelong battle with every kind of weapon, with prayers and curses, with cunning and strength. And he also knew that if he yielded as much as one iota now, he would soon follow where his wife had preceded him.

"It was just two days after Holy Rood Day, which is the third day of May; the jaeger had returned and the people of the parish had already paid their tithes. Right now, he

47

concluded, he must take the risk of winning or losing.

"Before setting out he fetched a harpoon from the boat-shed and sharpened the point and the barbs with his whetstone. Then with resolute denunciation he rejected all trumpery and magic; instead he simply checked to make certain the shaft was well fastened. He hid the harpoon under the seat and climbed into the boat. He cut loose the clock from the line and put it into his pocket.

"When Halvor rowed out that morning his expression was surly and sad—the look one sees on the face of a child who has been severely punished, unjustly. He had combed his hair and his beard, he had emptied the boat of sea water, and he had cleaned out all the rotting entrails.

"It was perfectly still. He could see the smoke rising straight up from the house. The sea around him was as clear as a mountain lake. The rocky crags—all have one face or another here on the Nordland coast—lifted their heads in the fresh spring air. They rubbed the melting snow out of their furrows and stared blankly at the insignificant creature Halvor Mikkelsen.

"As soon as he reached his usual fishing spot he pulled up the oars and let out the line. At the same time he placed the harpoon halfway up on the seat beside him within easy reach. Thereupon he settled down to the job of fishing. He kept his face turned downward to the water, but out of the corner of his eye he also kept contact with the sea beyond.

"Within minutes the porpoise appeared. First it circled the boat a few times and then it sneaked up slowly, as if preening itself and caressing the surface of the water. Halvor's eyes followed it. As he sat there alone in his boat watching that massive shimmering blue-black hulk rolling and turning, he suddenly felt strong and solitary and sovereign. God had abandoned all the islands and the whole

48

expanse of ocean, and he, Halvor Mikkelsen, had taken over His position on the Nordland coast.

"When the porpoise swam slantwise past the stern and sidled up to the boat, Halvor grasped the harpoon carefully in his right hand while he kept his left on the line so as not to invite suspicion."

Governor Florelius hesitated a moment. The morning sun shone directly into his eyes; one could see the deep wrinkles in his face, obviously traces of weariness or prolonged suffering. He had reached a point where the story would not flow freely on its own impetus but had to be nursed along by contemplation and moralizing. Perhaps the narrator's realization of his own incapacity accounted for his tortured expression. He took another drink, forced a low growling laugh, and continued.

"Standing there in the boat, harpoon upraised, Halvor exemplified both the fool and the hero. In this solemn instant he felt as if he had accepted both God's and man's responsibilities. He gritted his sharp pointed teeth, and the brown eyes that in happy times sparkled like clear water were glazed with tension. But exactly in the very second when he swung his arm out to plunge the harpoon into the back of his enemy, he caught a cod on his hook and it pulled so violently as to make him lose his balance. The harpoon went down, barely grazing the tail fin of the porpoise and ripping the skin only slightly.

"When Halvor managed to get back on his feet, both the harpoon and the porpoise had disappeared in the water. The sea described circles where they had gone down.

"As he rowed to shore that evening, Halvor sat bent over on the seat, like an old, old man. He pulled at the oars as hard

49

as he could, but it was as if someone behind him were tugging in the opposite direction. His eyes were bloodshot. It took him an hour to cover a distance that usually demanded ten minutes.—I shall eventually wear out the brute, he reasoned, and fumbled with the oars, but the sea was thick as mush. In the bottom of the boat lay all his fishing tackle in a jumbled heap.

"On reaching the landing and starting to climb out, Halvor was aware of someone clinging to his boot. Laughing derisively, he turned halfway around, slashed the air wildly in every direction, shrieked, cursed this devilment to the fiery depths, and grabbed for his sheath knife. The hold on his foot relaxed. But the sea was laughing. It flowed over the rocks, chuckling. It bubbled under the tangled weeds. It tittered in the sand.

"That night Halvor was awakened by the arrival of summer. Out there at the mouth of the sea they are likely to come hand in hand, spring and summer, in one and the same night. So Nature has wisely saved the poor an entire season, and those wretches ought to appreciate that disdainful concession.

"Awakening, he heard deep sighs all around him as the last clumps of snow slid into the water. Now and then he felt cold drafts through cracks in the walls and got up to go outdoors to look about.

"The moon was almost full. It shone directly over Landego and cast its beams out toward him, but beyond the cone of light the water was black and shiny like polished slate. Halvor trudged along making his way wearily up the side of the mountain, his face furrowed and ashen. Nothing happened. He could wander undisturbed wherever he wished, looking after his lifeless possessions: his house, his boat-shed, patches of sandy soil, an empty stone barn with

50

two empty stalls and a sheep hutch, fifteen partially covered drying racks, and a stone fence where the ground sloped down toward the sea.

"The children were asleep. The hush of peace lay over the sea and the mountains. But Halvor paced back and forth all through the night hours. He was like Christian II that dreadful time when his mind was torn between attack and surrender. The enemy had built bastions in his brain that harassed him night and day. But Halvor Mikkelsen tramped about on stretches of granite. Now and again he shook his fist at something in the air: 'I shall never give up! Never!' "

Florelius stopped talking. The lines in that bony face clearly showed to the minutest detail, just as the fissures in the side of a mountain expose the true nature of the rock when the morning sun fills them with light. He half-closed his eyes as if trying to hold fast to a dream of bygone days, and when he resumed his story Pastor Celion was surprised to see that the governor's face was young and ecstatic and that its ruddy hue was effected by something deep and wholly different from the mere reflection of sunlight.

The governor opened his eyes. He shook his head slowly and laughed in his usual satirical way, melancholy, yet defiant, like one who knows well the inconstant stuff of a dream but nevertheless is reluctant to let go of its precious fool's cloak. "It's characteristic of islanders," he remarked, "that they have to move in a circle when pursued. They are not able, like other people, to run in one direction, as, for example, to escape into the heart of a forest or to set out toward another town. They are bound by the oldest and the most evil of all figures, the circle. A shoreline, be it ever so treacherous and rugged, always ends at its beginning. Of course, one may cross an island and imagine he is taking a new direction, but the determination to deceive himself

51

can never prevail long; and if anyone seemingly does manage to hang on to such deceptions, then it is either because he has become broken in spirit like a regal lion behind iron bars or because he has always been a monkey and therefore by his very nature thrives in a cage. Otherwise—yes, otherwise he must always stagger, heavy-hearted, on the rocky coast like a tragic sphere linked to an ellipsoidal solar system. And in his deeply conscious moments of greater enlightenment, perhaps he catches a fleeting glimpse of a linear world, a world in which one doesn't forever meet himself coming back—by that I mean a world of freedom, real freedom, where good and evil don't exist, like earth's gravity when one gets far enough away."

The governor laughed. "Well, now once again I have betrayed Halvor Mikkelsen, for he was never one to prolong, belittle, or enlarge his problems by making them valid for the entire universe. He shouldered them with bold obstinacy —like Sisyphus the stone-roller. They were his alone, and he would carry them personally to lay them at the feet of his Lord.

"Night wore on. For a while he stayed indoors, seated on the bench near the fire. Then he ripped off a strip of dried fish.

"He wandered about, chewing and thinking, and by the time the sun rose over the mountains of Ranen he had begun to take down his fish from the racks."

Rough Sailing

"By noon the following day Halvor's long-boat, a black six-oared one, stood in the shed ready for launching. In the stern he had put the plow; he had cleaned and polished it free of dirt so that it glistened in the sunlight, and if viewed from just the right angle it looked somewhat like a sharp-nosed dragon's head. All the tools were also on board, together with two benches for sleeping and three stools with heart-shaped cut-outs in the middle of each seat.

"Near the stools stood his grandfather's chest. It held all manner of fishing gear as well as a moldering book of household sermons that smelled of guano. The chest was really a depository for life's greatest essentials on an island, a sort of crudely built Arc of the Covenant. Midships lay his personal belongings, clothes and the like, the total of which required little space. Halvor had removed the rear thwart and fashioned in its stead a kind of tent of two sealskins for the children.

"He had also loaded as much dried fish into a small rowboat as he thought it could carry so that the water came close up to the washboard. When the sun was at its height directly to the south he made one final round of the buildings. Then he lifted the children on board, tied the towrope to the smaller craft, and set sail.

"What a glorious day for sailing! The sea was perfectly calm, and Halvor's two boats left a wide gentle wake that closed again slowly behind them. The breeze filled his square sail evenly and steadily.

"The islands off the Nordland coast are indeed a heroic breed of people who long ago severed all connections with geography. They stand shoulder-deep in the Atlantic Ocean. I visualize them squatting on the ocean floor so that only their bald heads can be seen. In the winter darkness when day is merely the reverse side of night, they stand with their trunks immersed in icy water, locked in from all the world, with faces as dead as the pharaohs' stone colossi. But in May when the birds come to screech at them to hear the echo of their own joyful spirit and when men on shore sow lice in their beards, then they brighten up momentarily and one can see who they actually are."

The governor emptied his glass and smiled. "Yes, indeed, Halvor observed all this—it just came to him—as he turned to look back. He saw that his island bore a face on the side of the mountain above the house, a face lighted up by the sun. The forehead, the deep dark mountain, was rugged and grooved, the temples sharply receding. The eyes were set close together, two depressions in the rock with overhanging shelves where pale grass grew; the whites of the eyes were bird excrement, for a pair of gulls roosted in the corners of the eyes. He, himself, had climbed up there to get eggs. These eyes consistently spied on each other, they never worked together, and in the hatching season just before the young were born white wings darted persistently like peevish glances back and forth above them.

"Halvor bared his sharp teeth and laughed. The nose was a boulder-strewn slope; he knew its every pore, but occasionally when the giant sniffled he dislodged heavy rocks that tumbled down to the grass-covered ground. At times they had crashed into his stone fence on their way to the sea; and at times they had become so imbedded in the ground that he had to use a crowbar to pry them loose and send them pell-mell down to the shore.

"His face turned to the sea, Halvor Mikkelsen roared with laughter, and the two little blond heads immediately peeked out of the tent to stare at their father.

"The island behind them grew smaller and smaller. The buildings shrank to tiny black dots like a rash on the lighted mountain. The north side of the island lay in shade, its profile etched clearly against the pale sea as if cut out of black paper.

"All at once Halvor had the feeling the island was retreating from him. It was moving westward in the direction of Röst, and he was frightened because he reasoned that if he turned to sail back he would never overtake the island again.

"'We must wait for next summer to see whether it's still there,' he thought half-aloud to himself. 'We must go out to get the rest of the dried fish,' he added in an effort to reassure himself—though he knew he was mouthing pure nonsense.

"He turned to the east and then realized they were off course. He straightened the boat and pointed the plow directly toward land, to a spot he knew to be the beginning of the Salten Fjord.

"Presently he ripped off a strip of dried fish; then he remembered the children and called to them to ask whether they, too, wanted a bite. They accepted, but as soon as they had tasted their father's offering, the little boy snatched his sister's piece and threw it along with his own into the bailing dipper. They had made themselves a make-believe cargo boat out of the bailer, and now they sent their catch south to Bergen over a sea of darkness under the seal skins.

"They sailed on hour after hour, but the wind was gradually dying down. Eventually it grew so calm that Halvor didn't even need to steer. He settled down in comfort as if cruising for pleasure in a soft sunny breeze, and when eveing brought deep rolling swells in from the sea he fell asleep over it all.

"At midnight he awoke and sensed immediately that something had gone wrong. The boat was completely motionless, its prow pointing north, its sail hanging limp straight down from the crossbeam, and all the usual noises of a craft in movement had been silenced.

"'Oh well,' he mused, and spit out the dried fish. 'It isn't the first time this has happened to me.' He sat bolt upright and peered around. The sky was dark, but out on the water shone a yellow-gray light, for it was precisely that moment in the course of the twenty-four hours when the sun disk takes a bath. The children were lying on the deck floor sound asleep, and when he spread his jacket over them he noticed they both had hold of the bailer. Then he settled down to wait, rudder in hand, for gripping a rudder gives a feeling of security even when there is no wind blowing.

"A few minutes passed. Suddenly there was flapping of wings overhead, and just as he glanced up a big gray gull flew over him. It circled the boats twice and then came to roost on the pile of dried fish.

"'Help yourself!' Halvor issued the invitation with his back turned. 'But where you come from you are no doubt accustomed to fresh meat.'

"The gull made no answer. Halvor sat quietly for a while; then he whirled around and glared at it fiercely. But the bird sat motionless on a dried fish, carefully surveying its surroundings as is the habit of sea birds when they light on dry land.

"'Perhaps you're only tired and want to rest a bit,' thought Halvor suspiciously. 'In that event I'll give you five minutes, but then see to it that you move on if you're not the one I suspect you are.'

"Thereupon he turned his back to the gull and began counting. When he got to 200, however, he had the impression someone on the sea was laughing at him, and he realized he was in the act of making a private fool of himself.

"'Well, then!' He wheeled around again. 'You'll have to fly! Whisst!' But the gull stayed. It did, indeed, move enough to perch on a different fish but gave no indication of any intent to abandon the boat.

"Halvor had a dozen dried cod heads in the bulkhead. He stooped down, picked one up, spun around, and flung it at the gull. But when the bird was aware of an object hurtling through the air, it simply hopped onto another dried fish and perched as resolutely as before.

" 'You have a scar on your neck,' observed Halvor. 'Who gave you that?' Then he snatched all the cod heads, one after another, and bombarded the gull. But every time a head came whistling through the air, the gull hopped nimbly out of the line of fire.

" 'I have never been one to torture birds,' he yelled, 'and if I have stolen gulls' eggs now and then, they likely weren't your eggs anyway.'

"Halvor Mikkelsen sighed. It was as if every bad experience he could remember from the time he was a mere child up to this very moment were coming to life and demanding that he live through it once again.

"He caught hold of the tow rope and pulled the rowboat toward him. With oar in hand he let loose on the gull. But the bird flew up, and all Halvor accomplished was to dislodge some bundles of dried fish so they fell overboard. On discovering he was about to lose his catch, however, he regained his self-control, recaptured his dearly learned business sense, and with it recovered the fisherman's judgment and understanding. He laid the oar aside, sat down, and again took hold of the tiller.

"A narrow rim of the sun appeared in the east. 'A new day will dawn,' thought Halvor, 'and tonight we shall land at Salten. If only a good wind would come up!' He looked up. The sail was still hanging limp as before, and the sky was bare of clouds as far as eye could scan.

"Suddenly it seemed as if a blood vessel had burst on the horizon, the sun rose out of the Mosken Stream, and its reddish light bathed the West Fjord, filling every inlet and cove along the shore. Golden mountains sprang out of the sea."

57

At this point the governor was interrupted by a discreet cough. Pastor Celion smiled, somewhat puzzled, and made an obvious effort to look across the water's surface. Florelius followed his glance and presently realized why he had been interrupted. He had been carried away with his love of storytelling and had burdened the narration with a vivid description of something they all could see with their very own eyes from where they were seated.

"Good Lord, Celion," he thought to himself, laughing inwardly, "how little you have in common with your great ideal from Alstadhaug. Your sense of proportion and restraint is certainly a blessing in a storm-filled parish, but isn't it probable that your own story will feel itself smothered by such precision?"

He continued. "Halvor remained seated a while squinting into the sun; then he turned halfway toward the gull that still stood on the pile of dried fish. He laughed again for he felt the crimson-colored morning inspiring him with new vigor and fresh courage.

" 'Well, well!' He addressed the western sea. 'No wind! No, that's evident. There's no wind. It's going to get the better of me eventually. I shall likely lie here and waste away to nothing but skin and bones. Indeed! But don't you see I have a half year's supply of food in the small boat, and the fish is still raw enough so that we won't suffer from thirst—not at first anyway.'

"Halvor Mikkelsen sat two long hours waiting for a breeze. Then he got to his feet and hauled down the sail. He drew the rowboat toward him, tied it alongside, and began to transfer the dried fish into the long-boat. When he had cleared enough space to work the oars, he fastened the tow-line to the long-boat, sat down between the heaps of dried fish, and started rowing in toward Salten.

"At intervals he had to stand up to see where he was heading because the fish shut off the view when he was seated. Nor could he tell whether he was really moving forward since he had no other landmark than the horizon.

"He rowed steadily for two hours, but the mountains on the east seemed just as far away as ever. When he again seized the oars, he noticed straightway a low-hanging bank of clouds toward the north in the direction of the West Fjord. Darkness spread like black ink over the surface of the water.

"Halvor rejoiced and immediately pulled in the long-boat, climbed on board, and cleared a place for himself near the mast and the rudder. Again he tied the tow rope to the stern of the long-boat.

"At that very moment came the first gust of wind, sudden and violent, but he was ready. He had reduced the sail to the size of a tea-towel, so as not to break the yard. Now he hoisted it very carefully until the two heavily-laden boats moved at a fair speed.

"Halvor exulted in his might over the sail and the sea. The children awoke and stared in wonderment at this father of theirs who bared his teeth and scorned the storm, and he shouted to them that they must be sure to hold on tightly because now they were about to sail with a devil out of the northwest. Along with the wind came the rain. It whipped across the sea and beat down with pounding force before the square-sail got soaked through.

"Halvor Mikkelsen jumped halfway up from his seat and shrieked flashing curses into the air. 'Come, Satan's weather, come storm and gale, smash every boat that lies in port!'

"The storm battered the boats with a veritable drubbing out of the northwest. Halvor turned and looked benignly at the cresting waves.

" 'I'll let out more sail!' he yelled in sudden glee. At the same time his eyes and ears were missing nothing: the creaking of the mast, the billowing of the sail when the blasts struck, the size and contour of the waves breaking under the keel, the cargo in the rowboat, the taut rope under strain.

"They were moving fast toward shore, but off and on he could feel the boat slowing down. He felt it most when the waves rose up under the overloaded little boat lifting its prow high into the air. It was left hanging behind, the tow rope gave a singing whine like a tight string, the sailboat was held back, and the crossbeam groaned under the pressure.

"When the gale was at its worst Halvor growled in a loud and threatening voice and broke again into raucous laughter. He mimicked the sounds of the boat and the ropes as if teasing them with his dogged obstinacy.

"After an hour's sailing time he sighted land. Mountains and coastlines appeared through the spray. He lost no time in getting his bearings and set his course straight toward the Salten Fjord. The children lay mute and cramped underneath the seal skins. They saw their father's face, and the wild triumphant expression frightened them into forgetting the sea and the weather.

"By now Halvor had become so brazen that he again took time to strip off a bite of dried fish. He sank his sharp teeth into it and then shifted it impatiently from one corner of his mouth to the other, and the little brown eyes were almost black with delight and contempt. But when the boat ducked in between the two islands that together form the Salt Maelstrom, he turned ashen with fright, and the fish fell out of his mouth. He had forgotten about the Maelstrom. It was raging landward, and as if to remind him the wind lulled for an instant to let him hear the roar ahead in the channel.

60

A mile away from the farmstead of Bodö
A river flows forth so frightfully swift
Its power can scarcely be equaled.
When high tide and low tide in midway meet
Then it comes charging so rampantly on
That boats have to swerve to get out of its way.

"Instantly Halvor shifted the tiller. Better to run aground than to get into that. The long-boat responded for a second, it twisted, the boards creaked, the prow and the stern wanted to go their separate ways. Then it settled back slowly on its course and continued—like a horse in the instant its wild nature prevails over obedience to reins.

"Suddenly feeling the full force of cold, hunger, and fatigue, Halvor slumped down. He felt as if they were all heaped upon him, a wicked threesome that had robbed him of strength all his life, but he had always spurned them. Now they weighed down on him and demanded his total awareness.

"He realized the boat was gaining speed. The wind had almost stopped blowing and the sail fluttered loosely. He heard it flap against the mast and felt the boat quiver as if a palsied hand had taken hold of the keel. He saw at a glance that the children were no longer watching him because he had again taken on his lost expression so familiar to them. Their attention was on the sea and on the land they were rushing past. They were listening to the roar constantly growing louder in front of the bow, and Halvor felt doubly dismayed by their disregard of him in this crucial moment.

"He looked at the younger one. Now she was completely well. God had sent him a sheep; now Satan was reclaiming it. Or, when all was said and done, was it perhaps something altogether different? Was the whole matter nothing

61

but mockery and double-dealing? Only a chance happening? God and the devil? What guarantee did he have, after all, that they ever involved themselves in his affairs?

"Halvor had previous acquaintance with the Maelstrom. He had stood on the shore and had seen the whirlpools suddenly form in the rough water, now here, now there, and had seen the breakers crest and froth and then vanish.

"As they sped in toward the first whorls he pulled himself to a half stance. He held the tiller firmly with his right hand; with his left he took out his knife and cut the tow rope. He shouted at the children to hang on tightly.

"All at once his mind was calm and clear. God and Satan disappeared; they had upset his thinking much too long. He grasped the tiller with both hands and headed directly into the main channel.

"Then he felt that something reached under the keel and lifted the boat; it shook violently and rocked precariously as if riding on the back of a gigantic hand. Then it slipped down, pitched and bounced forward. Halvor steered where the water was smooth and shining, but almost at once he saw a whirlpool churning directly in his path, a boiling cauldron a short distance ahead. Then he drove straight into it with the rush of a mighty current at top speed.

"Halvor Mikkelsen uttered a curious sound—something between a cry and a laugh—got a good grip on the tiller and guided the prow into the Maelstrom. The boat was heavily loaded and had sufficient momentum to sail right through the cauldron. The rudder-stick jerked out of his hand and struck his thigh, but he quickly retrieved it. Again something touched the keel; the boat moved suddenly sideways as if skimming over rough ice, and then it straightened and rushed ahead. He was in a lane of glassy black water with foaming borders on both sides as if a plow had cut a trail for him.

" 'I'll make it!' he screamed. 'I'll make it! To hell with it!' Just then another enormous whirlpool opened in front of him, but this time he tried to turn aside. The long-boat skirted the rim, but immediately the current turned it half-way around, and again the tiller jerked out of his hand. The stern was held back but the front end was free, and now, strangely enough, a new swirl pounded at the bow while the other lashed the back. For two or three seconds the boat was pulled from both ends in opposite directions. Thus Halvor Mikkelsen came to be known as the first man on the Nordland coast to have been rescued by virtue of a showdown between the Two Mighty Powers.

"For a prolonged instant the boat stood still, quivering, but it had been built by such men as know that a craft must be pliant to withstand shock and strain. It groaned and creaked, but it held together and slowly moved out into the river and then inward to the Skjerstad Fjord.

"When Halvor knew he was safe on his course, he turned to look for the rowboat just in time to see its prow lifted high into the air and then plunged deep into the sea. 'There goes our winter's fare,' he mumbled. 'No man survives without cost.'

"He spied three fishermen on shore and eyed them as inquisitively as if they were his initial encounter with the human race. They stood on the side of the mountain, their attention fixed intently on him as well. They didn't wave, just stood there gaping, motionless, arms hanging at their sides—a triune revelation sprung out of granite, born this instant directly before his very own eyes."

The governor smiled and hesitated. "Well, Celion, you look skeptical, but—" He glanced down into the bottom of his empty glass. "My friend has a tough grip on life. To be

63

sure, he lost his faith on entering the Maelstrom, but not his life, and moreover—now listen to the rest:

"As Halvor turned to make ready to sail again, he caught sight of something strange. In the foamy wake behind him the little rowboat bobbed up, filled with water indeed, but floating; and, what's more, the dried fish torn loose in the whirlpools jumped up again, bundle upon bundle, one after another, like flying fish. They leaped up from the river as if spit out by an altogether too selective palate down there in the deep."

"That's right," Mylady broke in, smiling distantly. "That's no lie. I've heard a similar tale myself. But please go on and forgive me for interrupting."

"So now they were through the channel. Halvor Mikkelsen righted his boat. He tacked a couple of times and got hold of the tow rope. The gunwale of the rowboat was just slightly above water and he began bailing. Within an hour it was empty. Then he took the oars, climbed into the little boat, and rowed round and round to gather as much of the fish as he could reach. The wind had died down, and he ventured as far as he dared in front of the long-boat and managed to salvage half of the cargo he had started out with.

"It was now past the noon hour, the sea had turned gray, and a light rain was falling. Later in the afternoon, however, the skies cleared, a sea breeze came into the fjord, and at eight o'clock that evening they came to the entrance of the Salt Valley.

"Immediately afterwards Halvor saw a big gray gull flying high above the fjord."

ON REACHING LAND

"Halvor landed near the mouth of the river. He devoted the evening to unloading the boats, and since he no longer

64

lived on an island, he stashed the fish in some alder brush well out of sight. He pulled the light rowboat up on land and hid the plow, the beds, and his household goods under it. He covered the chest—the family altar out of the sea—with fresh leaves, to hide it well but for no other reason.

"Because as yet he had no house he left in the boat the book of household sermons, but he took great care to unload the best fish hooks and lines. Since he could not beach the long-boat by himself, he dragged it a hundred yards up the mouth of the river and tied it in a spot where the branches hung low and thick out over the bank.

✻ ＊ ✻

"That night Halvor Mikkelsen and his children rested under the squaresail; the little ones fell asleep each with a strip of dried fish sticking out of the corner of the mouth. He spread his jacket over them and covered himself with branches. There he lay awake a long time, inhaling the fragrance of the fresh foliage.

"New sounds and a new stillness. Rustling in the saplings and sighing in the quiet when the breeze died down. A new smell: the earthy smell of growing grass and moss on the edge of the shore. The smell of sand and of swamp. The shuffling of curious little animals in the brushwood. The aroma of night coming down from the hillside behind them. And the sound of water, two kinds of water, when the river met the sea in small splashes at the outlet.

"For a while he lay thinking about the buildings he had abandoned and about the everlasting noise, night and day, of water flowing along the foot of the mountain and of the pungent smell of salt and decay at low tide.

"Eventually sleep overpowered him. He felt intoxicated —and free. He slept and snored lightly under the coverlet of leaves; his mouth fell open and exposed the little sharp

65

teeth. On his lower lip lay a tiny alder leaf, moving up and down with every breath, trembling and hissing with each exhalation.

"The next morning they wandered into the valley in quest of new land. Halvor loaded himself down with all the things he felt they couldn't do without on their first trek: ax, fishing tackle, dried fish strapped on his back, a few cooking utensils in a leather bag. In addition, his little girl rode astride his shoulders most of the way, holding tightly to his tousled, salt-grayed hair that resembled nothing so much as a deserted bird's nest. All the while she offered a running commentary on their new life in such a way that Halvor, who couldn't himself survey the surroundings because of the burdens on his back, gained all his first impressions through the child's eyes. Now and then her outbursts into peals of laughter startled him and made him curious. The boy followed quietly at his father's heels, holding on to a rope tied to Halvor's belt.

"They progressed slowly, and if anyone had seen them from a distance at dusk in among the trees, he might well have mistaken them for an old, sick legendary beast skulking about waiting to die.

"Occasionally Halvor had to stop to raise his head because his neck ached. The weight of his little daughter forced him to bend his head forward, and having lived on a rock in the sea all his life he was unaccustomed to this posture. Nevertheless, he made many new discoveries in this way—the soil, sand, flowers, grass, bracken. He trudged onward, earthbound, and became a farmer all at once on his very first inland excursion.

"When the sun had moved around to the south, they turned down toward the river and set up camp on the bank. Halvor kindled a fire, fetched water, and cooked porridge with a handful of rye he had saved. Then they stretched out on the warm sand to rest and to sleep.

"Halvor awakened to a day of bright sunshine; the whole valley was drenched in light—this exquisite valley, the most beautiful in all Norway. The birches themselves exuded light; the leaves had taken on an eager, impatient green.

"Halvor waded into the river and climbed up on a rock to take possession of the valley. In two places he saw smoke rising out of the woods—tall, straight spires of smoke that dispersed quickly under a tranquil sky. 'They are farmers,' he concluded, 'ordinary native farmers. Here they live in peace, beyond the realm of the Powers. The Devil! They do indeed! God has forgotten them up here in the woods. They don't carry dried fish on their backs; no one is tracking them down. I must see to becoming a farmer immediately. There is room here for me, too.'

"Trees covered the floor of the valley—birches and alders. Higher up there were pines, strong old giants rooted in sand and heather.

"'There is an abundance of everything here,' Halvor thought further, 'and to top it all the river is full of fish. All I have to do is begin to work.'

"Wading back to shore to rouse the children, Halvor caught sight of a squirrel sitting in the top of a birch tree looking down at him. Its testy little grin exposed two chisel-shaped rat teeth. He paid it no more heed but picked up his possessions quietly and awakened the children. Nonetheless, the furrows on his brow had deepened; there were two of them, highly arched, patterned after two prodigious ocean swells —Halvor's cast mark.

"The three continued on their way up the flat floor of the

valley. Occasionally their approach startled birds, and Halvor was already mentally making traps out of cord and fishline. He followed a clearing at the edge of the valley, his head bursting with plans. Salmon nets were already hanging up to dry between trees bordering the river, the house stood ready—complete with windows and chimney—and there were barns and sheds of sturdy pine logs. A tall column of smoke rose to the sky, a symbol of perfect peace, pointing a path for him on his way home from a long journey. Sheep and cattle, horses and chickens scattered all over the valley.

"Halvor lifted his head to listen. The little girl cried out and pulled several hairs from his crown. Something rustled in the leaves. Were there people, animals, or ghosts prowling about in the woods in the very middle of a bright afternoon?

"'I must reach that open space by evening,' he reminded himself, quickening his pace. Once in a while the boy whimpered as he stumbled along over roots and stones, still clinging tightly to the end of the rope.

"An hour before sundown they came to a sandpit. Below, on both sides, the valley floor leveled off toward the river, and above were the pine-barrens.

"'Here we are! And in Heaven's name,' thought Halvor as he sank to his knees, not so much in an attitude of prayer as out of need to unload like a camel—child, dried fish, and gear.

"He cut out a site and put up a spacious shelter of leafy branches on a dry spot. This served as a home for Halvor Mikkelsen, a settler from a skerry in the sea, and his two children while he built a house in the course of the spring-time.

"The days were busy, he was a carrier of cargoes. He pitched like a freighter back and forth between the sea and the clearing, staggering under a load so big as to make it hard to push his way through places where the forest was dense. Early in the morning, before the devil got his feet into shoes, he gave his son orders for the day, and at dinner time he would come plodding out from among the trees, doubled under the weight of earthly goods. One day as he came with a bed on his back, his little girl cried out because the bed was loaded to such an extent that it looked as if it were the hull of a capsized boat approaching through the foliage.

"Fortunately the weather was in his favor, all kinds of weather—rain, wind, sunshine. Now that he was in the process of becoming a farmer, all kinds served him well.

"He placed nets in the river and seined fish; he set traps in the woods and caught birds. One day he overcame his shyness and went to seek out his nearest neighbor farther up in the valley, where he managed to barter five fish hooks and twenty yards of fishline for flour.

"Eventually one day Halvor got to the point where he could begin cutting pine logs. He lopped off the branches high up on the slope and tipped the logs down beyond the sandpit, so of their own momentum they rolled almost all the way to the building site. He laughed when he saw that; then all of a sudden it came to his mind that he had forgotten the chest with the book of household sermons down by the mouth of the river. He looked toward the heavens. The same deep blue sky had canopied the valley for days. 'Someone wishes me well,' he mused, 'someone who knows I live here in this thick forest.'

"One day he discovered a tree that looked exactly right for a ridgepole, but two magpies were nesting in it. From the time Halvor had started chopping they had put up a terrible fuss, but he decided to spare their home for the sake of his unidentified benefactor who wished him well; in his imagination he incorporated the tree, the magpies, and their shrill cries into his new kingdom.

"These were warm, dry days and blue-white nights when the trees were filigreed in delicate silk. Halvor worked and ate and slept in the stillness. The woods received and muffled all the noises of breaking ground, chopping trees, crying children, and shrieking magpies. At night when he was too tired to think, Halvor smiled to himself. And he kept it up."

✿　＊　✿

Florelius suddenly stopped talking. He closed his eyes as if searching for something within himself, and when he opened them again they had acquired a hard expressionless stare as if steeling themselves against the inevitable.

"One day when sitting astride his new ridgepole, Halvor saw the squirrel. It had climbed the opposite end of the pole, and now it was sitting there eyeing him. It sat on its hind legs, its forepaws in front of its mouth, hiding a sneer.

"Halvor lowered his head and shut his eyes. 'Tomorrow I shall fetch the chest with the book of household sermons,' he promised himself secretly. 'But I had to have a house first of all. God of the sea, the woods, and all eternity—it has been nothing but a struggle and still I don't own anything, and my only concern has been to provide food and shelter for my little ones. So help me! A man can't kneel and be humble and pray when he has to cut logs.'

"He looked up. The squirrel was still there rubbing its nose with a forepaw as if in deep thought.

" 'Heaven help me, if I can stand you much longer!' Anger was building up slowly and he mumbled to himself. 'You have the whole area up here and I have only this one little clearing.' Halvor moved cautiously along the log while he trimmed off twigs in order to look busy. But as soon as he sat up and threw his ax, the squirrel jumped down on the roof and with two long leaps was safe in a treetop!

"That night Halvor didn't sleep well. He dreamed he was sailing up the Maelstrom at flood-tide. All the fish in the sea had come to watch: cod, haddock, coalfish, lumpfish, and porpoise lay with open mouths on the surface of the water gaping at him. He dreamed he was sucked into a whirlpool and tossed round and round the edge of a greenish-black hole in the sea. He spun faster and faster like a little cyclone until at last the prow hooked itself onto the stern so his boat turned into a wheel.

"On awakening, the first sound he heard was a steady gnawing at the roof. He darted out, his heart pounding, screaming the strongest swear words he knew—Mylady knows what I am referring to if she remembers her childhood—and threw a stone the size of his fist right at the squirrel.

"There was no further disturbance the rest of that night, but the next morning he saw two deep teeth marks in the ridgepole.

"For days Halvor worked with his pockets bulging with stones, but he didn't succeed in keeping the squirrel away. When he was occupied on the roof, the squirrel got inside the house and made a vandal of himself. Objects designed to stand upright were tipped over, and before long the whole house was engraved with a new identifying bench-mark: two parallel dents met his eyes at every turn—on the walls, the bench, the bedposts, the door jambs, everywhere. Each morning the children's shoe laces were gnawed off so their father had to sit like an old parish pauper with trembling fingers tying the pieces together. And when they went to put on their clothes the buttons dropped off. Scraps of dried fish sprinkled the ground all about, and one evening his

71

very best salmon net fell apart when he was about to lay it.

"Halvor become an insomniac. At night the squirrel ran back and forth at the top of the sandpit, and the grating noise of crumbling grit kept him awake. He developed a nervous twitch and could not even lie still. 'Time is passing,' he reasoned, 'and soon summer will be gone. But I shall never give up,' he barked half-aloud into space. 'I shall never give up, and a sheepshed will be standing here before the frost comes!'

"The night-time sun shone blood-red between the tree trunks, and the same grating noise went on night after night. He got blue pouches under his eyes from lack of sleep. He stuck his fingers into his ears, and in his bitter loneliness he mumbled a new verse:

> Deviltry and storms and curses,
> Follow me from land to land.
> Dead men's babble and dead men's bones
> We'll still and crush with steel and stones.

"One night a scream startled him. He jumped up and grabbed the ax propped against the bedpost. His little girl was sitting up in her bed, her hands clasped over her mouth, blood oozing from between her fingers, and when he tore her hands away from her face he saw two deep bites in her upper lip.

"Halvor gasped and made a dash for the door. He seemed to explode internally; he completely lost his self-control, stumbled over his own feet on the stairs, and fell headlong on the grass as if an assassin had slugged him from behind.

"For a moment he lay face down on the ground sniffing the fragrance of wet grass, swearing heartily in a muffled tone at the earth beneath him. When he looked up, he saw the squirrel sitting on a stump, its bushy tail straight in the

72

air, and its round black eyes staring at him without any hatred. Halvor fumbled behind him for his ax, grabbed hold of it, and without benefit of either prayer or curse swung it defiantly above his head, and then hurled it with all his might directly at the culprit. The ax whirled around a couple of times, gleaming in the light of early dawn, and then struck the stump and stuck fast. The squirrel escaped, rump in the air, smacked contentedly, and scampered off into the sandpit.

" 'Now I've got him,' thought Halvor, and took off in the same direction, jerked the ax out of the stump in passing, and continued in hot pursuit.

"When he saw the squirrel in the middle of the sandpit, he flung the ax in an arc above it. The weapon disappeared in the sand, but the landslide he had expected didn't follow, and with a long succession of exultant cluckings the elusive reprobate escaped over the edge.

"Halvor's anger overpowered him, prostrated him, blinded him, and drove him to climbing and pawing in the sand, for he knew that if he were to preserve his sanity he had to rid himself of this plague by some kind of insane means.

"Then came the slide he had wished for. He was pinned and kneaded like a pine cone down into the sand. His eyes and mouth were filled, and that made him never worry again about the sound of crumbling grit.

"When he regained command of himself, he was standing imprisoned up to his neck, unable to move a finger. He spit out a mouthful of sand pellets, that rolled down to the bottom, and by blinking his eyes several times he cleared them enough to get a view of the valley. But he was incarcerated and powerless. He wept; he could do nothing else in his situation and he swore loudly and clearly so there shall be no doubt. The Devil! The Devil! He wept a little more and then quieted down. 'Deliver us from evil,' he mumbled, twisting his head to both sides to determine whether he had broken any bones.

"The hours passed; and the night-time sun shone for a moment on Halvor's bald crown. It seemed as if a severed head sat in a sandpit and wept, surrounded by an expanse of gold dust and gilt. The birches shimmered rosy-green when a breeze stirred them, and the pines stood up tall and rust-colored like pillars under the darkened ceiling of the forest.

"Halvor felt wordless and empty. Where he could see across the valley, the river flowed in a blue light toward the sea, and the tree-covered mountain ridges stretched upward. Clouds drifted along the mountains.

" 'Here there is no hurry about anything.' Halvor was pensive. 'There is ample time. Will I just stand here until I crumble away wi‘h the sand? So here we live, a family from the sea, and when this sandpit has sunk a half yard over my grassy plain, then we will have vanished.' Trunkless as he had now become, he realized the full meaning of loneliness and of eternity. He had indeed experienced this feeling before whenever he looked into the pale gray eyes of a dead fish but never so keenly as now.

"Only his head was alive. Arms and legs were locked in six feet of sand. They were of no concern to him now; they would never be crippled by rheumatism or lamed by muscular atrophy. But his spirit became still; it was enclosed in a cube at the top of his skull and scanned the beauty of the summer night. Centuries passed like chains of clouds drifting above the valley. Five hundred years swept by, gigantic pines withered, moldered, and turned into earth, new ones sprang up astoundingly fast, the annual rings circled like whirligigs within the trunks. In a minute's time the whole valley changed its dress. He caught the fresh smell of sun-warmed wood and resin. Two thousand years had sped by, and the valley lay there new—just as it is to-night—just as now.

"'Deliver us from evil,' he was mumbling again. 'Here one must accept things willingly,' he thought, 'here one must be shrewd and patient; otherwise the valley will have none of us.'

✿ ✿ ✿

"Halvor Mikkelsen's head stood there, collared by sand, until morning. It had eternity to draw upon. Now and then it slept, bobbing up and down, making a sinister picture with the dark woods all around, for it looked as if a person kept walking incessantly on the very same spot.

"With the dawn of a new day Halvor struggled to twist his neck and to move his jaws, so it seemed that his head had fallen victim to an onset of Saint Vitus's dance.

"'Forgive us our trespasses,' he murmured through closed lips. The prayer seemed to issue from a human torso deep in a bed of sand.

"He wondered whether to call the children. He shut his eyes and tried. 'Bertinus! Hanna!' Suddenly he stopped, astonished. It was the first time he had ever called them by name. Never before had he done that, and at once memories of the island they had come from swarmed into his mind, and he remembered the sea forever girdling the little skerry out there. This night the island had been bathed in sunlight. Now in summer all the birds were silent at night. He thought about birth and death, about children and drowning, and about all the turmoil through the years—about frost and salt-water sores on his fingers. 'Bertinus! Hanna!'

"Presently he discovered the children in the doorway staring at him. Cautiously they crept nearer, the boy holding his sister's hand.

"When they got to the lower edge of the sandpit, they

75

stood still, in tears. 'Is it you, Father?' Bertinus looked down.

" 'What are you doing there?' cried Hanna. 'Why are you crying?'

" 'I got sand in my eyes,' Halvor barked, shaking his head. 'There was a landslide last night. As you can see I am in it up to my knees.'

" 'You're in it up to your neck, Father.' This was the first time Hanna had dared look up at him.

" 'Come and dig me out, son. Don't just stand there and stare! The spade is beside the house.'

*　*　*

"They worked for an hour, the boy with the spade and the girl with a piece of board, before they succeeded in extricating their father. They had to rest at intervals and sat down on the sand to survey the valley and the surroundings.

"Halvor didn't begin his work until the sun had climbed high above the mountains toward the south. Suddenly he had come to feel he had ample time ahead of him. He prepared trout and pancakes for their breakfast—a completely new meal none of them had tasted before—and they sat on the doorstep a long time, just eating and listening to the deep rumbling of the river that flowed into the woods.

"The next morning Halvor Mikkelsen was unusually quiet while he pattered about putting things in order. Then he chopped his ax deeply into a pine log, thereby establishing this spot as his home. He looked long and intently at everything around him to fix it all irrefutably into his very inner being.

"So far the squirrel had not appeared. Halvor had begun to think far into the future, he had already started being a farmer, and he knew that intervals of peace afford the

76

Powers opportunity to brew trouble. Consequently, he instructed his son to keep careful watch over his little sister and the house while he would be away from them for a day or two. He must also guard the dried fish—always the barrier between them and starvation.

"Then he went down to sea to borrow a gun."

HALVOR AND THE COWARDLY CURATE

"Halvor had already trampled his own path to the sea. It meandered through the woods following the same winding course as did the river, and the valley had sanctioned this new thoroughfare. Battalions of ants crossed it and fought wars on its borders; corpses lay like spices sprinkled on the battlefield when Halvor's seven-league boots crushed them. Animals stopped on the path to sniff the tracks— human footprints. Halvor Mikkelsen's from the sea, they guessed. A Christian man's! If we follow them up the slope, perhaps they will lead to a chicken coop.

"The woods speculated, too: some of our trees are gone— there—and there—Halvor Mikkelsen's boots—and even long after he had disappeared his footfalls echoed in the marrow of their trunks. The path had taken on the familiarly secure brown of the forest floor. Surely a man with serious intentions had made this route, a man whose footsteps did not falter.

"And so to the coast, to the sea once again! Halvor quickened his pace. He caught the tang of salt and the feel of raw chill a half mile away. 'I am going to visit the sea,' he reflected. 'God protect all who live on the sea.'

"He dragged the long-boat to the mouth of the river and rigged it for cruising. Then he fetched the chest with the book of household sermons, placed it in the bulkhead, took his seat at the helm, and shoved off—keeping close to shore.

"At dinner time he anchored outside a farm that lay some distance from the fjord. It was the home of his mother's brother, and he thought he might be able to borrow a gun.

"The family were eating their meal when he approached. With the book tucked under his arm, he walked directly in, greeted them, said grace, and sat down on a box with peat beside the stove. As they all turned from the table to look at him, he noticed fat dripping from the corners of their mouths. They've butchered a sheep, he observed. He told them who he was and that he had just moved into the valley, explained that he had been bothered by a bear that made off with his livestock, and asked whether he might borrow a gun to rid himself of this marauder.

" 'Halvor Meikkelsa, eh, eh? Nothing but a child the last time I saw you!' The farmer smiled derisively and continued eating. 'How long has my sister lain in her grave by now?'

" 'Fifteen years Saint Olaf's Day. She died when Father was lost.'

" 'Oh, yes, you've always been stubborn, you people out there among the skerries. Now then, you've perhaps come to your senses at last and pulled up on land—eh?'

"The farmer went on eating, the fat running down his chin on its well-marked course into his beard.

" 'It was about this gun—' Halvor reminded him.

" 'The gun—well, yes, I have a good gun for shooting bears, but how can I be sure it will be brought back?'

"Halvor's face got white, and the two furrows that looked like magnificent swells on his forehead threatened to break the skin. 'Your sister was my mother, but I have discovered here on the coast blood is thinner than water. So I brought with me my mother's book. You've perhaps read it, too, at one time, and if not, then you may read it now; perhaps you'll find a little message there.'

78

"The farmer smirked again. He sucked the fat up out of his beard with a smacking sound—a sound that as much as said to him that his frugality had made him what he was today.

" 'Take the gun. And I don't need your book. I've managed without it up to now. But if you don't return the gun—may the Devil get you!'

" 'That he will in any case,' Halvor answered and got up to leave.

"At this time the rector at Bodö had two assistant pastors—or two resident curates—under him, and it was one of their churches Halvor visited after taking leave of his well-fed uncle. The sun was still high and warm in the late afternoon when he trudged westward along the coast. He carried the gun on his shoulder and the book under his arm—a crusader in the Arctic, fortified against both visible and invisible powers.

"The church stood on a barren mountain crag, its north side gray and weather-beaten by the caresses of hard winter storms, and its low spire askew like a clown's hat on the ridgepole.

"Halvor looked all around and saw no one near the church. 'It's a sunny day and the sea is calm,' he reflected, 'but when the boats begin to float by with keels upturned, then they come trickling in—widows and orphans.'

"He laid the book on the grass and propped the gun against the wall. Then he climbed up and pried loose a seven-inch strip of lead from around the window frame, but just as he was about to climb down he happened to look into the church. There was a figure kneeling at the altar—a small, thin man, bald and ashen like a frozen bubble on top of solid ice, with long, sand-colored tufts of hair around his ears.

79

"Up to now Halvor had fared very well, good luck had made him humble, and he clasped his hands around the strip of lead while trying to bring to mind a suitable prayer. But since he couldn't manage to hold on securely and pray at the same time, he tipped backward and fell down from the church wall.

" 'The Almighty is in high spirits today and He's making a fool of me,' he concluded, getting up on his feet again. At that moment the door opened and the man came out. He was colorless as bone, sallow, and beardless, and while he stood staring at Halvor he kept rubbing his chest and his hips.

"His voice was hoarse. 'Who are you? What are you doing here?'

"Halvor stuck the strip of lead into his pocket, stooped down to pick up the book, and clapped his other hand over the muzzle of the gun as if he were afraid it would blurt out something.

" 'I've come from far away and don't know whether I even belong in your district.'

" 'Good Lord!' The man shifted nervously. 'I didn't mean to offend you, but I am the pastor here.'

"Halvor tucked the book under his arm. 'That may well be. I didn't mean to offend anyone either, but where I live we are very far away from a church. Anyway, I think God has seen that I have chopped out a clearing in the woods by the sandpit, so the pastor must forgive—'

" 'Certainly, certainly. I, too, favor a direct approach. It was only out of human curiosity that I asked.'

" 'Of course. I am Halvor Mikkelsen from over in the valley, and now I have stolen a little bit of lead from your window frame because a bear is raiding my sheepfold.'

" 'Oh, yes, yes, we all have our troubles—I, not least.' The pastor sighed, scratching himself with his long, bony fingers.

" 'If the pastor has lice, the best remedy is sulphur. I learned that from my mother.'

" 'Not lice, not lice, my good Halvor Mikkelsen! But it may be we should be prepared for sulphur some time in the future—, but Good Heavens! I am a miserable creature.'

" 'Well, I suppose that's what makes us brothers and equals, though I wouldn't dare suggest that my misery—'

" 'Not so humble, not so humble, Halvor Mikkelsen,' cried the curate, putting his hand to his ear to smooth down the tufts of hair. 'I am the one who must be humble, I who cannot do well in my calling.'

" 'My calling consists of two hungry children and a pile of dried fish,' Halvor answered, 'and I don't feel humble but I get angry when I see them suffer.'

" 'God doesn't tolerate anger.' The curate spoke hoarsely.

" 'He has given me a tough lot in life. I am not just suddenly angry. I have been angry a long, long time. The sea makes one that way.'

" 'All anger shall sometime be silenced, remember that.'

" 'I forget it every time the children have to be fed.'

" 'You must bear your burden.'

" 'Yes, my burden, but the children are not in the least equipped to bear their burden.'

" 'You mustn't pronounce judgment.'

" 'I'm not pronouncing judgment. I am simply saying that bad weather and poor fishing are to blame.'

" 'Everything rests in God's hand.'

" 'Yes, in His fist.' "

" 'You have an answer for everything, Halvor Mikkelsen.' The pastor looked around nervously, restless and uneasy. The different parts of his anatomy seemed to have been assembled awkwardly. 'You have a solution to every problem. That's false confidence.'

" 'Not confidence, I wouldn't say. Only a pretense. When

I have a good day now and then I carry on a game of make-believe with the Lord. Yes, I do, for who knows? To me it often seems that we are only His playthings. I can't help thinking so when I watch my children barricading the ants in the act of dragging pine needles to their ant hills. Eventually the ants crawl up on the sticks the children are using, only to be crushed underfoot or thrown aside.'

" 'You have hardened your heart, Halvor Mikkelsen.'

" 'It has always been so,' laughed Halvor. 'It's soft in good weather and hard in bad weather.'

"The little yellowish eyes of the pastor darted in all directions. 'All the same, you're well off, Halvor Mikkelsen, but I'm an unfortunate soul.'

"Halvor shrugged his shoulders and put the gun under his arm. 'If it's not too prying, I'd like to ask the curate what his problem is.'

" 'Oh, Good Lord,' cried the little man, wringing his hands. 'No one can help me. I am lost—condemned.'

" 'Two lost souls who help one another create more joy in Heaven than ten thousand not in need of help.'

" 'Even if you have the courage to take fate into your own hands,' shouted the pastor, 'that gives you no right, Halvor Mikkelsen, to misquote Scripture.'

" 'I've always had a poor memory,' answered Halvor. 'Often I wander about for hours hunting my gear simply because I haven't a clue where I left it.'

" 'You have a wretched man before you,' the pastor said bitterly. 'You ought not ridicule his weakness.'

" 'I'm not ridiculing anyone.' Halvor was serious. 'And if I sound that way it's because of my clumsiness in expressing myself. I always try my best to help. That is a philosophy we have on the sea, so if the pastor will tell—'

" 'Oh, no, no, no one can help me. I am a complete failure. Nothing succeeds. I can't endure the sea. I can't stand the wind here. I pray fervently, but afterwards I feel nothing but emptiness.'

" 'Perhaps the pastor doesn't have faith,' suggested Halvor.

" 'Faith! Faith! It's not so much a matter of faith. I think it's rather the climate. Everything seems to blow away from me—prayers and thoughts and good intentions. No one comes to church to hear me. And what's more,' the pastor lowered his voice in despair, 'yes, what's more, I'm afraid of the dark."

" 'Afraid of the dark?'

" 'Yes, I'm afraid of the dark inside the church and of the dark outside in the winter. In this part of the country it's everlastingly dark.'

" 'But now we have sunlight all night. Doesn't the pastor feel that it is God's eye watching over us constantly?'

" 'But the darkness is within my soul, my good Halvor Mikkelsen and,—' The pastor broke off as if suddenly hearing something. He craned his neck, and the tufts of hair hung like wilted straw around a barren island. 'Listen.' He turned. 'Hear the Maelstrom. Now it's rushing again. I can't stand the roar of that current. Every time I hear it, I get a nervous itching. Four times in every twenty-four hours my body gets all scaly.'

" 'This is really a serious situation,' thought Halvor and shifted the book of household sermons to his other arm. 'I have sailed that current when it was coming in.'

" 'No, no!' The pastor was screaming wildly. 'That's not possible. No one could do that! Did you pray constantly?'

" 'I lowered the sail and steered the boat where the water looked smoothest.'

" 'I believe you,' the curate answered in a muffled voice. 'An experience like that either makes a man a believer or destroys whatever faith he may have.'

" 'I held her a little to the inside of the foaming edge

and then let her go right through the whirlpool,' said Halvor thoughtfully. 'But my boat is like a person—most like a woman,' he laughed. 'Submissive—so that you can tack her against the northwester.'

"'Don't jest, Halvor Mikkelsen. Don't talk like that about the sea. I can't stand to talk about the sea. In my prayers I include everyone who sails.'

"'In my haste I forgot all about that when I plowed into that current. All I thought of was my rudder and my sail.'

"'Now you're joking again,' the pastor answered. 'I never stop praying, but still I feel this bitter emptiness.'

"'Has the pastor tried cursing?'

"The pastor hesitated. 'I've done that, too, a couple of times.'

"'What did the pastor say then?'

"'I said—What the Devil—! I was busy repairing the steeple up there. It's falling down, and my parishioners give me no assistance whatsoever. They don't pay their tithes either,' he whimpered, 'and I'm often hungry.'

"'It's a shame,' said Halvor, 'that the steeple is toppling. It must be a good seamark, for the church stands on such high ground. I would be so willing to help if I only had my tools here.'

"'Oh, yes! If you would! There's an ax and there's a saw, too, up on the roof.'

"Halvor set his gun against the door of the church, laid the book on the threshold, and climbed up to examine the leaning steeple. The pastor crawled up behind him and sat astride the ridge of the roof on the opposite side. He breathed hard and shut his eyes. 'I'm dizzy,' he whined. 'And the worst is getting down again. I've often sat up here many hours before I had the strength to climb down. At first I had to practice in order to get used to heights.

84

I'd go up two rungs on the ladder and then down. The next time I'd try three, and then four, and so on, until I finally made it all the way to the roof. Oh, it's a tough vocation to serve out here.'

" 'Yes, I suppose that's the way to faith here on the coast —one step at a time,' Halvor philosophized. 'But there are termites in your steeple. We'll have to remove that beam and those boards.'

" 'Yes, I see the trouble well enough,' the pastor sighed, but every time I'm about to start working, my tools all fall to the ground.'

" 'That's the way it is on the sea, too,' Halvor answered. 'You have to keep one hand on the rudder, the other on the ropes, and your eyes on the water.'

"The curate still sat puffing and clinging to the steeple. 'I wanted, God forgive my vanity, I wanted to inspire people here by taking the lead in this task of repairing, but I am too weak. And perhaps the hope of gaining their respect is the only thing that helps me control my dizziness. I am that miserable.'

" 'He who humbles himself will be exalted, I've heard. But here's a magpie's nest in the tower!'

" 'I don't humble myself. I'm being humbled.' The pastor looked carefully down at the ground. 'Everything that grows in nature thrives on my humiliation.'

" 'If we're going to save the nest, we'll have to go about this very cautiously,' warned Halvor as he began to pound loose the rotting supports.

" 'Not a sparrow falls to earth except by His will.'

" 'He has so many irons in the fire,' added Halvor solemnly. 'I think you and I will take this matter of the magpie's nest into our own hands.'

" 'You must be a strong unbeliever, Halvor Mikkelsen, who dares to scoff so loudly and openly.'

" 'I've eaten mussels and red algae for weeks when the fishing has been bad. I don't scoff at anything.'

"The pastor hung on tightly while they worked in silence. The sky was clear and blue as ice, the sun was high, and a few fluffy clouds came drifting in with the sea breeze, white and airy like foam on the vault of heaven.

"After a strenuous half hour Halvor stuck his ax into the beam and said, 'Now if the pastor will support the steeple with his shoulder while I straighten it, I think we can make this God's house as fit as any other here on the coast.'

" 'I'll try. I pray He will give me strength to stand it.'

" 'We'll have to exert ourselves in accordance with His will,' Halvor answered cheerfully. 'He has placed heavier burdens on weaker backs than the minister's.'

"Halvor stood up and tilted the steeple to set it perfectly straight, while the woeful servant of the Lord supported it from underneath. Then Halvor eased the weight down upon him and laughed. 'Now take a deep breath and hold it. Don't exhale or it will sag again.'

"Pinned between the steeple and the ridge of the roof, the pastor groaned and creaked like dry wood. The veins stood out on his yellow forehead like rivers on a globe. 'If only the Bodö rector had assigned me a sexton,' he moaned.

" 'The Lord's own father was a carpenter,' replied Halvor, driving a nail into the beam.

" 'I can't get loose,' cried the pastor. 'I'm stuck fast, and Sunday the rector from Alstadhaug is coming on visitation.'

" 'I've heard he is as strong as an ox.'

" 'Halvor Mikkelsen, you surely aren't going to leave me lying here alone!'

" 'Right now we are both closer to Heaven than we've ever been before. Now it's only a matter of your holding out until I can make a wedge. But it has to be exactly the same width as your shoulders, and I'll have to go down because I don't have a piece of wood here that's narrow enough.'

" 'Don't make fun of me, Halvor Mikkelsen,' cried the pastor. 'The Creator hasn't lavished much on me, I know, but just the same it isn't Christian to ridicule people.'

" 'Then He will have to forgive me. I didn't intend to ridicule, but I haven't any better measure to judge by than the curate himself.' With that, Halvor clambered down.

"In the boat-shed he found a suitable piece that he whittled down and took with him up on the roof. The pastor had become flatter; he lay motionless under the spire. 'I can't take any more,' he gurgled.

" 'Here I am,' Halvor answered and drove the wedge in. 'This wedge is to the glory of God. But being a minister is certainly a more demanding job than I had imagined.'

"The curate backed out of the vise. He drew a quivering breath. His forehead bore the imprint of a knot in the wood—as if now at last he had acquired a divine stamp.

" 'Now it stands straight,' Halvor commented appraisingly, his eyes tracing the rise of the steeple.

"The pastor murmured, 'I already feel much better. In fact, I can even bear to look down—how wonderful!'

" 'Yes, and the magpie's nest hasn't been disturbed,' noted Halvor. 'Babies and eggs won't roll out of there now.'

"The curate massaged his neck and felt his head. 'Actually, my good Halvor Mikkelsen, I do feel better.'

" 'Of course, and your parishioners will notice the change. They won't need to cock their heads to one side to get a straight view of the spire.'

"The pastor looked upward. 'It points right up to God's footstool now. I feel as if a load has been lifted from my heart.'

" 'It's five o'clock.' Halvor looked to the east. 'I see they are going in to the afternoon meal at my uncle's farm. The

87

shadow of your spire points directly at the cow-barn over there, so hereafter you can use the church as a clock out here.'

"Carefully smoothing the tufts of hair into place, the curate sighed, 'I owe you a debt of gratitude.'

" 'That can be turned to good account, for I, too, am in debt,' Halvor replied. 'But now I hear that pair of magpies over there in the pastor's rowan tree are getting very impatient, and I have a long way to go home.'

"They climbed down. Halvor took his gun and his book of household sermons and made his way east along the shore. He found his boat where he had left it, and very soon the sea breeze filled the square-sail and sent the long-boat swiftly and smoothly on its way."

THE SQUIRREL HUNT

"There you see, Mylady," said Pastor Celion, smiling. "Florelius hates ministers. He never passes up an opportunity to show it, and if no opportunity arises of itself, he goes to no end of trouble to create one even at the risk of interrupting a good story. His hatred of ministers surpasses his love of storytelling. For that matter, it's understandable also that he has never married. I'd like to see the one who could drag him to the altar."

The governor allowed Pastor Celion to speak his mind. Moreover, he pretended to listen with undivided attention and exemplary courtesy to what his friend had to say. But it was obvious that his politeness was intentional. He wanted the effect to be completely devastating when he continued his story without so much as a word of commentary on the pastor's interjection.

The sun climbed higher. It seemed as if the very atmosphere itself had developed greater awareness. The only

88

sound to break the stillness was the thin squeak of the rudder as it moved in the water.

Mylady sat lost in dreams. Sometimes she smiled, hesitantly, distantly, from deep within, as if the smile were a treasure she had kept hidden a long time and now was apprehensive about exposing for all to see.

"When Halvor came home that evening, he stood for a while at the edge of the woods surveying his domain. 'I am not asking for anything,' he thought. 'I am not begging of anyone, but if we are lucky enough to be allowed a long, mild autumn, I'll—yes, I'll use it to chop some logs and build a sheepshed. And I must cut the grass in the birch groves along the river and put out my nets and traps and build a roof over the dried fish. And then if the autumn stays mild long enough, I'll gather leaves and store them in a shed because I think I can barter for a sheep or two. And then— yes, and then I must certainly start breaking ground, too, down by the river so I can plant grain early in the spring.' He laughed as he looked up into the valley. 'Well, I suppose winter has come to stay by then, and then I'll have plenty of time to plan.'

"Halvor Mikkelsen went into his house; he stopped beside the children's bed and listened to their sleeping. When he leaned down over them, he noticed the little girl's upper lip was swelled. He laid the book of sermons at the foot of the bed and went out again at once. He walked down to the river. There he searched along the water's edge until he found a fern with hairy, succulent leaves. He took the fern with him, and while he walked back to the house, he rolled the leaves together and kneaded them into a soft ball. Then he went indoors and placed a glob of the sticky pulp on the child's swollen lip.

"Afterwards he took his gun and a bag of powder and

closed the door behind him. Just then the sunlight broke through a cleft in the mountains toward the east. Dawn took a shortcut across the river and through the woods and cast a shaft of sparkling light onto the very top of the sandpit.

" 'I see it,' Halvor was thinking excitedly, 'I see it clearly: the dawn of a new day. But I have eyes in all directions. I'm on guard. I know anything can happen—yes, indeed. While my back is turned, my little boy can chop an ax into his foot, my little girl can poke a knife into her eye, my house can burn down, we can starve and freeze to death, and one day a bear can come and kill the sheep that I don't even own yet. But I'll never give up. I'll never give up—never—even if the devil in person equipped with hoofs and horns appears at my door.'

"He stamped his foot into the ground, but the turf was soft and spongy and responded to his temper with forbearance. Gradually he regained his composure; his face assumed its usual expression of attentiveness and anticipation. Halvor Mikkelsen the fisherman had not yet become a full-fledged farmer.

"He took the strip of lead, kneaded it, and shaped it into three balls that he put into his pocket and one more that he put into his gun. Thereupon he adjusted the primer and laid the gun on the ground. Then he sat down with his back against the wall, pulled his hat down over his forehead, and pretended to be asleep.

"The valley was immersed in sunlight. To Halvor it seemed like a bowl, and in a few minutes it would be filled to the brim. He could watch day floating in above the mountain ridge in the east. He could see it especially well when a few low-hanging clouds filtered the light on the rim. This was just the kind of morning Halvor greeted with a welcoming nod. At this instant he believed in the Creator. Our

Lord is punctual. He races over the vast expanse pouring light into all the out-of-the-way places of the land. The very bottom of the valley was flooded with light so everything came into view: twigs, grass, moss, heather, and fallen pine giants. It was like a jungle at sunrise, steaming with compost and fresh plants, with newly formed mold of the last two years, and with the never-changing sour marsh that had preserved its deposit of sticks and vegetation through thousands of years.

"Halvor was looking at it all through half-closed eyes. Then suddenly he heard the crumbling noise of falling sand—a disintegrating sound—but nevertheless one that brought him quickly back to the immediate present, and squinting up from under his hat, he spied a squirrel scurrying down the slope.

"He fumbled around to get hold of his gun, and then, eyes fixed steadily on the little creature, he slipped quietly down into the tall grass and took aim. The squirrel was still too far away, but Halvor kept his gun aimed. The barrel followed the animal's movements, drawing hieroglyphs in the air, up and down, from summit to branch.

"Now it was coming closer. It was a big beautiful specimen, its coat thick and glossy. Halvor continued to sight it along the barrel of his gun. He aimed at a spot just below the little pointed ears, but it took a long jump, swung onto a lower branch, and then hustled off to another slightly higher. The gun barrel moved right along in the same pattern. 'You're making an S curve,' thought Halvor, 'but you continue to stay in this same tree. What does that mean?' And the squirrel really did seem to confine himself to this one tree. It leaped from branch to branch, now higher up and again lower down, sometimes close to the trunk and again sometimes near the outermost clusters of pine needles.

"'Indeed,' Halvor thought, 'it knows the alphabet. That's an A and there, straight up on the trunk and down the other side, that makes a T. Write some more, you little devil, I am reading letters in the air. Now we've come as far as SAT, and that may turn out to be Saturn, which my father said is the name of a star—but he was perhaps not always dependable—or Satoma, the name of a Lapp sailor in Beiarn who brought misfortune to a whole crew because they refused to ferry him across the fjord. If this is intended to be a riddle, you are offending me, you little demon; I was never any great genius, but I've been a fisherman all my life and am quite accustomed to figuring things out. And now you needn't sketch any more designs on the slate up there because my index finger is on the trigger, and now—'

"The squirrel streaked off like an arrow straight through the tree, and before Halvor was able to fire a shot, it disappeared in the brush on the other side of the house.

"Halvor jumped up, gun in hand, to give chase. He started off into the pine-barrens. The pine-barrens in the Salten district are the aristocrats among woods in our country, a proud race. Nowhere else can one find trees so solitary; each tree is a forest by itself. There are open spaces between them; they maintain their independence. The trunks are bare of branches a long way up from the roots, and the crowns sort of look past one another. Nonetheless, together they are a clan united. When the east wind comes howling down from the mountains in the autumn, a deep melancholy lament sighs through the branches, the pine-barrens' national anthem. The trunks, too, stretch to their full height and join in with a loud arrogant accompaniment, like a single strong battalion concentrated on a major effort.

"The squirrel darted through these woods, and all at once pine needles started to shake as if all the crowns were sudden victims of a violent headache.

"Halvor Mikkelsen kept running on the flat, slippery forest floor, his gun in his right hand. He had never been a champion sprinter—a fisherman seldom is—and soon he had to stop for breath. He leaned against the trunk of a pine, his heart pounding so one could have counted the beats through his shirt that stuck to his skin. The squirrel was resting, too. It sat, its profile toward him, licking its feet lazily, expertly. Now and again it smacked loudly and distinctly in the roomy woods and shifted its position as if to announce that it was sitting here now—a conspicuous target against the pale sky.

"Halvor stared up at the animal. The tiny close-set eyes glittered with a hard relentless luster, the sharp rat-like teeth were exposed, and a little circular muscle worked swiftly under the skin covering the hollows of the cheeks.

"Halvor kneeled and cocked his gun. Was there someone in the woods? Did a twig break? No—but he heard a faint sigh. Perhaps one of the pine-giants shed the vestige of an arm? It had taken three hundred summers and winters to incubate this little report of a branch falling in the stillness. He laughed to himself. The thought struck him that he was a fish on the ocean floor; up above was the bait. He raised his gun—this time steadying it against his face. Hsst! Pine needles fell, and the squirrel disappeared into the next tree.

"The pursuit went on. The object of the chase swung in wide arcs from the crown of one tree to the crown of another, and each time the stalker came near enough to take aim, his quarry found refuge on the back side of another tree trunk.

"The sun climbed higher, it was warm, and the woods smelled of resin. Every so often Halvor's foot would come down on an ant hill and demolish a whole summer's laborious building project. At last he fell on his knees against an uncovered root. He laid his gun aside and looked at the root, his chest heaving like a pair of bellows.

" 'One hand in the earth,' he thought—'to be a farmer! Yes, yes, that was indeed his intention, but that is apparently not to be accomplished in a hurry by one who has sat holding a fish-line all his life. Alone and free in the woods—perhaps the Evil One will allow this choice spot. I've never really hurt anyone, except the fish. Oh, well, maybe I have stolen a few gulls' eggs on rare occasions.'

"Halvor thumped his fist against the root. 'And then I have boxed the children's ears three or four times a year, I suppose, but after all that is recommended in Scripture. True, their mother did walk into the sea, but surely a person can't be held accountable for someone who steps into the water when she ought to stay on dry land. And then—Hell's Bells—I took a sheep, but it was so very thin and as light as a pitch of hay on a pitchfork.'

"Was there another noise in the woods?

"Halvor lay still, chewing his fingernails, looking in all directions, breathing slowly and unevenly. No, just one of the senior giants again discarding a useless limb. The stub would be left to hang on like a peg for another hundred years. 'By that time we'll all be under the sod—all of us here in the woods.'

"Halvor gripped his gun and cocked it. There was the squirrel sitting on just such a peg, relaxed, halfway up on the trunk, beautifully silhouetted. He pressed the stock firmly against his face—a butterfly flitted past—and psst! The culprit took off up the trunk, leaving behind him a trail of falling needles.

"Halvor dropped his gun and screamed, 'I'll get you! I'll never give up. I'll follow you over the mountains above the timberline and down through a new valley and over a new

94

mountain—for one day we will reach the sea again, and then I will kill you on the beach.' ✗

"Halvor ran on farther across the pine-barrens until he suddenly found himself at the edge of the forest. The squirrel leaped to the ground, sped over an opening covered with grass and bracken, and promptly disappeared in a grove of scrubby birches. Again Halvor set out after it, but when he emerged from the trees, the miscreant was nowhere in sight. Instead he saw a small building in the middle of a clearing. It was built of heavy pine logs, a square house, with a flat roof surrounded by a three-foot-high breastwork. The door stood open, and the interior was dark. There were no windows at all—only two small openings that looked like embrasures.

" 'Now I've got it,' he concluded. 'It darted in there, the little devil, so now I'll shut the door and set fire to the building.'

"He lowered his gun in readiness and approached carefully. He felt something catching his foot, and when he leaned down he discovered a tight wire around the edge of the clearing. At the same time he heard a ringing up above on the roof, a sound not unlike that of a bell-wether on the mountains in autumn, and the next moment a figure appeared in the doorway.

" 'Stop!' He had a big bow in hand, the arrow pointed straight at Halvor's chest. He was tall, slender, broad-shouldered, and erect, dressed in skins from head to foot. His eyes were ice-blue and clear, his curly hair hung down at the nape of his neck from under the fur cap, and his chin was hidden under the iron-gray beard that reached down over his chest.

" 'Get away! Make yourself scarce!' the man shouted, the bow bending menacingly.

"At first Halvor let himself be intimidated by this authoritative voice and instinctively backed up a step or two, but suddenly he stopped and stood up to his full height.

" 'If these are your woods, you certainly don't need to bark at me so fiercely.' He spit into the grass. 'Besides I see neither a trench nor a fence here.'

" 'Get off!' yelled the fur-clad gray-beard again, threatening anew.

" 'Well, well, well, old fellow, I was reared on the sea, and no man owns the sea,' Halvor replied angrily.

" 'Go away!'

" 'Ha, ha!' Infuriated, Halvor laughed loudly. He retraced his steps in among the trees, turned around very deliberately, lifted his gun into position along a branch, and took aim at the stranger.

" 'Now we're equals. Can you hear me, old man? I have you covered. I'm aiming at the third button from the top, and now you'll be so kind as to answer my questions.'

"The man made no reply, but Halvor saw him blink his ice-blue eyes and crane his neck as if sniffing the air.

" 'I don't have time to quarrel over boundaries in the woods,' Halvor said, 'but I'd like to know whether you've seen a squirrel go past here.'

"The fur-clad man appeared to be reconsidering; he lowered his bow and called, 'Who are you?'

" 'My name is Halvor Mikkelsen, and that's not so very important, but I live over there by the sandpit north in the valley, and I'd really like to find out whether you've seen a squirrel recently.'

"The old man took his arrow away from the string and put it into the quiver he carried on his back. 'This is a ridiculous situation!' he exclaimed. 'Let's be reasonable. Come over here closer, step across the wire, and lay aside your gun.'

"Halvor leaned his flintlock against a tree and approached the house. 'I'll have to trust you wouldn't shoot an unarmed person,' he said, approaching the house, 'but as yet I don't know the accepted practice down here in the valley.'

"The man dressed in skins stared at him a long time, lost in thought, troubled, with an expression of being displeased with himself.

" 'I've lived here in the woods fifteen years, and you're the first person to come so near me.'

" 'Well, I'm not in the habit of intruding on people, and of course where I come from that's hardly possible anyway, but this building stood right on my path, and so—' Halvor said.

" 'For fifteen years,' repeated the old man, pensive and a little sad, as if the fifteen years represented a hoard of money now suddenly lost. 'Summer and winter—that's not so short a time.'

" 'No, that's right to the very year the length of time my father has lain drowned in the sea.'

" 'The fact is I never let anyone come close to me.' The recluse spoke gruffly and extended his hand as if to shove off an invisible creature.

" 'I'd like to say the same, but I have a visitor steadily, and a wire stretched around my house would not do any good. But I'll leave you now,' Halvor said. 'It's a pity I trespassed because you're perhaps trying to set a record of being alone and I've ruined a game for you.'

" 'Solitude is no game, Mr.—'

" 'Halvor Mikkelsen.'

" 'Mikkelsen, solitude is a devoted friend. I wouldn't exchange it for anything. What's more, I can't understand why I admitted you here. That was foolish.' He was looking intently at Halvor. 'But there's something about your face.

I can't say just what it is, but it reminds me of something. Yes—yes—memories. It is just a farmer's face.'

" 'I'm still a fisherman though. Early tomorrow morning for the first time I'll be a farmer.'

" 'That doesn't make any difference. In any case you're a peasant, so maybe it doesn't matter so much that you came in here; what I'm afraid of is a visitor from the big noisy world—people of learning. They're the ones I must not let in. I saw from your face right away that you're a farmer. Of your kind I have no fear. So, now that the damage is done and you're here, you may as well sit up on the roof with me for a while. I have a couple of ptarmigan wings we can chew on.'

" 'But about this squirrel,' interrupted Halvor.

" 'Nonsense! I've never seen squirrels here in the woods. You must be mistaken. Follow me, and you'll see how a person lives.'

"The recluse laid his bow aside and led the way into the house. They entered a large dark room where light sifted in only through long narrow slits in the wall. Halvor noticed that the floor was carpeted with bear skins, in one corner stood a bench for sleeping, in the middle of the room were a rough-hewn table and two heavy stools, and on one wall hung two bows and a fur jacket.

"The man dressed in skins climbed a ladder through a trap door opening out onto the roof. 'Sit down, Squirrel-face.' He pointed to a rudely cut pine log. 'That's a hundred and fifty years old, so you can really sit securely.'

" 'We don't sit so badly on our splinter stools down on the hillside either,' Halvor said, 'but then, to be sure, we have worn out our seats more on thwarts than on parlor chairs.'

" 'A free man living in the woods is better off,' said the hermit.

98

" 'Certainly! I would perhaps also have been a free man now if this house of yours had not been in my way.'

" 'This house of mine? No tracks lead to it—neither of men nor of animals. All remain outside the wire.'

" 'No, but a squirrel moves from tree to tree. His course is precisely like that of a boat—no tracks. I've been acquainted with boats ever since I learned the sea is not for walking.'

" 'You poor fellow! You're surely dimsighted. There's no sign of a squirrel here. But do help yourself to a ptarmigan bone.'

"They chewed a while in silence, and then the host waved his ptarmigan wing taking in the whole valley in a fit of laughter.

" 'From here I can see you all. Look, Mikkelsen, there a little puff of smoke is rising, and there still another—and another. I have watched you all and have had fun looking at you struggling up through the valley with children and axes. The man whose smoke rises up there by the stream in front of the crag came two years ago. He crept like a snail with enormous sacks on his back; he entertained me for three days. Moving like worms—ha, ha,—and you call him a free man in the woods? The valley oozes with women and children. Free man in the woods? Look here! With this ptarmigan bone I can point out an opening in the valley bigger than any farm in this land. You're worms! Worms on a spongy marsh!'

" 'A marsh is better than the sea.' Halvor looked out over the valley. 'You can always crawl out of a marsh, and then you can dig a drain. You can't drain the sea.'

" 'You're a real creature of the soil, Halvor Mikkelsen, a genuine marsh-worm!'

" 'You can't grow rye on a rock, and you can't force a fish to bite. My wife was probably a worm—forgive my sinful words—Heaven only knows where she is now—but I have two children who have to have food!'

" 'Food! Food!' The old man cried contemptuously. 'I shoot what I need for food. Everything comes directly to me when I need it. When I'm hungry, presto—a rabbit shows up and waits at the edge of the woods. When I need a skin, then comes—Oh, oh—did you hear that signal?'

"Halvor turned to listen. A bell was attached to a pole on the breastwork, and from it four strings stretched out, one in each direction.

" 'Did you hear that, Mikkelsen? That was a weasel on my wire at the edge of the woods. I know all animals by the sound of the bell—marten, wolverine, weasel, rabbit, ptarmigan, fox—not to mention the devilish little lemming. During lemming years the bell rings night and day. Sometimes I get tired of it and disconnect it. Besides, the lemmings always come from the east, and there, as you can see, I have the brook between my house and the woods. They drown by the thousands and float down into the valley. Surely you get them in your fish nets sooner or later. So you see there's no dearth of things going on.'

" 'I've also tried chimes,' commented Halvor. 'That did absolutely no good.'

" 'And in the mating season, ho, ho!' The old man's face brightened. 'In the mating season they often ring to attract the females. A fox can run along for hours with his nose on the wire. I can tell by the noise what it's all about. And when the female comes, they immediately get into the act. On beautiful spring evenings the edge of my woods is one single extended bridal bed. So you see everything comes to me.'

" 'My wife drowned,' said Halvor, 'and I have really—may my sin be forgiven—not missed her much, but I do believe it would be quite dreary sitting here by myself listening for fox bitches.'

" 'Ha! You truly are a worm!' yelled the recluse, enthused. 'You creep on your belly and see nothing but muck.'

" 'I've considered going up into the valley in quest of a wife when my early spring's work is done,' Halvor said.

" 'Oh, that I'd like to see. I'll be on the watch next May. Worm Mikkelsen on a wooing expedition! It's far to the nearest neighbor. You'll have to spend the night in the woods on your way home.'

" 'I have done that before, and maybe we can find an empty fox den to crawl into.' Halvor felt his neck and ears getting hot.

" 'And besides, Mikkelsen?' said the fur-clad man stroking his beard.

" 'What do you mean—besides?'

" 'All the rest that could happen, of course.' The recluse was laughing. His ice-blue eyes sparkled with malicious delight. 'Think of it! Landslides and crop failures and the children getting sick and the river flooding your rye field, and maybe some day you're struck by a pine tree you're cutting down.'

" 'On the sea we say everything rests in God's clenched fist. We are all subject to His wrath.'

" 'Not I! Not I! My good Mikkelsen. If you will look around, you'll see that nothing can happen here. Look at that mountain. The way it stands, a landslide here would miss my house. I have food both summer and winter. I can hit an owl's eye within a thirty-yard range. The bell rings a warning whenever anyone approaches, and as you see I've leveled off the ground around the house and cleared away the underbrush in the woods so I can't stumble into something and break my neck. I've gone over the premises blindfolded to make a test. I have a little bridge across

101

the river, and every year I replace the logs. And there's a railing along the steps leading up here. Everything comes to me. Nothing can happen. I am alone. What more could anyone wish for?'

" 'Well, well, I suppose that's it.' Halvor tossed the gnawed-off ptarmigan bone over the breastwork. 'When a person can put up with fox bitches and shoot an owl in the eye at thirty yards, then he is pretty well fortified for the winter. But when my beard gets as long as yours is now, I could very well wish for someone to lend me a hand with the plow—and even for some little ones to get in my way when I'm the busiest.'

"The lone man rose up, walked over to the breastwork, and motioned for Halvor to follow him. He pointed out a rectangular elevation enclosed by a circle of stones down by the creek.

" 'Do you see that, Halvor Mikkelsen?' he said. He shut his eyes, his voice quivered, and the hand that was pointing trembled as if he were cold. 'There they lie—my loved ones.' He was whispering and the ice-blue eyes moistened. 'I visit that grave daily, and all summer I decorate it with flowers. Do you see I'm crying, Halvor Mikkelsen?'

" 'On the sea we have no graves, and if we cry no one pays any attention because our tears are brine. But when I become a farmer, I'll see to providing for myself a grave —when that time comes. It's nice to have the dead around, I think, but it's even better with the living.'

" 'Oh, you're a peasant and nothing more.' The fur-clad man was irritated and his eyes dried in a wink. 'Of course, there's no one buried in that grave; it's empty, but as often as I wish I can imagine that my loved ones lie there. Then I weep and think about them. So is not my sorrow as real as anyone else's? The dead are dead all the same. As you see, everything comes to me. And as far as the living are

102

concerned, I'll show you them. They hang on the north wall below. I've made charcoal sketches of them, and I don't think I'm such a bad artist. In any case, they're more alive than the living. I have three daughters and five sons: Birgit, Dolly, Gretel, Michael, Rex, Magnus, Amyas, and Negus. I talk with them as often as I like; in the evenings we sit up here and discuss things together.'

" 'Mine are named Bertinus and Hanna,' Halvor said, looking around for his gun. 'But then they come from poor parents, and the pastor could find no better names than those of my father and mother.'

" 'You're a stubborn mule, Halvor Mikkelsen!' The man suddenly shrieked at his visitor in a rage.

" 'Their noses run all winter. Often they have chest coughs. And I guess we've never—discussed—as you put it.'

" 'You're a worm, and you have about as much sense as a snail of what it means to live!'

"Halvor glanced around. 'Just so they don't get tangled up in my nets. The current is so strong right beyond.'

" 'If the river doesn't get them, they'll sink in a marsh,' the hermit yelled and stamped the floor. 'There's a marsh west of your sandpit, Halvor Mikkelsen, and it's full of cloud-berries in the autumn. The biggest and finest berries always grow on floating tufts.'

"Halvor was not listening. He had caught sight of two squirrel's ears protruding from the birch leaves at the edge of the grove.

" 'Good-by,' he called hurriedly and scrambled down the steps. 'Thank you for the ptarmigan wing. When I get to be a farmer, I'll invite my neighbors to a feast.'

"He dashed out of the house and ran, bent over like a weasel, across the grassy clearing clutching his gun.

"The squirrel scurried off right across the opening which was covered with ferns and tall grass. Halvor let out peals

103

of laughter as he ran in pursuit. By now the sun was almost directly in the south. Behind him he heard a bell clanging noisily, and the angry, intense sound followed him all the way to the pine-barrens."

The governor took a deep breath and looked triumphantly out across the sea. Then he chuckled. "Halvor Mikkelsen, stubborn mule that he was, was not a fast runner, and I can't let him jog around all summer on the pine-barrens of the Salten Valley.

"Now the chase continued in a northerly direction down toward the floor of the valley. Little by little the sun had dried the salt out of Halvor's hair so it blew wildly when he ran. Now and then his boots skidded on the pine needles carpeting the ground. Once he slipped on a root and fanned the air like a madman; when he regained his balance, he suddenly discovered a steep drop-off at the edge of the woods. And there, at the very tip of the outermost pine, sat the squirrel, only his tail and the top of his head within view.

"Halvor stopped opposite him and dropped to his knees. He lost no time in aiming his gun and was lucky enough to find a ready support against a dry branch of a fallen tree.

"The deserted forest was perfectly still; there was not even a bird—only the soft, barely audible little sounds of tiny creepers, as when one lends his ear to the busyness in an ant-hill.

"Halvor pulled the trigger. A loud report echoed through the valley, and he landed on his back behind the fallen pine. When he got to his feet, dizzy and bruised, there lay a torn-off squirrel's tail on the cliff in front of him. It lay on the ground beneath the tree, bloody at the root. At once a shower of pine needles fell like hail and covered it.

"Halvor ran to the edge and peered down. The slope dropped off abruptly to the river, and there below, where the valley floor began, was a bloody rat moaning and dragging its stub behind it.

"Halvor abandoned his gun, leaped down the hillside, and watched the animal run toward the river. He could follow the black blood stains on the fern leaves wherever it had slipped past.

"When Halvor reached the bank, the rat was standing on a rock in the middle of the river. In that place the water was shallow, and toward the east side there was a kind of natural pier, but between the rock farthest out and the opposite bank flowed a stream three yards across.

"Halvor stopped, leaned down, and picked up five sharp stones as big as hens' eggs. When the rodent discovered that the road back was blocked, it stretched forward and stared into the water as if to estimate the distance. The tail dragged in the river like a broken twig.

"Halvor advanced two steps and stopped again. Suddenly the animal faced him; its tiny round eyes were jet black, it bared its teeth in anger, and then it hissed loudly.

" 'Now I'll throw,' he thought, 'and afterwards I'll kick.' The first stone missed. The rat jumped a little, looked up at him, and moved its head up and down in fear and anger.

"Halvor went one step nearer and threw a second stone. This one grazed the back of the rat, and it took one more little jump and squealed, still clinging to its perch on the rock.

" 'Now you'll get this!' Halvor bellowed and felt great relief in working off his anger. 'This! And this! All my life—'

"The last stone hit its back, but the creature was still alive and plunged into the river in rage. Halvor saw it swimming with the current and ran out into shallow water in pursuit.

105

"They raced side by side two hundred yards downstream. Then Halvor realized they were nearing the spot where he usually put out his nets. A sandbar extended into the river just above it, and from that he got his bearings. He ran up on land, through clumps of birches, and out onto the point.

"When the rodent saw him it tried to swim across to the other bank, but the current was too strong. It went down several times, finally gave up, and came drifting toward him. Halvor saw its little bristles floating on the surface and the beady black eyes fixed on him, wide open.

"Right there on a little projection in the Salten River Halvor was able to catch it. He waded into the river waist-deep, grabbed its neck and rump with both hands, and held it under water ten long minutes. Afterwards he buried the corpse in a hole in the marsh some distance away because he didn't want it to lie where it could contaminate the water.

"He returned to the river, undressed, scoured his body with sand, and bathed. The sun hung high in the southern sky, it was a warm full-summer day, and Halvor allowed himself time to dry his clothes before setting out for home. He also examined his nets and found three good-sized trout caught close to the bottom. A little later on his way to the house, he remembered his gun and decided to go back for it after dinner so he could return it to his uncle the next day.

"The children were playing in the sand pit when their father approached and didn't hear him clear his throat and drop down heavily on a pine log behind them. Sunlight flooded the whole valley, and the sand looked like dust of gold all around them."

The governor said no more, and tense silence settled on the deck. Pastor Celion turned in his chair, half quizzically: "Yes, yes, speaking of rodents, we had a monstrous one at home in the parsonage two years ago. And do you know

106

what it did? We had a cured ham hanging from the rafters in the store-room; near it stood a barrel of flour. That rat jumped up from the barrel one night and fastened itself securely to the ham. There it hung like a pendulum and kept on eating until it got so stuffed that it fell down. This had been going on many nights before we realized what was happening. But then one morning, there it lay dead on the floor below the ham. What's more, it had tried to be ingenious and had gnawed off the rope, but when the ham fell the rat was unlucky enough to be caught underneath it and got killed.

"Well, that's punishment for greed and gluttony. But in the meanwhile it had had babies—about a dozen—and we have had rats in the parsonage ever since."

Florelius looked at his friend. "I sense you are not satisfied with my story. Perhaps you'd prefer to take over?"

"No, certainly not, Richard. I was only afraid you were going to desert your friend Halvor Mikkelsen. He was, after all, facing autumn and a long winter."

"Yes, then," the governor continued, "I can report that it was a long dry autumn, and Halvor was able to accomplish practically everything he had planned. He managed to shelter his dried fish, to build a sheep-shed, cut the grass along the river, gather leaves and store them, and to spade up a field thirty yards square before the first snowfall.

"Then one day he shouldered a big load of dried fish and set off with a hank of line and several fish hooks in his belt. He walked along the river until he reached his nearest neighbor—a distance of perhaps three or four miles. When he returned that night he had an autumn-born sheep in tow. They named it Reisa in memory of Halvor's grandmother who had eight children. That was the first animal on the

107

farm and became the ancestress of a whole flock of descendants now spread over the entire district.

"When spring came and things in the earth began to stir, Halvor picked the maggots out of the dried fish and went off with a new load. This time he got himself a sack of rye, and he was so frugal with the seeds that he didn't dare to scatter them; instead, he planted each one separately, and in his most arrogant moments he assigned them names as he pressed one by one into the ground—for example, Spri, Si, Kri, Tri, Bri, and so on.'"

At this point Celion snorted in laughter. "You will never listen to warnings, Richard. Now you're at it again."

"Well, well, at any rate Halvor acquired an acreage and some animals. And one spring he went up into the valley again, and this time he brought back with him a real live person with hair and skirts and all essentials.

"The children were standing on the cliff above the sandpit when the two came wandering along the river bank. 'We're almost out of dried fish,' remarked the boy. 'Did you see that load Father carried away with him this morning?'

"'Yes, I did. But look! That must be our mother.'

"Halvor didn't say anything. He seemed merely to be delivering her carefully—even though she followed five paces behind him—but from that day on a new kind of life was initiated in their home.

"Halvor was less often plagued by such nuisances as squirrels and rats, but he was never completely free of the sound of them. At night he frequently heard something patter around in the yard. At such times he would get up and go to the river where he would stand and peer into the foaming water that continually flowed to the sea.

"Two years later a new human being was born on the

108

farm. But in the summer the child died. Then Halvor climbed up on the mountain and was gone a whole day. When he came home, he carried a birch-bark basket with a few cloudberries in it, but no one on the farm seriously believed he had time to pick berries during this busy season, and, moreover, his eyes were red and bloodshot as if he had stared a long time at the western sun setting behind the islands in the sea."

When the governor had ended his story, there was not a sound to be heard except for the monotonous creaking of the rigging. The pastor's glass was empty, and soon his head dropped with a nod, sideways. He snored unwarily and lightly like a child.

"It's getting to be daylight, Richard," said Lady Sophie. "Your friend is asleep."

At that moment Celion awakened and glanced around, bewildered. "Oh, Good Heavens! I was dreaming. How long have I been asleep? Please forgive me! But you had finished your story, hadn't you?"

"Yes, indeed. And now it's your turn," the governor said.

"No, wait a while," the pastor replied. "I see we are just now opposite one of the district's richest parishes and that reminds me we perhaps need food and rest. My colleague Gregers lives right there north of the church steeple. True, he's in the city with his family, but there's a housekeeper, and I know we would be welcome. There wouldn't be any question."

On considering the suggestion briefly, they all agreed to accept the pastor's counsel and promptly dropped anchor outside the parsonage.

The house was spacious and low-ceilinged, and the voyagers quickly settled down to rest—Lady Tennyson in a large guest room facing south, Celion and Florelius in a smaller room facing west, and Berg on a sofa in the living room.

Later in the day the table was set with fresh salmon, cream porridge, trout cured in the earth, and generous portions of flatbread with butter and white cheese.

"Yes, this is how we pastors up north live," sighed Celion when they later were drinking coffee around a table in the garden. "Is it any wonder we turn out to be good shepherds? Moreover, this puts me in mind of a story a hunter told me some years ago. He came to me wanting to sell two red fox skins. I wanted the skins, but I had no money on hand. I asked him to meet me at one of the chapels next Sunday and I would pay him then. In the meanwhile we had a storm and missed having a service that Sunday. A few days later the hunter came to my home demanding payment for the skins. He had gone to the chapel because he did not think the weather too severe. He judged me to be a somewhat mediocre pastor. I didn't answer that accusation, but, of course, he was right, for with such an expression of opinion one can get at the truth from two directions. But I explained to him that when God appoints a man to a calling, He doesn't always make him a good sailor and that a pastor should not be judged by the weakness of his diaphragm.

"Thereupon he inquired whether I had heard about Pastor Bartholin. 'No,' I replied. 'In any case he is not of my graduation class.'

"'Oh, no,' he retorted, 'pastors these days are more comfortable in vestments than under a square-sail.' And then he told me the story of this man Bartholin."

Richard is easily carried away — follows strands a story away from main point. yet all is somehow connected.

110

The Tale of Pastor Bartholin

"Pastor Bartholin was the minister at Skumvik.

"And where does Skumvik lie? Well, you are not likely to find it on any map. It is the smallest and the poorest of all God's parishes in this country. But it is nonetheless in Helgeland, in an area where the land strip is the narrowest, where the width of a mere seventy yards separates the interior from the coast.

"Someone viewing it from above will find that Pastor Bartholin's parish resembles a hand—a hand resting on a table top, emaciated, almost like that of a skeleton. At the wrist it is attached to the mainland, and from there five groups of islands stretch out into the sea. The islands are pitifully barren, and the obstinate people who inhabit them have settled on the outermost points possible, on the finger-nails—so to speak. And that means that the pastor can't be a victim of seasickness when he goes to fulfill his mission in the chapels.

"A mighty river flows out from the interior. Near the coast it divides into two channels. The one flows into the sea at Skumvik where the main church and the parsonage are lo-

111

cated—on the map, therefore, between the third and the fourth fingers. The other flows out between the middle and the index fingers.

"During the spring thaw these two rivers are both covered over with blue-green ice, and many small streams, a roaring network of veins, run between the rocks. And in that season it immediately becomes more difficult for Bartholin to be a pastor because he is a widower and has a housekeeper to work for him.

"It *became* more difficult, I mean, because what the hunter told me happened many, many years ago. Now the islands have been abandoned—or evacuated, as one might say. The buildings at the finger tips now serve as fishermen's huts. The parsonage stands empty; it is gradually going to ruin, there isn't an unbroken window left, and the outer door hangs by one hinge.

"It was autumn. The hunter had just come down to the coast with the skins of the animals he had shot during the course of the summer. Within a half hour he had sold the whole lot and had ordered new salmon nets and ammunition. In the restaurant he had struck up a conversation with a man who told him about this fellow Bartholin.

"When the hunter repeated the tale to me, he emphasized it was no sportsman's yarn he was unwinding though he did concede that he had perhaps embellished it a little himself afterwards, for, as he said, it is the kind of story one can enlarge upon without spoiling it.

"Later I realized he was right because it was indeed a frank and plain-spoken tale in a shining setting of mountains and water. It could well resist crumbling in the retelling so that even you, Richard, for whom it is so easy to get carried away, even you would unconsciously stick to the original version if you were to recite it again.

112

"The pastor was a small man. That is to say, his legs were too short. His clerical gown covered up the disproportion somewhat, but when he walked behind the plow it was apparent. His parishioners felt unpleasantly impressed because the first servant of God was equipped with legs that were too short; therefore they never sought him out when he was at work in the fields. The pastor sensed this very keenly, and as soon as a boat came into view he unhitched his horse and went indoors.

"There he was always to be found, seated at his desk in the dark living room. He looked taller in a chair. His shoulders were broad; he could cope with their problems.

"His round short-clipped head looked like a continuation of his thick neck. His beard was dark, and his face always looked a little stubbly, because he never cut the hairs growing out of his nostrils. The brown—almost black—eyes had a glint in them like a rare kind of gem.

"The pastor was not especially articulate. There was a hard, forced quality in his exegesis, abrupt, as if he chopped the words into bits and pieces before he let them out. But the little weather-beaten congregations thought that was as it should be. The minister's voice had the sound of a mill grinding away in the stillness. It ground God's message directly out of their surroundings; the cadence of the mountains and of the sea issued from Bartholin's throat. They understood him very well.

"He did not preach fire and brimstone, nor redemption either. When he had finished the sermon, no one could say what he had really expounded. But that was not particularly important either, for their pastor's authority was, after all, mainly confined to this world.

"He was indeed their minister, but he was also their doctor because he had studied medicine. In judicial matters he was their counselor when on rare occasions they needed

113

legal advice. He taught them to fertilize their land, to dig trenches, to sow crops at the right time, and he brought them sketches from the Salten region to guide them in operating their boats.

"Pastor Bartholin was inexhaustible. Whenever they saw his black square-sail streak past, they got busy with a world of conjectures; and when he went back on board after having visited a neighbor, they felt resentful and sneaked around trying to find out what blessing he had effected this time.

"It was rumored that he had offended authorities in the south. After that he was sent up here 'not unsuited to serve a parish among poverty-stricken farmers and fishermen in outlying fishing stations on those islands collectively designated as Skumvig. Among those wretched creatures whose spiritual condition mirrors their environment, this Mr. Bartholin ought to be able to do some good.'

"Most assuredly.

"The pastor concerned himself very little with the state of their souls, but wherever he went he left other kinds of traces behind. When he stood in the pulpit the eyes of his congregation were on his hands, not on his face. His mouth was no revelation. To be honest, it was somewhat shrunken and drooping, and because he chewed tobacco every day except Sunday he couldn't avoid having brown stains in the corners.

"But his hands were big and coarse and tanned, like waterworn leather. When he ran his fingers along the edge of the pulpit, it sounded as if a grating rasp was being worked in the church.

"In this way he did leave his imprints, and after some years had passed he had also made a little dent on the flaps of their desolate souls. The island people began to judge an act by what their minister would have done in a like situa-

114

tion—first, the acts of their fellowmen, as one would expect, and later on, their own. Nor did they loiter around one another's buildings as much. Eventually stealing fence-posts from one another also became less common. For a long time they did persist in the age-old practice of gathering driftwood along the neighbor's shoreline, but even that—yes, one autumn day Bartholin himself had seen Mikkjel Nilsa, who lived on the point of the thumbnail, carry driftwood up to the neighboring farm. Now, to be sure, the woman there had just recently become a widow, but anyway—

"When the pastor sailed home that night he was preoccupied. He had begun thinking about his own miserable self. He had been a widower more than four years, and, as I mentioned earlier, he had a housekeeper. It is true that she was more capable than she was beautiful, but Bartholin knew very well that with such limited choices available temptation had few nuances.

"Last spring it had happened for the first time. In May. The river roared as usual, icy green. Over the bay at Skumvik the gulls screamed as if possessed. On the south side of the parsonage there was a garden with three tall birches, currant bushes, and thickets of alder.

"It was a Wednesday, the pastor was in the garden, and he saw one of the birch trees was sprouting. He remained there wondering why the one should sprout before the others; they were all equally tall, rooted in the same soil, and warmed by the same sunlight.

"Just then the housekeeper appeared on the doorstep. She stood there, broad, somewhat insipid, slow-witted; there she stood folding her arms across her stomach, squinting at the light.

"The minister had noticed the furrows in that earthen-gray face and the forlorn expression in those water-pale eyes. Had he become aware out of sympathy, out of kindness?

115

"Bartholin pushed these thoughts out of his mind with a quick motion of the hand that caused the boat to tilt and take on water. He felt his clothes getting wet. It was cold and bracing, and other things soon captured his attention.

"When the pastor got to the farmstead, he first made a trip to the barn, pitched some hay to the two cows, and gave the horse a drink. Then he went into the house, took off his boots, and emptied them through the window. He glanced around—feeling somewhat conscious-stricken.

"In the kitchen his meal of young coalfish, potatoes, and peppered liver floating in fat awaited him. The housekeeper was at the work-table washing the dishes. The pastor looked at her and sighed. She was wearing a blue wind-breaker and a gray skirt reaching almost to her ankles, and he could see she had holes in both her stockings. She was slopping the dish-cloth around in the basin.

" 'She washes dishes exactly the same way she eats,' he thought; 'she is a charitable sort, but simple and slovenly—May God have mercy on us!'

" 'It's coming from the west tonight.' She spoke without turning around. 'Has the pastor pulled the boat up on land?'

" 'No. Will you perhaps lend me a hand?' Bartholin addressed her formally. He felt that might make it easier for her to reconcile herself to some of the things that had been happening between them since spring.

"They put on their seaboots and went toward the boatshed. The wind had already begun to blow violently, and the pastor could hear the gale rushing in, making its way fast among the outlying islands. The housekeeper lifted her skirt and stuffed it inside her boots. Then they waded out and dragged the boat into the shed.

"There was another rendezvous in the housekeeper's room that evening. In fact, not a word was exchanged between

116

them. Bartholin set the candle beside the door. The wind rattled all through the old house, drafts made the curtain blow out straight, and the light went out. The housekeeper moaned softly; otherwise everything was quiet at Skumvik. Now and then the walls creaked when the wind swept around the corners.

"But during the night as he was sitting at the table in the living room reading, the pastor had a visitor. The lamp began to smoke, and the soot constantly puffed up into his face—almost like an admonition.

"A heavy squall had developed. Bartholin closed his eyes and listened. Through a hole in the wall right beside the window frame came the wind—now gentle and subtle like irony, then with a snort like a charger out of the Inferno, and then again with an evil sneer, grave and hollow.

"The minister was acquainted with all these noises from before. They had different tone qualities according to the seasons. So he sat with his head lowered, visualizing the months marching past outside the window: spring—raw and damp and cold with broken clumps of earth and all kinds of winter ugliness on the ground, but also the grass, the sedge stiff and tall and the trees whining in the wind; autumn—like this, the time of remorse, any morning now the river would be frozen over from the marker on the east side near the marsh, the voice of God drowned out by the storm on the fjord; winter—with black and white spots, and the distance endlessly long between chapels, between hearts.

"He sighed and looked at the clock. It was past twelve; it was Sunday, and he must begin concentrating on the text for the day.

"At that moment he heard someone click the latch of the back door; he sat bolt upright in his chair, and listened carefully. Indeed his light was visible from across the bay,

117

but surely no one would come at such a late hour. Suddenly the door opened behind him, and Bartholin felt a cold draft on his neck. A small thin man entered, wearing seaboots, black trousers, and a short blue jacket. His hair was wet; his face, worn but expressive. He approached the table directly and stood there shaking his sou'wester. It was dripping.

"The pastor broke the silence. 'Well?' There was no reply. The visitor looked around, and then Bartholin offered him a chair.

"Bartholin searched his memory. This man was hardly one of his parishioners. The face bore no trace of that gray weariness he was accustomed to seeing. On the contrary, it was vibrant and cunning; the eyes shifted all about the dark room and then fixed on the hole in the wall.

"The wind changed its tone, suddenly becoming loud and shrill as if stingy about air. The stranger listened and laughed softly.

" 'Next time I'll use that.' He nodded toward the hole. 'I'd rather not break the pastor's door locks.'

"Bartholin shuddered. The stranger noticed it and was delighted. Now the pastor knew who he was, closed his Bible, and placed it in the drawer to show his command of the situation.

"The visitor crossed his legs and assumed an authoritative air. 'Well, since we obviously don't need a mutual introduction: on my travels in this parish I have observed certain changes among people here since the late Pastor Vik's day.'

" 'Since the time of Pastor Vik of blessed memory,' corrected Bartholin, listening to the gusts outside.

" 'Well, if you insist, since the time of Pastor Vik of blessed memory. Nevertheless, you understand what I mean, and you also understand very well that it isn't to my advantage to see things evolve in this way.'

118

" 'For the most part the people are just the same as they've always been.' Bartholin spoke firmly. 'And if there has been any change for the better, it is certainly not to be credited to my work here but to the general improvement in their living conditions. As you well know, good conditions tend to temper behavior.'

" 'I've also seen the opposite result,' quipped the visitor. 'And in this instance I'm sure the pastor's influence has put this parish on the debit side of my account. This was once a flourishing district for me.'

"Bartholin took a plug of tobacco from the drawer and bit off a quid. Indeed it was already Sunday, but—

"The sharp flavor gave him a spurt of courage. He became almost insolent. 'Yes, and so what?' He peered into the darkness.

" 'I have learned,' said the visitor shifting his footing, 'that the pastor has certain inclinations in the direction of—' He glanced toward the loft.

" 'That's it,' thought Bartholin. 'I knew it all along but didn't want to believe it.' He said, 'I understand what you mean.' He heard the whistling of the wind through the hole. 'Either I must break off my connections from now on, or you'll see to it that a whispering campaign gets started about what goes on at the parsonage.'

" 'I don't think the pastor understands quite correctly. I have no objections,'—again he glanced at the loft,—'to attachments of this kind. A person's private pleasure doesn't arouse my jealousy and the individual's—hmmm—sin, even if it does involve a minister, doesn't alter his credit column in my account. I must always think in terms of the parish as a whole, you see. It's your disposition toward the congregation that I want to get at. You may continue as pastor ex cathedra, but your work as counselor, so to speak, I can no

119

longer sanction in the parish. These people threaten to become veritable saints if you continue.'

"Bartholin smiled coldly. 'Oh, they have a long way to go.'

"The stranger rose. 'I assume then that you will confine yourself to preaching, that you therefore do not put your doctrines into practice. Otherwise I shall have to make use of—the one up there.'

" 'I can so easily dispense with her,' the pastor lied as a last resort. 'And it would make no difference to me if it were known.'

"Again the visitor laughed quietly. 'No, perhaps it would not make any difference to you, but to her up there it surely would. Be that as it may, your line of reasoning pleases me.'

"When Bartholin glanced up the stranger had vanished. He heard a glupp-pp from the hole, like the noise of a cork being pulled out of a bottle. Immediately the wind lulled; it became perfectly still. 'That's so that silence will engulf me,' the pastor rationalized; 'in silence all ideas loom large and foreboding.'

"He remained seated there until the graying of early dawn. In the dull light of morning he watched the gulls in their melancholy flight back and forth above the bay and heard the sea flow along the shore until it splashed to nothing against the rocks. In stormy weather it made a loud splintering sound like the shattering of glass breaking. He recognized it now—the eternal pounding of the tireless sea against the rocks. Skumvik.

"Pastor Bartholin sighed. He then set about to work on the text for the day.

"Sunday morning breakfast consisted of bread and coffee and an egg. When he had donned his long black gown, he turned to the housekeeper and proposed marriage. 'I have

120

wondered for some time whether that wouldn't be for the best,' he lied.

"After the morning service the parishioners watched their minister stride off on his short legs into the churchyard. Bartholin sought out the grave of his late wife. She rested under a black granite marker. The gold lettering was gradually flaking off, and in distraction he remembered that he had intended once before to do something about that.

"His blessed wife had not been able to endure the climate in Skumvik, and moreover the incessant rumbling of the water unnerved her. She was a displaced, distraught soul, her face constantly looked frost-nipped, she couldn't bear the sea, and on land she was a delicate bird's wing buffeted by the wind.

"The long winter evenings in the living room came back to Bartholin. He felt her silence like a persistent hum in his ears, and again he reproached himself.

"They were married just before Christmas. The following day the housekeeper told her husband she was going to have a child. The minister was taken by surprise, though he had known it a month already.

"They went on a honeymoon trip to all the chapels; Bartholin brought reports of big schools of herring in the far north. Besides, he had with him a few trinkets for some orphans; they both entered the kitchen to deliver the gifts.

"Beyond that, everything went on as before. The first few evenings after their wedding the housekeeper sat in the living room in front of the window, diligently knitting something nondescript out of green wool. The pastor raised his head; he had never seen her knit before. The fourth day she moved out into the kitchen again, and Bartholin resumed his trek to her room—his way lighted by the stub of an altar candle.

121

"The winter of the new year proved to be the worst Skumvik had ever experienced. There came reports of shipwrecks, of sickness, of auctions. The entire parish suffered. Bartholin understood well. Eventually he grew restless and anxious and raced in and out of the fjords oftener than usual. Though he carried on his work regularly as always, he had become a little irritable. People wondered.

"In March one of the minister's cows dropped dead in her stall, and Bartholin himself buried her in an out-of-the-way spot. A man came wanting to get the carcass for feeding foxes, but he was not even allowed to examine it. People speculated about this, because the pastor was otherwise a practical man.

"It happened that the pastor would come to an abrupt stop while in the pulpit. He might stop in the middle of the text, as if he could not go on. People looked up and wondered. They observed that he had become thinner, that his hair and his beard—now left to grow like brushwood—framed an almost colorless face. Only his eyes were the same as always, yes, even more than ever they resembled a rare kind of black gem.

"The child would be born in April. Bartholin sent his wife to a hospital on the mainland. Many said the pastor's new wife was too old for childbearing. They proved to be right, and for two weeks the same ones nodded knowingly to those whom they met, and didn't say a word.

"The pastor buried the housekeeper and the child alongside the grave of his first wife. People said it was a nice thing to do. Later, however, it occurred to them for the first time what they had meant, and when they realized it, they felt illwill toward the pastor.

"Bartholin continued as before. His black square-sail darted in and out like a pirate's flag among the little islands.

It had acquired a white patch in the upper left corner. People were puzzled.

"He arrived regularly with seeds and pamphlets; he came with medicine and used clothing. One day he summoned them to meet on the tip of the middle finger and made suggestions about bigger boats and broader nets. He said they ought to join forces. Think about it! And then he rushed off.

"The disastrous winter finally ended. The usual number of misfortunes began to occur. No one thought much about it.

"Soon came May. A day in the month of May. Again the pastor walked behind the plow. The soggy earth steamed; the horses steamed. The pastor stood, his short legs wide apart, sighting the islands out in the sea. The furrows were straight as an arrow, so when snow fell during the night his field was like a blackboard marked with straight chalk lines.

"At twelve o'clock he unhitched his horse and went into the house. He ate bread and cold coalfish left from the day before, kindled a fire, and hung his clothes to dry.

"When Bartholin came out again, he found his horse lying on the ground; his front leg was sprained. He managed to get the animal up, and by pushing with his shoulder and lifting from underneath he succeeded in urging him, yard by yard, into the barn.

"Later in the day the pastor went down to the sea. A breeze was stirring. The weather was mild, and on the mountains toward the west the snow was melting. Then he saw a boat approaching land; a thin man, dressed in dark clothes, was at the helm. Bartholin stood there, lost in thought. The spongy earth gurgled under his feet. He sighed and thought to himself: 'Soon you can begin to plant. The wind is right.'

"The man in the boat stood up and cried, 'The baby at Garvik is sick!' Then he had to scud away immediately because the wind had suddenly become strong and was driving the boat out into the fjord again.

"The pastor had bought new seaboots. He jumped into them and made a trip to the table in the living room. There he stood, pensive, looking at the wall where he had used a cork to plug the hole by the window. He lifted one foot—the hole was hard to reach—and kicked the cork farther into the wall.

"On seeing the child, Bartholin realized at once that hospital care was needed. He bundled the little body into wool blankets, put it into one leg of a pair of oilskins, and fastened straps around it. He went down to his boat, set the bundle aslant against the bulkhead, and seated himself above it. Then he told the man to go home.

"Though the air was mild, the wind velocity had increased and the boat moved at full speed along the shore. Bartholin's mind was on his horse, and now he could fetch a veterinarian on the same trip. He kept thinking to himself that it could be arranged somehow, that in the night the last trace of snow would disappear, that tomorrow he could—yes. Presently he caught sight of the man who had brought the message. He was in a little Nordland boat, painted green, that came driving toward him from the northwest.

"The pastor looked up and smiled. Dark clouds had gathered and the wind had strengthened to gale proportions. Now the snow will melt, he concluded, and then he placed one of the oars under the seat in front of him. 'I must get me a new cow. I have too much fodder for only the one. But my horse—well, I'll have to wait to do the rest of the plowing. Tomorrow I'll repair the north wall of the boat-shed. "'Yes, by Jove! That I can do!' The pastor talked aloud to himself. Out of the corner of one eye he watched the stranger approaching from the side. He snatched the oar, jumped to his feet, lunged forward, and hurled it like a spear toward the dark figure. The oar struck with full force between the feet of the rower; the heavy blade pierced the floorboard and stood there like a broken mast. The water poured in, and the boat swerved.

"Bartholin walked up to the hospital, the bundled form in his arms. It was his second visit within a short time. When he left, the nurses were huddled in groups, smiling; he noticed them and laughed. They had never seen him laugh before and put their heads even closer together.

"By the time he got back to his boat, the wind had again freshened to a stiff breeze. Bartholin's pale face registered changes in weather like a barometer. He had felt countless winds and knew that no two are exactly alike; but this one—he thought he recognized this one.

"The minister steered his boat on a north-northwest course. He laughed and sat down securely, clutching the rudder like a sweetheart in his arm. Beyond the point the stranger was awaiting him; he knew that.

"Pastor Bartholin sailed on and on, a strong and steady wind pushing him. Out there lay Skumvik with the church and the two black-as-soot buildings of the parsonage. Above the roar of the wind he could hear the waves splash against the shore and spill like shattered glass back into the channel.

"The minister looked up and laughed. There, high in the western sky as far as eye could see, the clouds hung heavy and black. Then, half-aware, he saw the same small green Nordland craft approaching from starboard, riding the crest of a wave and bearing down on him. He turned his head a couple of times. 'Now everyone in the parish has kindled a light,' he thought; 'it must be after nine. I'm sailing as if I were going down the middle of an avenue with street lights on either side. And over there way ahead, at a point farthest west, there is also a light. But now it is jet black, and I must be getting home.'

"When the collision occurred, Bartholin was lifted up by a big billowy wave. He felt dizzy, and with the shock of it all he did not remember anything in particular worth remembering. He only saw lights meeting above his head as he was being pulled under."

Celion hesitated. His coffee had cooled. He left it standing.

"At a later date I myself visited Skumvik. How did I happen to go there?—Well, that is not really of any consequence, but it was an unusual day, like a day loaned to me out of the unreal, or was it perhaps just—?

"In any event, it was autumn, late in September. The tops of the many little islands were bare, with strips of anemic grass here and there and a scant border of brown seaweed like a fringe all around—like a tonsure. The sun shone and the sky was clear that September day when I visited Skumvik. A lustrous white autumn light lined the heavens, almost like a fabric one could touch. But I could imagine so vividly the winters here and the stormy nights.

"I walked across the marsh and followed the river to the sea. The coloring of the marsh out here is more drab, more blanched, than where I usually wander in my autumn vacation, in the inlands and up on the mountains.

"I spent an hour walking in the churchyard and around the parsonage. Tall coarse grass covered all the graves, and I couldn't distinguish one from another in that overgrown plot. It was as if a slow-moving, yet steadfast, will had tramped over every inch of it.

126

"The parsonage was going to ruin, little by little. The boat-shed was gone. In one upstairs room I found a long strand of green wool on the floor, and when I picked it up it crumbled to dust.

"On the east side of the farmhouse, sheltered from the wind and still warmed by the sun, there were wild raspberries growing.

"I took a walk along the shore. There lay great piles of yellow-white driftwood, big pieces, scoured by the water until they looked like joints of monsters.

"At noon I went back into the village. The birches shimmered, golden-red, as if feverish, as I kept walking eastward that afternoon."

"I agree with the hunter. He was quite a minister," said Mylady when Celion had finished his story. "He could well have been of help to your friend Halvor—don't you think so, Richard,—so he wouldn't have needed to run around in the woods in the Salten Valley in search of ghosts!"

"I don't know," answered the governor, "whether Bartholin could have helped Halvor any more than Pastor Celion could have helped me in a similar situation. It's my feeling that it takes a person of the opposite sex to bring lasting help to a man just as it takes one of the opposite sex to bring trouble. I'm not thinking of the common run of troubles; I'm thinking of the slowly developing problems that grow within."

Lady Sophie sighed. "You may be right, Richard, but let's not get into that, because if we do the steamer is likely to catch up with us before we have a chance to hear the beginning of the next story. It's your turn, Eberhardt." She addressed the merchant, Berg. "Since I'm the only woman passenger, I'll take the privilege of being the last. It's the same as in social life; one prefers to make his entrance

127

when all have arrived, and the initial excitement has calmed."

"That sounds reasonable," the merchant replied sportively. "And as long as we're speaking of a beautiful woman passenger, it's especially a good idea."

"Now, now!" Mylady pointed her index finger at him. "I'll catch you up on that one, Eberhardt. You mean to say only an exceptionally good story would entitle a person to the privilege of being the last narrator. But you know I can make a choice—I can indeed keep silent. There's no risk in an untold tale."

"I'm not so sure about that," Berg replied. "And in that case Mylady would break the rules of the game. It was her own suggestion that each of us tell a story."

At that moment the young helmsman came to announce that the boat was ready to sail. Lady Sophie smiled at him as she rose from her chair. The group dispersed immediately. Celion went up to the house, and Lady Tennyson called after him, "Leave a few shillings from me, too, Pastor." "Yes, and please include me, too," the governor and the merchant commanded in chorus.

Celion stepped over the high threshold and stuck his hand into his inner pocket—somewhat peevishly, unable to hide his irritation. "Don't they know a minister's state of finances—those three out there? Furthermore, this happens to be the county's most affluent district, and the dinner we were served was locally produced. I'm not stingy, but why does it always have to be one in a group?"

Thereupon he made his payment, wrote a thank-you note to his friend, laid it on the table, and then tripped down the hill behind the others with short, angry steps.

Ahead of him went the other three, arm in arm, Mylady in the middle, chattering. "Actually, she's a featherbrain," the pastor thought, "and Heaven only knows what those two—"

128

Half a yard of space separated the pier from the roof of the ship's cabin, and as they were about to embark Lady Sophie lifted her skirt a way above her ankle with one hand and extended the other toward the young helmsman to solicit his help in getting on board.

The sail was hoisted; the cargo-boat moved slowly away from land and headed south, making its way among the little islands. It was late afternoon, the sun was still high, and a gentle breeze came in from the sea out of the northwest.

On the round wicker table stood the four glasses from the night before. The pastor's glass was completely empty. As soon as they were washed, Florelius uncorked a new bottle. In the meantime Berg had fetched a leather portfolio from the cabin; he took out a slim pamphlet and began leafing through it as if looking for a particular entry, though his attention seemed not to be on what he was doing.

"I can't tell a story. It would be silly for me even to try anything like that, but once when I was in Copenhagen I found this little pamphlet in a second-hand book shop." He continued speaking without raising his eyes. "I don't know whether you, Sophie, will think someone like me is just putting on airs by displaying such interests, but nevertheless with the passing of years I have found great enjoyment in reading. It helps one pass the time up here in the polar night—as one says—though to say they fill the hours is, of course, the least one would say about books."

At this point Mylady looked as if she would like to interrupt, but Berg did not give her a chance to break in. He raised his voice a bit and went on. "Here is a story that I like. Moreover it has cost me dearly—I mean the purchasing of the book."

Fernando Riazola's Report

THE SHIPWRECK

"We set sail in the morning on the ninth of February, two months to the day after I had lost my wife. I was at the ship chandler Toris in Genoa that day and knew nothing of what had happened until I came home and found her.

"A week later the murderer was caught on board a barge, and I witnessed his hanging in the city square. Seated there between the aldermen and the old magistrate, I felt I could read in their faces a sort of thankfulness to me because my wife had let herself be killed. So few things happen here, even though wise people maintain we are living in an age when events are taking place that will change the whole world.

"I had a full view of the execution, and I sickened and went limp at the sight. For me there was no vengeance—merely justice, and justice provides scant fare for the human heart.

"He got his punishment—sprawling. What good is it all? My faith is weak. I believe only partially that everything is subject to God's will. For if such a thing could happen to us, there must be a rival power in competition with Him, one that operates unrestrained, in secret. Some people first become believers when God punishes them severely, but I will not crawl to faith under His rod. I know, too, that running far away is of little avail; the world is no longer that big. My father, who bought the *Beatrice I*, has circled the globe twice, and I know he never escaped the memory of a woman he loved. And yet she died of typhus—a slow wasting-away, as we know, and no sudden catastrophe.— At any rate, preparations were made, the crew hired, and, as I said, the ninth day of February we set sail.

"The *Beatrice II* was loaded with wine and Venetian silks of fabulous colors. We might well have been taken for a warning, for I'm certain that ever since voyaging first began with Captain Noah's remarkable cruise on the double-decked Ark few have experienced anything to equal what I, Fernando Riazola, am recording here. The fat men of the maritime court of Venice nearly fell victims to apoplexy from both laughter and indignation on hearing my story after I returned home.

"Strange people! One could show them a chestnut branch in the instant the buds are bursting and the sticky graygreen pod is opening toward the light, and they would believe it immediately—and yet my voyage was only an insignificant gesture on the map in comparison to that miracle.

"Nor is there one single sailor on the entire coast from Constantinople to Gibraltar who believes my story. For that reason I've come inland from the sea. Now I live right in the middle of the continent of Europe in a dull German village that inspires no exaggeration in any way. There is no rushing water for miles around, only hot and dusty pavements, and this is where I am writing my account. I pray the guardian angel of the city of my childhood, Saint Andrew, to give me a clear sign, for example a strong trembling of my right hand or even a throbbing ache in my wretched eyetooth, if at any time I should tell a lie or remember something inaccurately.

"The schooner *Beatrice* rode much too high in the water. She was a bit too elegantly and gracefully designed so as to put one in mind of the rice maidens on the plains, and in all likelihood she lacked the strength of character to carry a cargo of wine and silk. In contrast to Dante's beloved of the same name, she was not steadfast and shifted coquettishly with every breeze that blew.

"We were to unload in London. It was therefore not a long voyage, but at this time of year the weather is unpredictable, and the Bay of Biscay is known to be God's own witches' cauldron. Nonetheless, we crossed safely and successfully; the *Beatrice* flirted and babbled with the sea, and the gold-ornamented figurehead—carved of teak by Leovantis in Rome—never got wet above her knees.

"But one morning when we were in the English Channel, the horizon suddenly darkened. I immediately gave orders to steer for the English coast so we could at least take refuge in a harbor if we couldn't reach the Thames. Before we got that far, however, the storm overtook us. The gale splintered a couple of spars and tore a long gash in the mainsail. Old Pivante at the helm called to me that he did not like what he heard when the sail was torn to pieces. He had heard that noise six times before, but this time it sounded as if a hand had plunged a knife into it and shredded it to tatters. When he said it, he laughed the way he always did when he wanted us to accept something he himself didn't believe.

"We turned south at once and caught the last glimpse of land we would be privileged to see for two long months. The Cliffs of Dover showed their deathly white brow just twice when the storm clouds broke enough so that we could see through the rift.

132

"I still kept hoping we would get into calmer water near the south coast, but when we had sailed three days and nights I realized that England herself is nothing but a reef in the Atlantic and that God's wrath is greater than all the geography I had learned from all the old salts in Genoa. The storm gave no signs of abating and we were buffeted by wind and weather, without light of stars, and soon also without a rudder, for it had been smashed to pieces the fifth day after the storm caught us. Nevertheless, old Pivante refused to let himself be wrested from his place the first few days, and even after we had lost the rudder he had lashed himself to the wheel though it was of no more worth than would be a wagon wheel high up in the air. Where is he now in the great Nothing? Well, I say nothing because I know he was a pagan; he believed in nothing but ropes and rudders and decks of ships, but he taught me that man is greater than the sea, because the sea ends somewhere, and God's thunder will subside sooner or later when the beaker overflows with wrath. But Pivante's stubborn, mocking eyes will not be cast downward, no matter what comes. And I do not think he has yet heard of these new gadgets that have appeared between the heavens and us. For a long time, indeed, men have talked about one Copernicus who wanted to have the earth abdicate for the benefit of the sun and in more recent years about the telescope-inventor Galileo who peered more deeply into the heavens than anyone before had ever done.

"Thus we sailed for four weeks. The sea was black and rough and we must have been pushing northward, for the days got shorter and the temperature steadily colder. Eventually the rigging iced over to the point where we were unable to distinguish the ropes from the thin rags of sail that flapped in the wind. When we got up in the morning, Pivante's hair and beard framed his face like frozen shrubbery. He burst into laughter when we remarked about it, broke off long strands, and told us that's how men up north in Thule cut their hair.

"*Beatrice* had become a hideous sight. She had turned into an old glaciated ghost, covered with hoarfrost and ice, and whenever the waves rose particularly high all her spars creaked, and down rained big chunks of ice and icicles so long and sharp as to make walking on deck mortally dangerous. Leovantis's beautiful girl at the bow wore a mantle of ice, her midriff a frozen girdle of chastity; but her abdomen protruded large and shiny so that one would think the desolate waters up here had made her pregnant. The whole vessel was heavy and sluggish with ice; it had sunk deeply and no longer swayed so willingly.

"One night there was complete calm. The skies cleared, and for the first time in seven weeks stars shone overhead. I alerted every member of the crew so all would see, for they had begun to resign themselves to their fate, and I thought the cold dark and starry sky would give them—if not new courage—at least a strong awareness of the purity of the universe and convince them that in spite of everything there was no bungling in God's work of creation.

"At last the *Beatrice* rested motionless, glistening white, ethereal in the moonlight, and now all at once I realized a moment and eternity must be one and the same. I felt confused and anxious as if I had discovered something forbidden, and I didn't overcome that peculiar mood until two sailors from Catalonia began to sing very softly Thomas of Celano's 'Dies Irae.' Just then I caught sight of Pivante at the helm sneering to himself. Chips of ice flew out of his beard, and I wondered how advantageous it might be after all to have a pagan as helmsman.

"At dawn the wind came up. We kept moving further north and within a few days got into seas where there were icebergs. It was a strange spectacle, a veritable landscape of ice drifting all around, and in the dim light of early morning the shapes looked like story-book animals, such creatures as I have learned inhabited the earth thousands of years ago. Perhaps we were prowling about in God's store-room where He keeps samples of His creation which we have not yet seen. Actually I have faith in Galileo's telescope; by that I mean to say I don't put much stock in tales of evil spirits and witches riding broomsticks, but I know, too, that nothing is impossible. And while I haven't the slightest fear of pain and adversity, I do fear despondency from within. Indeed I can joke about seven-headed monsters that breathe out flames of many colors, but I am concerned about that little clammy leech in my own breast. I was certain all along that we would manage now that the wind had died down somewhat, and I was only waiting for it to lull sufficiently for us to repair the sails and to improvise an emergency rudder. Consequently I got everyone busy chipping the ice off the ship. The only one excused was Pivante. He stood stock still at a wheel that revolved in empty air, but I felt that must be allowed him because I don't think it does an old person any good to be deprived of a cherished delusion.

"Oddly enough, the *Beatrice* never collided with a floating iceberg. She maneuvered casually as if she were quite at home, as if she had discovered a secret in this world: to let herself drift, covered with ice, insensitive to wind and water.

"My major worry was our dwindling supply of food. We had a few fish-hooks which we baited with crusts of bread, but the fish up here—if indeed there were any—obviously did not relish crusts. Consequently we took to dipping them in wine, consuming them ourselves, and letting the hooks dangle empty in the water. I dreaded the time when we would have nothing left at all except wine. Of that we had

135

plenty, but I had consistently measured out no more than two quarts for each per day.

"Suddenly one day the wind stopped completely. There wasn't a stir. We set about promptly chipping ice off the sails. Then as soon as we had cleared and repaired them as much as was possible, we hoisted them to the tune of the somewhat somber chanty:

> Come wind from east, come wind from west,
> From anywhere, and drive us on,
> Our home is on a foam-swept deck.

"In the meanwhile the ship's carpenter had pounded loose the remains of the rudder. He fashioned a replacement, thinner, to be sure, and not totally dependable in a gale, but at any rate Pivante's importance was restored—in the eyes of the others.

"But now calm prevailed. The crew hoisted and lowered the sails several times to invite a breeze, but it was like waving a rag in the desert. There was not enough movement in the air to freeze a wet shirt on a man's body, and the song sounded hollow and flat in the arctic air.

"I brought out an extra quart for every member of the crew, for I realized this was a desperate hour. We stood huddled together in the middle of the deck and drank. Afterwards we resumed our efforts to court a breeze.

"For three days we did not move at all, and it was the season of darkness both day and night. Only at midday was there sufficient light for us to make out one another's faces, and then not light actually but something resembling a grayish shadow that crept in to where we were each time a door opened and closed on the rim of the world. At night, however, bright streamers ribboned the heavens, constantly shifting position and pattern, flashing and vanishing like fever flare-ups. The men had grown uncommunicative, and every noise sounded loud and sharp. Even when they whispered, it was as if they were breaking off fragments of silence to give to one another.

"The icebergs appeared and disappeared, made a circuit at night, and then returned. Now and again when they bumped, it sounded as if huge machines moaned and groaned in the blackness; the men stopped and stared at one another, and it occurred to me that if this is how the earth turns then perhaps we were in the neighborhood of the majestic mechanism that propels it. The sky and the ice and the sea were deep blue like dark metal, like a landscape set out to cool, the clanging of the craftsman's hammer still echoing in the room.

"Finally on the fourth day a wind came up, and we set sail in a south-southwesterly direction. Pivante's eyes sparkled with boyish confidence. 'There you see, captain! One must stay at the wheel,' he said. 'In a week we'll be in London!'

"For many days we sailed through dark waters with Pivante persistently at the helm. By now we had only a few loaves of bread left. I divided them among the crew and gave orders to allow each one three quarts of wine daily. They were to warm it and add cinnamon.

"One morning when I approached Pivante with a mug of steaming wine, I saw he had lashed himself to the wheel again. 'What's up?' I cried out. 'Is there another storm in the offing?' He laughed quietly while he drank.

" 'How are the men getting along, captain?' he asked.

" 'Not so well. Yesterday two of them stabbed each other, but now they're almost too groggy to fight. They're at their worst in the daytime. In this dim light they can't bear the sight of one another.'

" 'I need someone in the rigging,' said Pivante. 'We're in for a little storm. Besides, we're soon going to be near land.'

" 'Land!' I screamed. 'What land?'

"He emptied the mug and laughed. 'How should I know that? I only feel it. I feel it in the wheel. The wheel tells me almost everything that's going to happen. Look at my hands!' he said, holding them up in the filmy morning light. 'Do you see they're made of the same kind of wood as the wheel?'

"Now Pivante's laugh was a growl, as usual on occasions when he was especially pleased with himself. 'I relate to all things, captain: coming disasters, great festivals in Venice, old people at home in Genoa sitting on the steps in the evening, calm on the Indian Ocean. All come to me when my hands are on the wheel. But a dark and desolate wasteland lies ahead of us. I do not like it.'

" 'What land is it?' I cried again, forgetting in my haste Pivante's delight in making fun of me, for he really considered me to be only a naive, good-natured soul.

" 'Nothing but barren mountains without a harbor.'

" 'Ask the wheel! Then tell me what you feel.' I saw his eyes and the deep sneer hidden in his beard. 'Are you in that mood again?' I yelled in anger. 'Perhaps it's true that Saint Andrew spit on the floor when you were baptized.'

" 'Ho, ho! Saint Andrew's nothing but a poor specimen of handiwork, Fernando. In the thick of a crowd one Easter Day I stuck my knife into his backside, and he was rotten all the way through.'

" 'I'd like to know,' I retorted, 'you who can see everything—what will become of the likes of you in the end.'

" 'Well, I've wondered about that, too,' he laughed. 'So far I've not found myself any place. Isn't it odd, Fernando, that the best sailor in Genoa—who was a pagan besides— won't be assigned to a place anywhere? Do you know what

138

that means, Fernando? It means nothing. There is nothing beyond. But what is Nothing?'

" 'I know what Nothing is if it's the same as emptiness,' I answered, taking up my mug and starting to leave.

" 'Calm yourself, captain. You are young and have just suffered a great sorrow. My wheel also tells me that your grief will pass, but I am old and what befalls me won't have time to pass. On the other hand, when after a long life you finally put your faith in Nothing you will have peace of mind.'

"I went below and warned the crew to be on the alert, for Pivante's seamanship surpasses all witchcraft and hocus-pocus. Then I retreated to my own cabin and looked at Carmen's little portrait. Afterwards I knelt before the crucifix, and while I prayed I realized the storm was catching up with us.

"When I stepped out on deck again, the crew were already busy taking in the sails, and the waves were gradually rising higher behind us. I could hear Pivante's husky command above the roar of the storm, and when I came aft he pointed due west.

" 'Land, captain! We have to reach shelter before the storm breaks.'

"Through the driving rain I could see an island. It looked like a single mountain that had sprung up perpendicularly out of the sea—not unlike those icebergs we had circumvented earlier—and a wreath of foam encircled it.

" 'What land do you imagine this to be?' I was yelling as loudly as I could, directly into his ear.

" 'Don't know, captain!' He was laughing. 'But land it is, for sure—though you aren't likely to find a market for wines and silks here. Anyway we'll discover how seaworthy *Beatrice* is.'

139

" 'There might be shallows around it!' I shouted.

" 'I know that already!' he shouted back. 'Just so the rudder holds!'

"Presently we were so close to land that I could hear the water crash against the rocks. The sails were down, and we did only what was necessary to maneuver the craft. The crew stood around on deck holding fast to railings and ends of ropes. We sailed to the left of the island, and just as we passed a precipitous tongue of land I glanced at Pivante and saw him craning his neck as if to listen. Suddenly his eyes got big and unbelieving. He spun the wheel around and leaned on it with his whole weight. I ran over and grabbed hold to help him. In that instant a violent jolt went right through the ship, and then followed a prolonged succession of creaks in the bottom as the *Beatrice* ran aground on a skerry. The first wave caught the schooner and whirled it halfway around so it was left with its side toward the storm. The next wave swept over the deck and carried with it all that was loose on board.

"When the third wave struck, I was sitting with my back against the cabin wall. I heard the mainmast crack with a loud noise and watched the rigging collapse. The last I saw was Pivante being hurled across the deck and down into the sea, the wheel like a gigantic disk underneath him."

On an Island in the Sea

"When I regained consciousness in the ice-cold water, I was at once aware of a sickening odor that the sea could not dispel: a mixture of blood and native Italian wine. I lay there bumping my head against the edge of one of the big casks. The cover had come off. I lay virtually afloat in a bay of brine and wine. At the same time the thought ran through my mind that these oaken kegs of ours were extremely solid. If I could only manage to crawl inside of one of them, the jolt would be lessened were I thrown up on land.

"I kicked violently, the force of the water helped push me, and when I got myself into the bottom of the keg, I curled up like a frog and twisted around so my head was at the open end. Indeed I accomplished that just in the nick of time when a wave struck and set the keg in an upright position.

"Standing there in the wine barrel being driven to land, I kept hearing distant cries for help. Then I saw the *Beatrice* separate into two parts with a motion as graceful as if she were making a curtsy before slipping down off the skerry. Immediately afterwards sheets of foam flowed past me. I realized the sea itself were being smashed to bits and spewed back, and momentarily I had a false and fleeting sense of security at having come so near to solid ground. In the next instant, however, my head hit the side of the keg, and for one giddy second I tasted the salty-sweet blend of wine and sea water as I sank down lower in the barrel.

"On coming to my senses the second time after the shipwreck, I lay half-buried under seaweed and barrel staves on a narrow sandbar. My body had furrowed a deep groove in the sand where the sea had cradled me back and forth between the water's edge and the mountain wall. The elements had planned to bury me alive, and from that, I dare say, one could make a meaningful deduction. Above me I heard the wind whistling through the clefts in the mountains, but the sea pounded vainly against the rocks only to be churned into dazzling white froth. My whole body was sore, and I stayed there a long time, face down in the shifting sand. I heard mighty powers take hold down below, the ground under me quivered like a tensed muscle, a deep, persistent, and defiant tone filled the atmosphere all around

141

me as if an organ were concealed within the mountain, and in contrast to the music the noise of the wind and the waves sounded like little more than trivial bickering.

"When I recovered my wits properly, I realized I was lying prone in the sand laughing and crying at the same time, and for an instant a wild thrill of ecstasy went through me, an overwhelming zest for life such as I had not felt since that fateful day in Genoa.

"No bones were broken. The sea had relinquished me without ransom. To be sure, I had an ugly gash in my forehead as a reminder, but the cut was not very painful. On the contrary, it seemed the bleeding cleared my brain, and I decided immediately to seek shelter somewhere so I wouldn't freeze to death here on the sand.

"Occasionally the storm tore holes in the darkness, and I could see that this desolate land had a high sinister sky above it. As I fumbled my way along the mountain wall in search of a possible ascent, I caught sight of Pivante pinned under the broken wheel. I knelt down, took out my knife, and cut him loose, all the time wondering whether Pivante—the same as I—had no anchor in life and that we reached for the same kind of buoy; a scrap of wood, a picture, a few remnants of thoughts.

"When I put my arms around him to raise him up, he vomited quarts of sea water and soon afterwards opened his eyes. Obviously he didn't know me and he wasn't able to get up, but I succeeded in lifting him to a standing position. Fortunately he was not a heavy man or I would not have been able to carry him with me. I think I remember walking a long time—several hours—or perhaps actually only a few minutes—before I found a kind of gorge that led up from the sea. I climbed until I reached a plateau and then continued inland, the wind at my back. About two hundred yards beyond, we stood at the end of a precipice.

142

Below lay the interior of the island, a flat dark plain with no sign of habitation. I laid Pivante down on the heather and set out to find shelter from the storm. That was not easy; the mountain was a series of round knolls, bare of trees; all little protrusions seemed to have been worn away by the weather. Here and there grew a kind of gray-green moss that could hardly have covered a field mouse. But again I was fortunate, and I felt there was something almost uncanny about so many strokes of good luck being lavished on one who really had nothing to live for. I found a small hole, very much like a cave, in the side of the mountain and carried Pivante to it. His lips were blue and his body trembled. I pulled the moss to make a bed for him, but it was freezing cold, even though it neither blew nor rained in where we were, and then I hurried back to the shore to see whether anything might have washed up on land.

"The *Beatrice* was gone for good. I saw the top of her mast and a piece of the rigging sticking up near the reef and a flap of canvas beckoning to me. I spied a mess of wreckage on the sandbar, and I couldn't refrain from laughing in the very midst of tragedy. There lay a heap of exotic, luxurious objects intended for people in warm, magnificent houses—among other things a gold-embossed leather chair, a Chinese teapot, cups and a few bowls bearing my insignia, the lamp shade from my own cabin, and an empty window frame. Best of all, farther off in the shallows I found what I had most hoped for; I found two big bolts of silk, and hidden between them the little decanter of choice wine that I usually serve to my customers.

"I set about at once to drag the things up through the gorge, and before it got dark I had the two bolts of cloth, the decanter, and the two china cups in place in the cave. Then I took off Pivante's wet clothes and bundled him securely in yellow silk so he closely resembled an oversized, puffed-up cocoon. That accomplished, I poured a pint of strong wine down his throat, and as soon as he fell asleep I got out of my own wet garments and wrapped myself up in the silk of the other bolt. I also put on my wet clothes over the silk so they would dry on my body. At last—and by now it was completely dark—I made a couch for each of us, one of red silk and the other of yellow, and still there was sufficient yardage left for me to hang up a sort of curtain in front of the mouth of the cave. I also drank a pint of the heady amber wine, and since I had not eaten properly for a long time, I immediately got gloriously drunk. I barely managed to lift Pivante up onto his bed of red silk, and the last I remembered before sleep overtook me was a drapery sweeping across my face.

"Pivante slept on. He had drawn the heavy silk up over his face and obviously was living within it like a butterfly before it breaks a hole in its cocoon. (English nobility—and common citizens, too, for that matter—prize this material highly because it is satiny and exquisite and inspires pleasant thoughts on awakening.)

"I was faint, nauseated, and hungry, and two swallows of wine made me groggy. The storm was over, the curtain hung straight down, and through the red silk I saw daylight over a strange, hazy, reddish-blue world where sky and sea were intermingled in a gossamer-veiled fairyland. I lay down again, unable to destroy the shield between me and the mysterious world beyond.

"Had death come this night? Was death a gentle sleep, and had I awakened precisely in the first minutes of eternity? If this were true, then at least I knew now that we take with us across the threshold those things which surround us in our final hour. As I reached out I caught hold of the decanter and the bowl. I closed my eyes and prepared for eternity

144

to begin to pass. Then I heard Pivante mumble in his sleep: 'Come storm and calm, sun and frost—' And all at once the whole dream vanished. I turned over on my side and uncovered his face. He wore a strained expression, his jaw was set firm, and yet there was something childlike, distinctly different from the expression familiar to me, and when I bent over him I saw another face behind his face—a pair of strange lines at the corners of his mouth as if someone had made scrolls with a fine goose quill while he slept. Apparently Pivante kept his private soul veiled in daylight. This was not the face that believed in Nothing. To be sure, bitter, arrogant rivers and ravines ran down into his tawny beard from which he had broken off icicles in the cold, but when surrendered to sleep his face was also that of a child, a child whose feelings had been bruised and who needed to be comforted.

"Eagerly I leaned forward. He suddenly opened his eyes. 'What are you looking for, captain?' He spoke sternly but immediately laughed as usual. 'Did you think by chance I had departed for good?'

" 'You were so quiet; I wondered whether—'

" 'You shouldn't wonder so much, captain. That's not good for someone who is going to sail the seas and sell silks. Have I overslept my watch?'

"I told him what had taken place since the shipwreck.

" 'Splendid, Fernando!' (He addressed me as captain and as Fernando by turns and I think he did so by intent, though I was never able to decide on what occasions he preferred the one to the other.) 'And the others?'

"I threw up my arms and shook my head; it suddenly occurred to me that, after all, I had not given a thought to the ship's company since the mishap.

"Pivante raised himself up and looked around. 'You are

145

prodigal with silk, captain. I see you've lined the mountain. Your competitors will be pleased.'

" 'But not the widows.'

" 'Your soul is much too sensitive, captain. Your father's was, too. That's why he never acquired more than one ship in his time. Serentis and Menzolis in Venice are shrewd; now they own three schooners and one caravel each, but no one accuses them of being unfeeling. Moreover,' he said as he emptied the beaker I had given him, 'this place looks as if it needs outer clothing, but it could do with wool.'

"I got up and tore aside the curtain. Daylight flooded the cave, and I saw Pivante's eyes were burning with fever. 'You are ill, Pivante,' I cried. 'We must get away from here!'

"He laughed mockingly. 'Yes, see to it, captain, that the sails are hoisted, and then we'll shove off with the whole island.' He lay back again and I made a pillow for him so he could rest there and look out.

" 'Thank you, captain,' he said briefly. 'Now you can sail. It's good for an old man to lie still and be lazy. The wind is steady and the sea is smooth and we have worlds of time. The only thing we lack is food, but we're beginning to get used to that by now. If we had all the grapes that went into the making of this wine, maybe we could survive.'

" 'Survive!' I cried. 'Of course, we'll survive. Otherwise why do you think we came out of it alive?'

"He laughed and looked at me with those sparkling eyes. 'Oh, you're just like your father, Fernando. He, too, always found a plan in everything. You're so trustful, you Riazolas. And then he was always ready to help when God didn't act. Once an albatross had got caught in the rigging and we had to cut several good ropes to free him. Another time when we were driving down to the harbor, he stopped the horses to lift a beetle out of the wheel tracks. 'Surely you see it is on its way to the ditch,' he said, 'and aren't we on our way to

146

the sea?' On that voyage we lost our youngest sailor. He fell overboard in the Indian Ocean on a calm, sunny day. I recall how your father went around scowling at me afterwards as if he expected me to say, 'He is, of course, on his way, captain.'

"For a while no one spoke. Then suddenly he asked, 'Do you know what day this is?'

" 'First day of Easter.'

" 'Then it must be spring, Fernando. The air outside is milder. This catacomb of yours is not for Christian people.'

"I helped him to his feet, but when he tried to walk he couldn't. 'You've laced me in tightly,' he joked. 'When I'm dead I want you to prop me up there inside the cave so I can look out on the sea. I'll surely last. I'm of the same breed as the icebergs we sailed among.'

"I moved him forward to the edge of the precipice and stacked the bolts of cloth around him.

" 'Once I greeted a fat prince in Pondicherry,' he said, taking a sip. 'He was sitting on a white elephant just as I am sitting here on a mountain crag in Thule, swathed in silk, and when the elephant tramped by me the prince plopped a coin into my hat, no doubt because I was a poor white, the most despicable of men. He had a long pole with a spearpoint that he stuck into the elephant's ear when life became too boring. Apparently it quickened his senses to see red on white. To what extremes won't a person go to add excitement and meaning to life! Later I learned he did not fare so well. For years the elephant had endured these sharp stabs patiently, and now his big floppy ears had grown limp and hung like folds of dried-up skin. But one day when the prince was exceedingly dejected, he had stuck the spearpoint right through the one ear. Thereupon the elephant sighed deeply, shook the driver off like a cow getting rid of a flea on her back, and took off for the woods. The prince,

147

however, was securely fastened in his seat, and the wild ride continued far into the jungle until a big branch swept the chair with His Highness in it down off the elephant's back. The white elephant was going at high speed and made a circle of several hundred yards before turning around, then trotted back to where the prince lay, and sat down on top of him. When the servants came, all they found was a round depression lined with the prince and his silks. They agreed to bury him on the spot by filling in the hole to level the ground just as it was. On their return they explained that the prince had been spirited away by his gods.

" 'Why am I telling you this? Well, captain, you have been like a son to me, and now that I have grounded your ship, I have nothing more than this piece of gold to give you.'

"Pivante was struggling to put his hand into the bolt of silk. 'I want to save you the trouble of hunting for it your-self afterwards—things like that are always unpleasant—though I have certainly had a part in ransacking the dead without qualms.'

" 'What are you talking about!' I shouted angrily. 'Now just lie down while I find something to eat. In two days you'll be well.'

" 'Here it is!' he said, holding the gold coin up in the air. 'Every time I've caught myself feeling superior to people or animals I've taken it out and looked at it. You know very well, Fernando, that I believe when the end comes for me then I go to Nothing. But if you put yourself above me because I believe in the land of Nothing, then I also want you to remember that I couldn't bear to see people or animals suffer. This is the only thing I know with certainty now, and this knowledge I bequeath to you in compensation for the *Beatrice* which I ran aground.'

" 'You speak as if your hours are numbered.' I felt faint.

148

'You who have been shipwrecked five times with my father and twice with me.'

"Pivante smiled gently and looked out across the sea. 'Indeed, the *Beatrice I* was a remarkable vessel. The more she foundered, the better she sailed. She should have been a human being. A part of her always survived, and then we patched her up and put her out to sea again.'

" 'You are saying that luck does not follow me.'

" 'Don't get excited, Fernando,' he replied. 'In spite of all I am the one who sailed the *Beatrice II*. This is my seventh shipwreck, and it is said that one should not tempt fate; I have been like the Indian prince—not out of boredom certainly—but when I was younger I was very sure of myself. Your father had to keep his reins on me. So it's really not too soon—'

"I glanced down at him. Fever had burned the cloudy film from his eyes, and now they were big and bright above the sunken cheeks. His hooked nose stood out like a reef on a weather-beaten, tempest-torn shore. Pivante's face was like something without a port, and I was obsessed by the desire to know more about that other face I had seen when he was asleep. His hair and beard were grayed by the salt water, but I knew that underneath there were red bristles as when he had been on land a long time.

" 'You're not ill, Pivante,' I said and refilled his beaker. 'You have only a slight fever.'

" 'Ho, ho! You Riazolas could convince the devil. If there actually were a heaven, the order of reception into it would be: 1. Riazola of Genoa. 2. The twelve apostles and the Holy Father—. But someone may perhaps ask where is the mate Pivante. No, he won't be coming; he has gone back into earth; he has turned to mold; now they are harrowing his skull; now they are sowing rye on his chest. No, my boy, I am not ill; nor do I have a fever. But I have been sent a summons from the land of Nothing. I know this wretched old hulk well enough to feel what's going on in the framework. Captain, do you feel how mild it is up here in Thule? A blessed Easter morning without bells. No, Captain Fernando, what I feel within me is not the ringing of bells. I feel the earth working itself up into me; my muscles are crumbling. The earth is saying: That mate Pivante is a stubborn fellow. He doesn't want to come down to me, so I will go up to him.'

" 'Lie down now, Pivante,' I said and pushed him back against the bolts of cloth, but he sat up with a jerk.

" 'I'm in no hurry to lie down,' he said laughingly. 'No, let's rather take a good look around this island. Have you ever seen anything so absolutely barren, Fernando? And you would accuse God of having created this? This place is nothing but the leftovers from Liguria. Look at those bald crags. From behind, they resemble our fat monks at home when they stand mumbling in the rose garden. And that black place down there—is it a bog? I don't want to go there, Fernando. You must see to that. Slough worms! No, I want to be put down into the sand where we were tossed up. I'm tough. I'll go on living a long time after my heart stops beating. My muscles and my senses will live on. I want to hear the sea, captain. You can surely understand that.'

" 'I think this is a beautiful spot!' I said, trying to divert his thoughts. 'Look, here comes the sunlight over the mountain. Down below the wet marsh sparkles. And the side of the mountain has already turned green even if there is still snow in some places.'

" 'Fernando, there's not one tree here; nothing grows; people can't live here.'

" 'I see both heather and moss, and look how bright the colors are!'

" 'Rocks, heather, moss—those are nothing to fasten one's hopes on. Such things will disappear in the time I have ahead of me. The sea is the only thing that will endure. If I hadn't already decided on the land of Nothing, I would just as soon become water. Don't you think it might be possible to siphon a barrel of brine out of me considering how much I've swallowed in my lifetime? Then I would rest idly on the beach in the warm sunshine or skim over the globe on the crest of a big swell in the moonlight across the Pacific and turn somersaults like the ocean spray when the breakers crash. Roll up along the coast of East Africa— feel the shark's fins scratch me. You'll never be a real sailor, Fernando. You use the sea to freight bolts of cloth. The sea is a person, not a warehouse floor. You have offended the sea, and now it has rid itself of you by throwing you up on this crag.'

"Pivante moaned and lay down again. 'May I have a little more of your wine, captain? I don't understand—but it doesn't affect me much any more. It's exactly as if someone taps it out of me while I'm drinking. Maybe there's a little devil sitting at the base of my throat absorbing it. But at any rate wine is still our best pledge—wine drunk to seal a bargain. Shall we make a bargain, captain, that you don't pray for me afterwards? In return, I'll give you this coin.'

"Pivante placed the gold piece solemnly into my hand and sighed. 'You have experienced a truly great sorrow, Fernando. You have been fortunate. But you must not brood so much over it. Your grief will take care of itself without your concentrating on it. You must stop reproaching yourself for visiting the dealer Toris that day. My sorrows have been only minor, such worries as dogs and donkeys have. Such griefs are nothing for a grown-up man to keep going on. I've always been bothered with cricks in my back.

151

They come and go. That is about all my sorrows have amounted to also—cricks in my soul.'

" 'Don't you want me to pray with you anyway?' I asked, bending over him.

" 'Listen here, captain!' he said, and his face was distorted in pain. 'Understand that I don't want any godliness sneaked in on me the last minute when I have invested a whole lifetime in the effort to reach the land of Nothing. I see it before me now—sleep without dreams—peace at last—rest from it all.'

"Suddenly he fell back against the rolls of silk and closed his eyes. I leaned forward to listen. His heart was beating, he was breathing a little unevenly, he was asleep. But now the other Pivante came back in that taut face, the Pivante in sleep. The lines shifted direction; he became unrecognizable as a landscape changes its appearance in a flood. I looked at him a long time, but it was as if I were watching a strange face in a crowd, and my memory drifted back to the games with masks at home during Easter time. What can a face reveal?

"Then I walked down to the sea.

"The tide was rising. The water came way up to the mountain wall; the wreckage lay partly submerged, but I got hold of half of Pivante's wheel.

"The day was calm, the weather bright and sunny, and a mild breeze blew gently from the south. I had expected to find shells and other creatures in the seaweed, but now I had to wait for low tide; I laid the wheel aside and waded along the edge of the mountain in quest of gulls' eggs. Above me, the big gray birds circled in their melancholy flight over the island—homeless—and I found nothing at all.

"When I returned, Pivante was sitting upright, staring out upon the sea. I noted at once that his fever had soared, and the thought came to me that he would die at high tide.

152

It was as if he had read my mind, for a quivering smile crossed his face. He said, 'The tide is on the rise, isn't it? I can feel it. My body is getting lighter. Soon I shall really be afloat, captain.'

"I could hear he was trying hard to be cheerful, and I had to fake an errand to get behind him so he wouldn't see my tears. Afterwards I took the broken wheel and stuck it down into the heather next to his legs so he would have something to brace himself against. Then I poured him another drink of wine, and he managed to hold the beaker himself. 'Is it true that you are clairvoyant?' I asked, sitting down beside him.

"'Certainly,' he answered as he drank, and then he laughed mockingly just as he had always done when he was at his best. 'Yes, I'm clairvoyant, but not in the same way as fortune tellers and star gazers are. I see all that is happening, but I don't always believe that what I am seeing is what is actually taking place. What difference does it make? I see big things and little things, all that lives and all that has lived and all that will live. But, of course, it is not always certain that everything is really happening as I see it. But what of that! I have made many long voyages, as you well know, and when I'm at home I'm also on a voyage.'

"I leaned forward, and I thought I felt the warmth of his feverish face in my own. 'But beyond, Pivante, beyond? Can you see anything of what is beyond?'

"'Are you still at it?' He laughed gaily. 'Have you turned into a fisher of souls? Or do you perhaps think I'm so near the door now that I can peek behind the curtains? I'm going home to Nothing, Fernando, and that is nothing to make a row about. I haven't said no to either joy or sorrow, and it has all been wonderful except that devilish sciatica—

153

but time eventually runs out—Don't talk nonsense, captain. I'm hauling in time now—'

"Suddenly he spoke excitedly and fumbled with something in the air. 'What are you hysterical about, Fernando? This is my affair, but if I were ever able to return from the land of Nothing I would surely come back to tell you something or other.' His breathing was rapid and shallow, and I heard a strange rattle in his throat. 'Guard yourself against all kinds of brooding, Fernando. All thoughts that cause one to sit still are poisonous.'

"All at once he shook violently and slumped over, but he was still in a half-sitting position. For a while he did not look at me, and his eyes began to roll upward. I thought he was dying, and I grasped his shoulder and his arm and shook him, crying, 'Pivante, come back!'

"He turned his head slowly toward me and I could see he was on the way. 'Soon there will be a spring flood,' he whispered with mold on his tongue. 'Then the *Beatrice* will drift to shore. Cut the little boat loose or take the hatch covers and tie them together. Use the sailspar for a mast, the silk for a sail, head straight east—I have seen land there—'

"He lifted his hand in an effort to point, and then he died.

"He sat upright between the bolts of cloth; it was high noon, and the sun shone bright and clear over the island.

"I closed his eyes and wrapped him well in the yellow silk. At ebb tide I buried him in the sand close to the rock wall.

"He lies facing west, in three feet of sand, for I had only a board to use as a spade. I respected his request and did not pray over him. Where is he now? Has he turned into sand? Or mold? Or has he been resurrected just the same—against his will? Or does he still hear the sea? Twice every twenty-four hours the sea rolls over him. Does he hear a song from all the seas he has sailed? Twice also he lies dry under the sand. Does he hear the sand crumble through him? Does he hear time—the first difficult moments of eternity? Or does he perhaps lie down there chafing and fretting in grand style and using ugly words?

"This is an orderly and boring city. Occasionally a couple of carriages rumble across the pavement. People like it; it is a safe and hard sound. Nothing can happen here. In the tavern the burghers sit with big, dull eyes and with froth in their beards. They don't believe in anything, not even in their own death. And in the meanwhile time is passing."

IN THE PEAT BOG

"That night I slept fitfully. I dreamed about Carmen, my wife, and awakened often; each time it seemed as if she had just died. Who can defend himself against thoughts that come to one in sleep? It's difficult enough during the day. Finally toward morning I fell into a dull, blank state of drowsiness. When I woke up, it was already late in the day. The sun shone blood-red through the silk, it was as if the whole world were drunk, and several minutes elapsed before I could make out the dim contours of reality. But at the same time I had a distinct feeling I was no longer alone, and when I sat up and supported myself on my elbow, I caught sight of a young girl squatting near the opening and staring at me. Beside her stood a white goat.

"'Nonsense!' I thought and closed my eyes. 'Hunger makes you have hallucinations.' With that, I remembered about a gifted young monk of Verona who fasted through the Advent season in order to 'see' the Gospel. Unfortunately he fell ill and died as a result. Perhaps by now he has become eternal and permanently clairvoyant. But when I opened my eyes again, she smiled at me, raised her hand, and

155

seemed real indeed. She was, however, also a vision, a revelation—a lovelier creature I have never seen in any land. Her golden hair, lighter than amber, hung all the way to her waist. Her mouth was like a rose, sparklingly alive like running water—that much was plain to a starving man —and her bright blue eyes were fixed directly on me.

"On discovering I was awake she stood up. It was as if a young sapling shot up in front of me, and I saw she was slender and limber like a stone pine.

"I stood up, too, and must have looked strange with silk billowing in all directions, for she pointed at my drapery and burst into laughter. I tried to speak to her in Italian and in French and in English, but she merely shook her head in amusement. Then I stepped out of the cave, pointed to the sea, and charaded a shipwreck with my hands. She understood that, nodded vigorously, and confirmed the affirmation with a grimace.

"I was very faint and sick with hunger, but since I had been well reared among the elite of Genoa, I went back into the cave and poured two beakers of wine. 'Welcome!' I spoke in Italian and bowed to her, and then the bright and happy thought flashed through my mind that I ought to make the most of it because this also would still be only a dream. But she did not vanish in a mist after all. She smiled, imitated my welcome, and bowed to me in return. Then she broke into laughter as if she thought me a fool, but on tasting the wine she let out a cry of surprise and promptly emptied the whole beaker.

"Apparently people really lived here, and for a moment I wondered whether Pivante would have still been alive if we had discovered that earlier. Although—the old helmsman had a will of his own about everything and perhaps wouldn't have favored a delay.

"The girl must have read my thoughts because her expression suddenly grew sad, and in order to offer some sort of explanation I used my hands to tell her of Pivante's death. She nodded comprehendingly but then immediately pointed to her mouth and her stomach and looked at me inquiringly. I shook my head and nodded and made all manner of signs to indicate hunger. She turned and motioned eastward; there on the other side of the island I saw gray smoke rise over the marsh. At once she started walking across the rocky ground and beckoned me to follow.

"We took a narrow path southward along the ridge. Occasionally she would stop to wait for me; she nodded again, and her eyes told me she didn't think I had always been such a weakling—only now for lack of food. She tripped along in her fur moccasins with a spring in her step—a delight to see—most simply dressed in a short homespun tunic with a sleeveless jacket of the same material.

"Somewhat farther on, the path veered to the east and disappeared in a cleft. When we began the descent she took hold of my arm and steadied me over the steepest places; her natural grace prevented my feeling the least bit embarrassed at being guided. Soon we found ourselves on the marsh at the base of the island. On turning for an instant to look up at the mountain, she let out a quick, gay shout and motioned toward the cave. At once I understood the reason for her joyful outburst; up there the silk draperies were waving as if a big red and yellow flower had unfolded its petals to the light.

"We continued our eastward trek, all the while slogging through marshland, wet and spongy underfoot. Heather grew profusely everywhere and a few scraggly birches. Sara (she had pointed her index finger between her breasts —without so much as a hint of flirtation in her eyes—and repeated her name three times. And because of my hunger

157

I had pointed to my stomach and told her my name. I discovered later that she thought Fernando meant 'hunger' in Italian, all kinds of hunger—also the kind that sets in when hunger for food is satisfied) showed me the buds were about to burst. She regarded them tenderly as if they were her own offspring and then she made a sound with her lips, and I still had enough sensitivity left in me after the shipwreck to realize she was saying something hands could not communicate.

"As we neared the sea and the marsh became more firm, we had to detour around peat-ponds. (Up there people live off the sea and burn the land.) On every hand stacks of peat the height of a man were standing up to dry. When I happened to bump into one stack and knock down a few turfs, she quickly went back to replace each one carefully.

"At last we reached the sea. Protected by a rock wall stood a small low building of stone and earth with a sod roof. Acrid gray smoke rose from a hole in the roof and settled heavily over the marsh. At the shore was a boat-shed, and a long narrow boat with tall prows had been pulled halfway up on land. Beyond that I did not notice much, for I was so weak and famished that I had passed the stage of hunger in which one's eyesight is reputed to be exceptionally keen.

"As soon as we had stepped inside, Sara fetched a wooden bowl of milk and a piece of black bread. The milk was bitter, and the bread sour; I felt as if I were sampling the very nature of the island itself—a sort of sacramental fare—and I devoured everything she set before me. She stood watching the whole time. She showed me to a couch that looked as if it had been nailed together out of flotsam and jetsam. Fully clothed as I was, I climbed onto it and fell promptly asleep.

158

"On awaking the next morning I heard rain pelting down. I lay in a half-dark hut with earthen walls, the floor was also of earth, yes, even the scant bit of daylight that sifted in through the hole in the roof seemed mixed with earth. The sour bread had that same dingy color—perhaps they milled earth for flour. I had heard tales of the people in Thule, but wayfarers, of course, exaggerate with every passing mile, so I ought not take any stock in what I had heard. Damp smoke filled the room and made my eyes smart. Embers still smoldered in the open fireplace in the corner, but the rain was coming down through the opening above it so I climbed up and covered it. At the same time I poked the fire and added two squares of peat, but then the inside got unbearable. I went out and left the little door standing open. The outdoors was not much better, however, for a thick blanket of fog hung over the marsh, and the mountain was hidden in a heavy mist coming in from the sea. God had closed His damper over this world. I suddenly heard a bird screech and I imagined I could see it rummaging with its wings in the impenetrable air. This place was desolate and fallow—as the void must have been before the Creation, and the sky and the sea were one.

"Just the same—was I dreaming? I went over to the hut and leaned against the wall. I wanted to pick up a stone and toss it into the fog but I couldn't find one, and all at once I grew tense with worry that I would never see the sun again. Had I not been convinced the earth is round, I would have suspected we had been shipwrecked beyond the edge and had been thrown up on one of those dismal ledges leading down to the great Nothing. Just then the stacks of peat on the marsh began to move. They paraded and shifted places, they came and went in the fog, and then they came back again.

" 'Sara!' I could see my breath form her name in the fog.

'Sara!' I called again. I felt her hand on my arm. She smiled, but then she shook her head vehemently and pointed to the open door. I felt my knees trembling. The past few days I had subsisted solely on wine, now the effect had worn off, and there was nothing but low-grade blood left in my veins. I returned her smile and tried to look brave, but my pretense made her laugh so heartily that her breath formed a cloud around her mouth. Then she took my hand, drew me back into the hut, and pushed me down onto the couch.

"The next few days I lay in a stupor, and I think I ran a fever, but then again it is just as likely that this new world, which was indeed a dream, affected me as would a fever. There were sunny days and rainy days. I heard sea birds scream at dawn; others came, strange birds whose calls were not familiar. The weather turned milder, and when the rain fell the sound of it was loud and distinct as if it dropped from a lofty sky. The fog dispersed. Spring was coming to Thule, and with that realization my fever mounted.

"In the midst of all this Sara wandered in and out like a goddess. Three times daily she brought me food. Wherever she walked the goat tripped along at her heels, she milked her outside the entrance door, gave me the milk to drink out of a wooden bowl, and under her surveillance I had to force it down my throat, warm and distasteful as it was. When I wrinkled up my nose, she pursed her full soft lips and nodded determinedly. I drank slowly and turned up my nose between swallows. For my dinner I was given fish—head and tail intact—its liver swimming in grease. Occasionally she would bring me a piece of the sour bread, and eventually I came to understand she was offering me a great delicacy because I never saw her eat any of it herself.

"Sara was very young. When she leaned over me, I always

160

caught the spicy perfume of fresh heather and the tang of salt water that seemed to be a part of her.

"She was completely innocent. At night she undressed in the middle of the room and did so in a manner so charming as to make her simple garments shine and glow. This gave me ideas and I grew eager with the anticipation of being well and strong again. During the day she wore her long hair tucked under her belt to keep it out of the way, but in the evening she often stood in the doorway, stark naked, grooming it carefully with a comb fashioned out of bone. When the sun cast its rays slantwise across the island, she was like a figure of shimmering gold, and I could perceive dimly the fine network of veins in her delicate skin. Then she would shut the door, close up the smoke hole in the ceiling and lie down under a fur coverlet in the farthest corner of the room.

"When she wasn't stacking peat on the moor or catching fish on the sea, she would sit on my bed and teach me the names of things that surrounded us. I was soon aware, however, that she was learning Italian much faster than I was learning her language. She absorbed words as easily as parched ground drinks up rain, and within a few days we were able to converse without having to draw pictures in the air.

"The days were steadily lengthening, the hours of darkness diminishing, and even in the night I could see light sifting in like colorless water through cracks in the wall.

"One warm night I got up to open the door. Sara's bare arm hung down over the side of her bed, she was breathing evenly and softly, and I fancied I could hear the same gentle sound of growing that one can hear in rare moments when he presses his ear to the ground in spring. The fur coverlet had slipped to the floor, and I wanted to take it up and spread it over her. She lay on her back, outstretched, with the lower part of her body slightly twisted, one knee resting on the other as if she had fallen asleep in the act of turning over. Under her long hair I could see her breasts lift like two white mountain peaks rising out of the sea. I have seen such mountains in the Orient, shrouded in golden mist at dawn. Not only is it a beautiful sight to behold, but it also creates a desire to see, to know and to experience. (Are you laughing, Pivante? Do you think I'm simply inventing this to cover up a vulgar longing to stare at her body?) I leaned over her closely, held my breath like a true believer in accepting the Bread of the Sacrament, and even though I had seen her breasts every evening, I now cherished the wish to look at her while she was asleep. As I carefully brushed her hair aside, I discovered a tiny birthmark between her breasts. It was golden and shaped almost like a hoof print. I stooped down. Suddenly her eyes opened; she smiled and looked at me. Then she closed her eyes again, sighed, and breathed deeply. I covered her with the fur coverlet and went back to my own bed in deep wonderment and joy at what I had witnessed.

"She had already left the next morning when I awakened. I got up, dressed, and went outdoors. Big patches of the marsh were covered with newly cut rectangles of peat that stood supporting one another in pairs.

"Sara was busy stacking them. She waved and greeted me 'Good morning' in her high resonant voice, seeming not to know anything of what had taken place during the night. I cleared a space beside her and set about to stack the peat in a circle just as she was doing. I tried my best, but a seafaring man is hardly any good at standing still picking up bits of earth, and when I was half through, my pile collapsed. Sara laughed aloud, clapped her hands in childish mirth, and then squatted down beside me to show exactly how one builds peat cocks, piece by piece.

"She was completely absorbed in this monotonous job. Indeed I have watched the pawnbroker in Genoa fondle coins in his little cubicle after closing time, but to see Sara bend down to lift the turf easily and tenderly as if she were picking flowers was something different. She is a child, I thought, and yet some instinct or other (Pivante always maintained we Riazolas had no instinct for anything else than buying cheaply and selling dearly, and that was really no instinct at all) told me there must lie a deeply hidden experience underneath the appearances.

"When we had finished rebuilding my first stack, she looked up at me and blushed, and I did something foolish: I grasped her hand and kissed it. She withdrew it slowly, laughed a little bewildered, and looked first at her fingers and then at my lips. Her face wore the same expression as when I spoke words she didn't understand.

"By now I had recovered completely from the fever and was beginning to think about the future again. ('The future!' Pivante would have said with disarming irony. 'Do you think your father thought about you when he planted the seed in your mother?') Of course I could sail to the mainland, but what should I go home for! Nothing but a grave awaited me at home, and wasn't I really too young to sit beside a grave the rest of my life? The *Beatrice* lay on the bottom of the ocean. Creditors would be my only visitors, and the name Riazola would have been forgotten or be mentioned only out of pity because good luck had not been with me.

"But could I discuss this with Sara? Her eyes would only get big and sad and she would be more beautiful than ever, and it would be twice as hard for me to leave the island.

"I weighed these thoughts while I stood poking at a slab

163

of peat. 'Such a bit of turf,' I mused, and without my being aware Pivante's reflections were becoming my own—'such a bit of compressed earth, Fernando, look at it. You imagine it has no value, but it is more precious than all the books in the Vatican. What you are holding in your hand is a part of eternity. Perhaps your thoughts are drifting back to Carmen, and you can't forget that she begged you to stay at home that fateful day. But what are you and Carmen fifty years from now? You Riazolas are given to brooding and don't accomplish anything. You are like blind horses moving in a circle turning a mill-wheel. Now is the time for you to live, Fernando. You don't have so many breaths left— 20 x 60 x 24 x 365 x 50—what does it add up to? Nothing as over against a beetle in the earth. Figure it out, you who are a tradesman, and you'll see how little it amounts to. Nonsense, Pivante! You old joker, you clown! You spoil things for me.'

"Suddenly I dashed the slab of turf to the ground in anger. Sara looked at me, shocked. Then she put her hand on my arm and said sadly, 'You are not well yet, Fernando. Go indoors and lie down.'

"But now, oblivious to everything about her except her beauty and her youth, I forgot all my old inhibitions, threw my arms around her, and drew her close to me. I did not kiss her, only stroked her hair and whispered into her ear a host of words she didn't understand.

"She said nothing, but when I released her she immediately returned to her work, and in her face, which was more expressive than spoken words could ever be, I read wonder and confusion and also a kind of sweet shyness.

" 'Now you have committed a sin, Fernando,' I reproached myself. 'You have destroyed her innocence.'

"We worked a while in silence. I glanced in her direction

164

a couple of times and then I noticed she had botched her peat stacks in one or two places.

"During our meal I pointed to the two couches and inquired whether she lived alone. I questioned her carefully and learned she lived with her father, but he was out at sea and wouldn't be returning for a few days. As she was telling me that, the sad expression came back. She didn't look at me, and I felt there was something she didn't want to disclose.

"And her mother?

"No, she had never had a mother. She and her father lived here by themselves. They cut peat to supply the inhabitants of the other islands where there were no bogs. In exchange they got fish, tools, and a little flour.

"That evening she did not stand in the doorway to comb her hair even though the weather was mild and sunny. Instead, she undressed in the dark in a far corner of the room and went directly to her bed without bidding me goodnight.

"I lay awake a long time, looking through the cracks and seeing how the night light invaded the house. It was still. I smelled the ocean and the seaweed. The flow of the water was like deep sleepy inhalation along the shore. Now and then I held my breath and raised my head to hear whether she was asleep. But each time I heard nothing; perhaps she, too, lay listening to my breathing. Much later in the night she sighed deeply and fell asleep.

"Then I got up, dressed, and went out.

"The island lay fresh and moist in the shimmering light, as if it had just come up out of the sea. Dew lay heavy on the tall grass, bending the stems with its weightlessness. A cobweb of haze bordering the shore soon blew away, and I saw how the water came up to the shifting coastline.

"I walked to the cave. The gigantic flower still flamed,

165

for it takes the sunlight many years to fade this kind of material. I rolled up some yards of the silk, tucked the wine cask under my arm, and returned. In the marsh I sat down on a stack of turf and took a drink of wine. The air was cold, the peat ponds looked black and silent. Such a marsh is indeed a place to make one feel insignificant, but it also has a strong invigorating atmosphere that should enable a person to decide on the right course of action. Should I take the boat now while she slept and sail to the mainland?

"Quickly I rejected that idea as too idiotic. I realized without further shilly-shallying that Sara must be mine, cost what it might, here on an island in the sea or wherever else in the world.

"As I got up to continue on my way, a black bird flew over me. It resembled a raven though its black hue was even more glistening. It shrieked and circled around and around, and I could not see that it had a nest anywhere; at last I picked up a clump of dirt and threw at it. But the bird returned presently, with no sign of anger, and persisted in shrieking above me steadily until I reached the hut. Then it closed its beak and winged silently westward over the marsh.

"She was sleeping. I did not look at her for now I knew I loved her, but I placed the silk and the wine cask in front of the bed. I do not know whether such an act is an accepted token of love in Thule, but if I had cut off my little finger at the first joint and given it to her I could not have loved her more truly. (That should tell you, Pivante, that I am beginning to come to my senses little by little. We Riazolas are not so neurotic as you think.)

"I prepared a meal and sat down to anticipate her waking up. After some time had passed I saw she was beginning to stir. There were little twitchings in her pale skin, her color came and went, she smiled and wrinkled her nose amusingly.

166

It was like being present at the Creation, and involuntarily I got up and stood beside the table. (Be careful, Pivante. Don't say anything.) Then she opened her eyes. At once they were big and wide awake. That is the way of sleep with animals and with people like Sara; they are born anew each morning, and while still asleep they overcome that flaccid transitional state that exposes itself in yawning and in surly eyes.

"It turned out to be a happy morning—by that I mean there was no worry about anyone's returning from the past. However, if someone thinks this is a little too simple to be called happiness, it is because he equates happiness with being well off. From down at the ale house I can hear silly, noisy happiness. That is not what I long for, but neither do I reject it either now that I know one must awaken in the pungent air on an island in Thule in order to feel happiness that is pure like sparkling water.

"I unrolled the silk, and when I had explained to her what I had in mind, she shouted with delight and threw her arms about me just as I had taught her to do the day before. We had no time to eat, but I filled two wooden bowls with wine to take out with us. Then we spread the silk out on the grass and cut it with a knife, and I had to fit the garments on her several times. At last she stood before me, barefooted, her hair tumbling loosely, dressed in a brilliant red skirt and a yellow jacket. The whole effect was unbelievably ludicrous, for the costume made her look like the courtesans in Marseilles, and everything about her that had previously been concealed now became silhouetted. This was not what I had intended and actually it was regrettable, but then I am not a tailor and I am a genuine bungler with my hands. Moreover, I raved about fetching Leovantis's figurehead, for they had somewhat the same bosoms and hips—but Sara's waistline was smaller—and we

167

might nail a pretty dress on it. Perhaps we could even find the mirror from the *Beatrice*'s lounge. (Do you see, Pivante, what love can do to a shipwrecked man?)

"Afterwards we sat on the stone doorstep, and I described to her the ways of life in my world. But when I tried to explain about Galileo's telescope and all one could see through it, she seemed distracted, and then she emptied the bowl in a single gulp and laughed uncontrollably. I could see the wine inflaming her every pore.

"In the evening she again milked the white goat. This creature seemed to have an inexhaustible supply of milk though I never saw her eat. She had none of the cuddly, flighty qualities of her species. She had a beard and resembled one of the old sedate gentlemen who come to the Bay of Genoa every year for their health. She always followed in Sara's wake, and when Sara stopped the goat stopped five steps behind and cocked her head. On the whole, she moved with far too much awareness befitting a goat—as if rhythmically joined to her mistress. To an outsider, they might well seem to be one and the same creature, separate, but governed by one impulse. I didn't like the goat, but perhaps that isn't so queer, for in Sara's presence I would have been jealous of a snail. Once or twice I stole black bread to secretly lure the animal away, but then it was as if she smiled at me. There is something uncanny about pets that see through you.

"After the evening meal Sara went outside, and I watched as she disappeared southward along the coast. I took the bowl she had set before me and emptied it into the grass beside the back wall. Some days later I noticed the grass had withered and yellowed, but at the time I didn't think about the milk. My mind was on something else entirely, for a man in love interprets no signs.

"Then I went in search of her.

"Here along the south shore the mountain towered like a mighty inpregnable coat of armor against the sea, shining like gold in the evening sunlight. Tall pink flowers poked their heads out of crevices; I observed that some stems were broken and concluded that Sara must have picked them. She usually went out every evening to gather a bouquet, and when she came in she simply dug a hole in the sod wall, inserted the flowers, and poured water into the hole. These were flowers of a shy, pale hue, almost without aroma, but they grew just as profusely in spite of the darkness in the sod hut, and eventually I had a whole vertical garden above the head of my bed. Everything is different in Thule, and what you formerly held to be right and proper is completely reversed.

"Then I discovered a flock of gulls flying very low, back and forth above a hollow in the mountain. I went to the edge and peered down into a long narrow dip close to the sea. It lay above the high-water mark but not high enough to prevent its being filled when the sea rose during a storm. At this time it was a little crystalline lake with polished walls, and in the clear greenish water Sara was swimming like a big golden fish in a pool.

"On seeing me she laughed and waved, and all at once the gulls swooped down toward her, one after another, so together they formed one long undulating arc in the air above her.

"In the same instant she dived underneath the surface, and I saw how the graceful arching of her back and the movement of her hips were in harmony with the soaring of the birds above and the swelling of the waves beyond. It was an enthralling scene, and I couldn't help thinking of the strong but yet gentle lines in Palestrina's madrigals. (This constant restlessness of mind may perhaps be a result

169

of the atmosphere up here which has the effect of light intoxication. A man's thoughts almost become physical, like flickerings, but I think, too, it readily makes one go astray. And the thoughts you dismiss half resolved always come back, just as sea birds return to a familiar spot after their flight over the island.)

"Presently she stepped out of the water and ran up the side of the mountain, untamed, sparkling. She didn't approach me; she only snatched up her clothes and darted up the slope to the left.

"I called her, but not until I had shouted her name three times did she stop. She turned halfway around, hesitantly, and now her face wore a new expression: shyness and passion. I went to her immediately, and as I came near she regained that proud, controlled demeanor that I knew so well. When I was so close that I could have caught her in one jump, she laughed that high resounding laugh and ran off in an easterly direction across the plateau. I delayed a second or two, and in that short interval all my indecision vanished. I set off in pursuit, and as I ran I had the same feeling as when I saw the *Beatrice* lying dazzling white and ethereal in the moonlight: an overpowering sensation of being alive at that moment. The atmosphere around me was brimful of the immediate, and I knew that everything else was wasted time, a mere imitation of life. (You would have enjoyed the scene, Pivante, that would have met you had you come sailing in to land that evening. Sara, naked from top to toe, radiantly white, hair streaming like a banner of gold in the sunlight. And your apprentice and foster son in his studded boots striking sparks against the rocks.)

"Now and then she looked back and laughed up there ahead of me, and in the ecstasy of that moment I could have sworn that golden dust fell from her lips. But then suddenly she disappeared into a cleft, and when I reached that spot

170

I saw it was a creek bed with lush grass. There she was running along it, and it looked as if she had jumped into a trap intentionally because the cleft ended under the steep mountain wall.

"I gained on her with every step, for here my boots caught hold better than did the bare soles of her feet. I heard her shrieking laughter like that of a child, and when she got to the wall of the mountain she attempted to climb straight up. She succeeded in catching a foothold in one or two places, but by then I was directly below her. I grabbed her ankles and pulled her down with a jerk. In falling she spun us both around so we rolled in an embrace several yards down the grassy slope.

"Finally we came to a stop, side by side, and when I kissed her for the first time her eyes grew wide and full of merriment. But soon afterwards they narrowed and glistened, and when I tightened my arms around her, she responded with a fervor and intensity that almost frightened me. In this instant of complete transport, I imagined what the earth must feel each springtime when it is bursting with the force of new shoots. In comparison with this miracle, the ecstasy of saints and the exaltation of warriors must be like only a minor spasm.

"A long time later when we got up to leave, she put on her clothes, guilty in every pore, and yet still innocent, proud and free in every movement, and I knew that if I had to live without her, the rest of my life would be a never-ending fall from a high, shining pinnacle.

"As we walked homeward along the mountainside, half of the sun had sunk into the sea. It shared a part of itself with the sea; it boiled up a frightful red potion out there, and Sara had a delicate blush on her forehead and cheeks.

"The goat was standing on a rock on the incline. She stared at us, nodding her head. That devilish creature seemed

171

to amble about, wise to something. What did she know to make her nod so affirmatively all the time?

"When we had finished our work in the marsh the next evening, a boat with a black sail approached. 'It's Father,' said Sara. 'He has been far away. We must go down to help him.'

"He was a stooped, undersized man with long arms and little brown eyes, and it surprised me that he could be Sara's father. On seeing him closely I got a violent start. I was staring at him, for this man's expression reminded me of Carmen's murderer. He had a tiny pinched face under a growth of black beard. There was something unfinished about his face, it lacked unity, as if it had borrowed a nose here and a chin there—not fully created, but tossed together hurriedly, so if a part had been lost in the process no one would have noticed. The mouth was gray like clay, and when he talked the lips turned inside-out and exposed the red inside of his mouth. He was bald and had a big yellow spot on his crown.

"He would have seemed insignificant and a little comical had it not been for this dreadful resemblance. I became instantly ill-at-ease in his presence. He moved about quietly, bent-over, without saying a word, but there was something about him. In moments of nervousness, you can have a feeling that things are seeing you, knowing something about you. A stump, a sharp stone, the outline of a mountain peak, can stand there knowing who you are in your innermost self. He was like such a knowing object in nature, almost like a broken tree.

"When Sara had explained who I was (I didn't understand much of what they said), he extended his hand—but only the tips of his fingers—hesitantly, as if he were embarrassed to have a fine guest in his home. His hand was

172

small and hard like a claw, and I noticed his knuckles were scaly.

"A tied-up sack lay in the boat. It appeared to be heavy, and I had a mind to carry it for him, but before I could fetch it Sara slipped ahead of me and picked it up. When he saw her do that, he smiled so broadly that the red inside of his mouth showed, and his melancholy face took on a cunning, almost cheerful, expression.

"Now that Sara's father had come home, I wanted to move into the boat-shed, but they wouldn't consent to that. Adjacent to the hut stood a shanty where they housed the tools. Sara placed the sack there and also made a bed for her father there. Apparently he didn't think it odd that she and I slept in the same room. Everything here is like the flower bed on the wall.

"During the days that followed we all three worked in the bog, and soon such an array of peat stacks had been set up that one could lose his way among them. Her father always stayed by himself, a distance apart. Sometimes I felt his eyes upon me, but whenever I looked up his back was turned. But why did his back shake so often? Did he cough, or was he laughing?

"Two things especially disturbed me. One was the frightening resemblance. It was most evident when he straightened up; he would turn his head and draw a whistling breath through the corner of his mouth as if trying to relieve a pain in his neck. It came to me every time, and all the horrors of the murder descended on me—hate, revenge, the wish to destroy. Here, for example, stood hundreds of peat stacks!

"Then I grasped at a way of release by picking up a piece of turf and tracing with my fingers the thousand-year-old projections of a branch that spread itself out like a dark vein in the earth. But it also happened that it affected me

173

so strongly that I pushed in the side of the stack I was working on. (What does one do, Pivante, in his struggle against feelings that rob him of control? I missed you as never before those days in the marsh and wished I could be more like you and laugh off everything—from slivers in fingers to death itself.)

"The other thing that disturbed me was that mysterious sack Sara would not allow me to carry up from the shore. One evening after we had finished our meal, I sneaked around to the back of the hut. Sara was occupied with the washing of the wooden bowls in the stream, and the father was sitting in front of the boat-shed mending a net. The shanty door stood ajar; I threw a quick glance around the corner and slipped inside. The sack stood at the foot of the couch. It was secured with a piece of string tied in a knot no seaman on our shores has ever tied. I tore at it frantically and broke two fingernails, and when one contemplates what an impossible knot can drive a man to doing, it was perhaps the best thing I could do to take out my knife and cut it; so that is what I did. In the sack lay an executioner's ax and a store of hangman's tools."

The Escape

"It became clear to me immediately why Sara had not allowed me to carry the sack. The poor child did not want me to know of her father's bloody occupation. She most likely thought that if I knew I would regard her as one tainted. I had also learned that up here in these northern regions an executioner is shunned like a leper. Therefore he was forced to live alone in the marsh and be summoned each time his services were required. These men, all poor fishermen and farmers, do not share the sense of the sublime that a few of us have about an execution. Their

174

imagination stops at death's threshold, and they regard it, moreover, to be an unnecessary waste of human life in a sparsely settled land; but that does not deter them from punishing a transgressor in an exceedingly clever way. Sometimes one condemned to die may be permitted to live on the condition that he will agree to become an executioner. Thus they let the damned be his own slow tormentor. Each time a new head falls by his ax, he suffers again the anguish of the condemned. Each time he saves his own life anew by taking another's.

"I thought at once that Sara's father was a man like that who had bought his own life at so evil a price. But he did not terrify me. This man lessened the significance of death by his own insignificance.

"During the time I lived on the island he was fetched twice. They came at night in blood-red light: two men dressed in black, in a four-oared boat. Neither of them went on shore. The executioner saw them and came on his own, carrying the instruments of death on his back. He took his seat in the bulkhead, and they sailed away without speaking a word.

"Occasionally, too, people came from the islands to get peat, but they never spoke to him either. It was eerie to watch them gesture and count on their fingers like a group of deaf mutes.

"As time went on I became more and more determined to take Sara away from this place. This way we kept going about trying to hide a dark secret from one another. This mute dwarf of a father was casting a shadow over our love, though, to be sure, he never interfered in our affairs and did not show the least bit of curiosity about where we spent our nights.

"Sara was just as delightful each evening, and when she stretched out in the sunlight, she was radiant from tip to toe without one blemish. And the thought occurred to me that up to now the sin of man had not touched her, and indeed it would be a crime to move her into my world where love feeds on flirtation and deception.

"On one occasion the idea did come to me that there was something odd about her 'experience.' From the very first it seemed she knew all about love. Her innocent artifices enraptured me completely. She would surprise me suddenly with a little touch that I am certain highly sophisticated mistresses in the South would have given years to know. The small firm hands that stacked peat during the day constantly awakened new sensitivities, and every move of her fingers set my body on fire.

"But now and then when I lay awake in the sod hut thinking about Sara, breathing so deeply across the room, I could hear her father arranging his tools in the shed. He had a long-handled spade for cutting turf which he had to sharpen each night to make sure it was ready for the next day. That grating noise drowned out the screeching of gulls and oyster catchers. At regular intervals I heard him spit on his whetstone. To avoid listening I stuck my fingers into my ears, but I heard him just the same; and one day I casually set a wooden bowl of water outside the door, but apparently he did not notice it because the following night he spat again.

"Nor was I able to put him out of my mind during the day. Every once in a while he made a grimace that made Carmen's murderer come alive. I always had the feeling that he knew something.

"One day in his presence I asked in Italian, 'Sara, what does your father do when they come to get him at night?'

"Did they exchange a quick-as-a-flash glance? Or was it merely a chance look?

" 'He goes fishing,' she answered. 'Poor Father! He's so

unlucky. He seldom catches anything.' She looked at him sadly and tenderly.

"When I saw how protective she was, I doubted whether I could persuade her to leave the island, but gradually I also came to realize life here would be impossible for me. This miserable executioner went about accusing me in silence. He had made himself the spokesman of my dead wife's power over me, and I would never find peace as long as we lived under the same roof. Certainly I was not directly guilty of Carmen's death, and more than likely it was only a chance incident that she had looked at me so strangely that morning and had asked me to stay at home because she had a sweet secret to tell me.

"Does anyone imagine I haven't guessed what the sweet secret was!

"Day was now brimful of light. The island was like one huge crystal that caught and intensified all shifting rays. The sun moved like a glowing wheel around the earth, and I, who am virtually a heretic at heart and believe in Galileo, got a very strong feeling that the earth stands still while the sun revolves, and I began to wonder whether this barren island in Thule was turning me into a Papist of the worst kind.

"Pollen drifted in from distant islands; the atmosphere was so satiated with perfume that you wanted to open your mouth to taste it. And when you did so, you got a strong flavor of the sea and the bitter-sweet spice of birch and blossoms.

"A few more days passed. We cut peat and stacked it. To slash the earth up into little cakes in this way is blessedly monotonous work. I tried to concentrate all my attention and energy on each single slab in order to forget everything else. Sara continued to work beside me in a pure, wholesome void. She hummed and smiled and every now and then

177

threw a clump of turf at me when she thought I was brooding.

"But neither Sara's beauty nor the wonderful nights I spent with her could expel my worries. Constantly I heard the executioner inside his shed whetting his instruments. Sometimes it sounded as if he were honing thin hard metal. These must be stiff-necked people among whom I had been cast. And by daylight he took on the gruesome expression showing that frightful similarity. Except for that, he was friendly and helpful. He taught me to lay nets and to fish in deep water, and at such times he was nothing but a down-and-out fisherman on a lonely island. There are, after all, scores of people who resemble one another, I reasoned. You must use common sense, Fernando.—But common sense is like ice in spring, with warm currents underneath.

"Eventually I began to hate him—so now I knew what it was, and for the first time I understood fully that people are completely justified in harming one another. (Do you hear, Pivante, how clever and hard I have become?)

"Then something happened that prompted me to make a decision. One Sunday morning I was walking alone in the marsh. A somewhat strong offshore wind was blowing that day, and suddenly I heard the faraway tolling of a church bell. I stood still, listening devoutly; it was as if tender, barely audible calls were coming to me from my own world. I walked further westward across the marsh, my heart heavy with homesickness. In the exact spot where Sara and I had descended the mountain the first time, there was a sunken place with a big peat pond. I approached the edge, and while I stood there gazing at my own humorously distorted reflection in the water, I caught sight of an oval patch in the mud at the bottom. When I got on my knees to examine it more closely, it began to rise slowly to the surface, moving back and forth in the

178

water as it kept rising, like a flat lid that is sinking. Then I saw the shining patch was a face. It reached the surface and lay there floating beside my own reflection. What I was looking at was a hideous, sinister face, but at the same time an anxious face, and while I stared at it a ripple disturbed the surface of the water. As soon as the pond was black and calm again, the image only slowly smoothed itself out. It was still furrowed and twisted, and the eyebrows were grown together to a border across the forehead. In the same instant our eyes met, and I saw in the flash of a second a great many familiar expressions in that face—among them the executioner's, my father's, Carmen's, Pivante's, and my own. Suddenly it gave me a great and serene smile, an almost condescending smile. I heard a splash like that of a stone falling, and when the rings had disappeared, the face in the water was gone; nor was there any trace either of anyone on land.

"I came back to find Sara's father seated outside the door mending nets. I observed that he had mud on his hands and knees, but that perhaps was of no significance, for here in Thule Sunday is no different from any other day—that is, if one doesn't live directly under the minister's scrutiny.

"But now my suspicions were aroused in earnest, though you would hardly think this disheveled mite of a man had strength for anything more than to chop the head off a poor criminal with his hands tied behind his back, and I don't consider that to be great in a time when human life can be sold for five lire.

"Pivante maintained that we Riazolas are no good when it comes to action because we commonly suffer from a bad conscience. We had a hard enough time making transactions in wines and silks. (The stubborn old fellow always enjoyed this bad joke.) Well, well, at any rate listen to what hap-

179

pened next—whether you are now crumbling in sand on that beautiful accursed island or riding the crest of a wave across all the oceans.

"In the evening I went into the hut and embraced Sara a long time; I fondled her and aroused her passions, but no more, because momentarily I had need only of her desire and longing.

"I asked, 'Shall we go for a sailing trip tonight? I'd like to see how this island looks from a distance, and perhaps we can disembark on one of the golden reefs eastward close to shore.'

"She responded with a completely new kind of smile. In a way it was deliberate, almost flirtatious, restrained and cunning, sudden and without inhibition as if she had kept it hidden all the time until now. 'But we won't leave until midnight when the sun is just this high above the sea.' I indicated a space with my thumb and forefinger. (Galileo ought to have been there with his telescope that night. The sun was no farther away than I could have caught up with it within three hours sailing the *Beatrice* at top speed.)

"Sara smiled and said nothing, but she unbuttoned my jacket and laid her ear to my heart. That was a tender gesture which I think procuresses and duchesses have in common; I have observed it in Madagascar and in Mexico, and the heart must be made of sponge that fails to beat faster when someone like Sara applies her sweet ear to listen.

"Then we went to bed, and a little while later I heard rustling and creaking in the bunk of twigs within the shed.

"On the island all was perfectly still except for the washing of waves against the rocks, the incessant screeching of gulls, and the strange whistling of the airy void itself that you hear when you lie quietly on a bed of earth. There was a faint light in Sara's flowerbed on the wall; a few blooms hung limply out of their holes; others stood erect like tiny faces glowing in the darkness.

"Presently I heard Sara breathing softly and easily like a child. She was drawing in more than mere air; she was inhaling peace, rest, earth, sea. For a moment I grew weak because of all the pleasing sounds, and since I heard none of that awful whetting of tools from the shed, I began to regret my decision. My intention was after all in no sense criminal, and I think it would have passed the law court of my conscience. I simply wanted to bring Sara to the mainland and then ask her to continue farther with me. And if she really loved me, as I had reason to believe, she would indeed be willing without my having to impart to her my suspicions of who her father actually was.

"At midnight—I could tell the time by the rays of light on the stone wall—I got up and dressed quietly. Then I took the wine cask (I had forgotten about that completely during the happy days I had been there) and a piece of bread and slipped down to the boat-shed. Moreover, I found a couple of dried fish in the boat-shed which I had stowed away in the stern of the bigger boat. Thereupon I covered the provisions with a bit of canvas and returned to the hut.

"Sara was still asleep. I could see that even in repose her body had kept the ardor I had aroused in her—and that perhaps is no mean accomplishment for someone who has never pretended to be any sort of great lover. I looked at the queer little birthmark so nearly resembling the innocent footprint of a miniature fawn, and for one brief second I had a slight misgiving, but it did not develop into anything more than just that for in the same instant she awoke. Immediately she dressed and followed me. As we emerged from the hut and I could see her in full light, shiningly youthful and guileless like a tall unfamiliar flower on the hillside, I felt the way Marco Polo must have felt

181

the morning his eyes beheld the Orient for the first time.

"We climbed on board. Sara sat on the thwart behind the mast; I shoved off and hoisted the black square-sail. A strong steady wind was blowing from the northwest that night, and when we had slipped out along the shore past the headland, I turned directly east and let the wind fill the sail.

"Then I heard Sara's goat bleating. I had never heard that before, and when I turned around I could see it running back and forth on the rocks south of the boat-shed. Now it will alert her father, I thought, as I tightened the ropes.

"Sara sat erect, her face lifted upward, her eyes closed, her hair blowing like a flame up along the mast. I had no problems now with the wind and the sea, I could watch her freely, and while the boat bobbed playfully from one wave onto another, I began to think about the future—something I had not done since I was shipwrecked. I envisioned our arrival at Genoa one glorious day with the harbor full of ships. The lustful little Italian charmers would turn to look at us and most likely be jealous and shout words at Sara which she wouldn't understand. But I would hold her hand and lead her through the crowd and hire a carriage to take us to our house.

" 'I exchanged my boat for her, rigging and cargo included,' I would say, and after a few days my friends would throng to my garden and wait to be invited in. Serentis and Menzolis, the two fat shipowners, would sail around all Italy and puff their way up to my house.

"Then she suddenly opened her eyes and looked at me. 'Our little island, Fernando!' She laughed and pointed to a small skerry at the right.

"I shook my head. 'Too small, Sara. Too small for you and me. We must get closer to the mainland.'

"Soon we approached a new island. It was round and

182

green and inviting. Sara twisted around on the thwart and cried out exuberantly, 'That's where we're going, Fernando! Lower the sail!'

"I avoided her glance. 'No island for us tonight,' I thought to myself, 'but soon we shall be on the mainland and then nothing will separate us.'

" 'There is no shelter from the wind there,' I yelled back to her and steered around the island. She closed her eyes tightly so I could not see what they were saying. At the same instant the wind gusted. I got busy with the sail and the rudder and had to veer to the north in order not to take in water.

"It occurred to me that I ought to bid farewell to the island. When I turned to look back I was shocked to discover we had not moved farther. From out here, the mountain where Pivante and I had managed to save our lives looked like the beak of a vulture. A churning scroll of foam ran along the shore; all the colors of the island were blazing. I could also see the stacks of peat in the marsh, and the thought flashed through my mind that I was perhaps committing a crime and maybe she would wither away in a land other than this.

"Then I caught sight of a boat heading out from the island. Immediately a sail shot into the air. Well—I thought, and I felt of the ropes. Deep within you, you had perhaps expected this, and he may be a better sailor than you are, but you will outwit him just the same if you only keep your eyes on the sea and aim for the point up ahead.

"At once I turned the boat even a little more toward the north to get more leeway, and at the same time I maneuvered our position so that the sail was a curtain between Sara and the other boat. I heard her chuckle to herself; she pointed out across the water, and by following her finger I noticed a small bank of dark clouds dispersing

183

as they approached from the west. 'Now it is a matter of who gets the benefit of that first,' I thought, and at the same time I felt a joyous thrill at being involved in a race for life.

"The other boat was moving faster and soon came so near that I was able to see the outline of a bent-over figure at the helm. Again I estimated our distance from the point ahead and steered a little more to the north because of the drift. Then I saw the black boat suddenly shooting forward. The storm caught him first, but in less than a minute it struck us, too. The boat groaned and quivered before it straightened itself from the effects of this new blast.

"We sailed on. Each sailed from his own direction, both on a course heading directly toward the identical sharp point. I watched his boat riding high on the crest of the waves and thought he must be a very clever sailor even though he looked so unimpressive sitting there hunched over at the rudder, just as he sat when he mended nets in the boat-shed.

"By now I had progressed so far toward the point that I decided I could set my course straight east. I would have the current and the wind pushing me from behind and could move at full speed down toward the low headland. But just as I was about to turn the rudder, I saw the other boat going more to the south, racing in the froth toward land, and I knew he would succeed in intercepting me.

"He raised his head and looked at me, seemingly shocked at the very idea that I would think of competing with him. In that moment his reason for pursuing us became clear to me. He had no intention of taking Sara back with him. What he wanted was simply to follow us. He did not want to let us go. He wanted to be at our heels wherever we went, over land or sea, in cities or on ships. In other words, he was attending to his business as executioner, and I was

the victim who was to be scorched with glowing tongs.
"Then I was aware that Pivante was in the boat beside
me. He grinned and bowed deeply. 'You Riazolas! You ought
to know that everything that is to happen, will happen.
Do you pretend to be mightier than God by dreaming up
so many thoughts? Now it is a matter of sailing into the
wind, Fernando.'

"He was only fifty yards from me. A tremendously high
wave rose between us. We climbed the crest, each from
his own side, and there was still time for me to steer away.
But I didn't turn aside; I urged my boat farther forward into
the wind, and within seconds we collided so violently that
my prow cut right through to the mast of the other boat.
I was thrown full force forward just as the rigging fell
overboard.

"When I got to my feet, I saw splintered wood floating
all around, but our boat was completely intact except that
the uppermost plank at the front was smashed in. 'Sara!'
I shouted proudly and triumphantly.

"Then I saw her in the stem of the boat. She was balancing
with incredible dexterity on the edge of the broken plank,
laughing, her face radiant with strength and beauty. 'Sara!'
I yelled. 'Come down from there!'

"She jumped. I dashed forward and leaned out toward
her. She came up directly in front of the boat, and I
reached out my hand and caught hold of her hair. She
grasped the splintered prow with her left hand and lifted
herself halfway out of the water. Then with a big radiant
smile flashing with malice, she slapped my face so hard that
I tumbled backward and lay sprawled across the thwart.

"It was late in the day when I awakened in the bottom of
the boat. A few black birds were winging over me but flew
away on seeing me come to life. The sky looked distinctly

high and deep blue. Above floated one lonely elongated cloud. I lay still a long time watching that cloud. There was a slight breeze, but perhaps not up there because the cloud didn't change—unless it was made of especially solid stuff.

"On the whole, what is one to think?

"After a while I sat up and felt of my face. It was swelled and sore, true enough. I looked around but could not get my bearings. The boat had drifted a considerable distance; there was the mainland, not many hundred yards away.

"I stayed seated for some time feeling of my bruised body. Apparently I was all right. I was tired, bereft—and very happy. Every detail took on great importance. I set about to examine the smashed rigging, investigate the ropes, and study its trim structure—including the bailer, a crude hollowed-out piece of wood. When I held it in my hand, it turned into a treasure. I sat laughing to myself. (What did you say, Pivante? Did you say I had become queer because of the treatment I'd received?)

"Perhaps so. My whole body felt tender, especially my right shoulder. It was as if I had gone a long time with a dislocated shoulder and then had suddenly had it jerked back into place. And if I now should try to describe what I mean, you would likely doubt me or think I am crediting myself with some kind of retrospective wisdom. And while I'm sitting here that makes me wish we had a telescope like Galileo's, only that it might enable us to look inside human beings, for I do think there are countless multitudes of worlds and wonderful scenes within us.

"Oh, well! I repaired the rigging as much as possible and then sailed southward along the coast for two days. I reached a little place where I could stay, and a week later a ship came by to take me even farther south. Eventually the topography began to change: the land grew flatter, rounder,

186

inhabitable-looking, all covered with trees. One morning we arrived at a little village. There I loaded stockfish for a month, and that's unpleasant work because one tends to take on the qualities of the fish—to get woody, tough, and dry-as-dust. And if a man continues long enough, he can finally get to thinking there is nothing in the world that is noble, beautiful, or great. Therefore I was glad when the ship was fully loaded and we set out to sea on our way to Spain.—

"Now I hear the waiter asking the last guest to leave. He's locking up, and that's a good thing—so I'll have a chance to read through what I've written. I don't want anyone to see it until after I'm gone. I did not report all this when I appeared before the maritime court.

"But perhaps I will not be able to keep silent anyway. In any case, I think when I am very old I am likely to reveal that I once fell in love with the devil's daughter, and then for the sake of the young at the same time I shall add that everything else—deliberations, doubts, guilt, pride, vengeance, and riches—everything is only a worthless pastime compared with love, and that to pass up your sweetheart's invitation to go ashore with her on a little island is to commit an unforgivable sin."

187

Regine's World

1

"I am sitting here thinking of those two friends of yours, Halvor and Fernando," remarked Mylady after the glasses had been filled, "and I am glad they fared well, though I really feel it was a big mistake for a person to try to run away from his isle.

"Now note I am saying 'isle,' not 'island.' 'Isle' sounds more solitary, more difficult to escape from, and for that I am directly indebted to the inventor of the alphabet, because this is the way it came about—though you may not be aware of it—when Our Lord wanted to endow the first people with the ability to speak, then His—yes, I must say— inspiration was almost exhausted. He looked around all over the world, and while so doing He arrived at the Nordland coast. But the land there was still warm from the process of creation, and when He breathed on it to cool it, it took the strange topography we see all around us. Thus, God's own breath shaped the whole region, and among the rocks and fossils He also found the makings of man's vowels and consonants."

188

Mylady smiled mischievously at Pastor Celion. "I trust the pastor doesn't consider that explanation to be a mere flight of fancy. It is actually true, every bit of it; to be sure, the account is not recorded in Genesis, but I have a suspicion Our Lord began the alphabet at Brønnøysund in the south and then completed it somewhere in Vesterålen in the north. And here is where we get to the point of my story, for what I am going to tell happened precisely on that spot most closely resembling the letter Ø, at least if one views it from above. Moreover, I think He Who must have felt the loneliness of the creative act must have rounded His lips in gentle wonder at the sight of this place—especially if He came at dusk—and, presto, there a new and essential vowel lay ready for use during millions of years in the future. Thus out of His loneliness and wonder it has derived its being. The pastor must forgive me for having acquired the bad habit of discovering a meaning in almost everything.

"Yes, indeed, an isle. And it does lie somewhere in Vesterålen, jutting out a little into the open sea. But from the very bottom of the letter itself—if I may phrase it that way—it is only five minutes' smooth sailing to one of the larger isles, those forming the major geographical pattern up here.

"On the older maps, the ones in use at the time sections of the country were mapped on a reduced scale, the isle itself was no bigger than a dot. However, we need not fret about a reduced scale so long as we have God's own standard right outside the door. At any rate, the isle has found room for so much of nature as to be a place nearly perfect in itself. It need not borrow from its surroundings, and the only neighbor it acknowledges is the sea.

"It is bordered by an evenly sloping shoreline except on the southwest where a nesting cliff rises straight up a hundred yards out of the sea. The north coast has many bays and inlets. In some places the sea flows in deep narrow

189

tongues almost all the way to the heart of the isle. There is a mountain in the center where it is said that if one puts his ear to the ground at flood tide he can hear the sea whisper evil verses in the little depressions leading to the very marrow of the isle. A fisherman named Jeremias was the first to learn of something secret going on here between the land and the sea. But he also had an especially frisky wife, and furthermore he always ate the bloody parts of the cod which, as you know, are very stimulating.

"Aside from this, the isle has two visible attractions: the one, a cave that a person can visit at ebb tide and be drowned in at high tide; the other, two stone pillars.

"What a geologist would call these stone pillars I have no idea, nor do I know what God intended them for. They are simply two columns rising perpendicularly out of the water fifty yards from shore, directly to the west. They are of equal height—about six yards at low tide, I would guess—and at least a yard square. For the fisherman Jeremias, however, they might well have had a meaning of one kind or another. And to someone who has lived from infancy to manhood in their company, they must have seemed like two of life's confidants, a pair of silent wise men who could be entrusted with secrets to be hidden in their granite cloaks. They have stood there a thousand years, just as they are, lathered by foam, washed so clean that not even shells lodge in their cracks, slippery green, oily from seaweed, gray with salt, and fissured in hot summer days. And I imagine if a depressed, frustrated person who could find no meaning in life ever sailed past them, he would suddenly burst into peals of wild laughter at the sight, or perhaps he would experience profound inner relief, a fantastic devil-may-care feeling, even unexplainable security. And later when he would think back on this special moment, he would not remember the stone pillars and would not entertain the slightest suspicion of the

190

two obelisks beyond the shores of an isle on the Nordland coast.

"I deem that to be waste: to set a pair of stone columns so deeply meaningful in a place where perhaps only every fifth year at the most one lone observing soul might pass by.

"But had they stood in the midst of the big noisy world, they would, of course, have been called Adam and Eve or Per and Kari, or pillars of love, or something else nonsensical—and people would have crowned them with orange peels and newspapers on Sundays and thereby tapped them of meaning and wisdom. So we had rather rejoice at the fact that there is but one person who knew them: the dark-haired Regine Beck, the heroine of my story. And as far as I know she is no longer alive, but when I heard about her I made a voyage out to the very spot. I found everything that was said about the columns to be true, only that I was no longer able to see them precisely as she must have seen them.

"I climbed the mountain and lay down behind a sharp rock in the heather, for when one sets his sights from that particular stone and takes aim between the two columns, as with a gun, on clear days he can get a view of eternity far beyond in the west, out where the earth starts to round off.

"I did that, and while I lay there staring, inhaling the spicy, pungent perfume of heather, I felt as if all restraints on my soul suddenly burst.

"The east side of the isle where the inlet is the narrowest was the site of the old trading center, now long since deserted. The only one who lives there still is Lola, the old housekeeper who told me the tale of the Beck family. I doubt she is more than ninety, though I can't be sure because she is one of those people who seem not to show their age beyond sixty. Now she has yellowed and shriveled and become wooden like the gateposts at Becksgård. She

191

herself is like a precious hard sort of tree, not likely to decline noticeably. I believe rather she will crumble away to mold in the lapse of a few morning hours, perhaps some day in springtime when a strong wind, heavy with rain, is blowing across the isle from the south.

' "The docks and warehouses stand completely empty; fishermen long ago stripped them of chests and iron bands and nets and barrels, and not defiance but only an old habit can account for their still being there at all.

"The windows are broken; spiders spin their webs in the openings. The seagulls often sit wing to wing on the ridge of the roof nodding to the ruins, for now nothing drives them away—no rumbling of wheels on the dock, no noise of cranes in operation. Each spring when the snow melts, more broken roof tiles clutter the ground near the buildings. And if you come sailing up the bay at dusk, you will hear tedious plaintive sounds from the pier and you may be frightened by big gray-black fans that move. Those are the large double doors of the warehouses flapping and wailing in the wind—as if summoning and pleading with cracked voices: 'Come back, old times! Come back, Regine!'

"But no one comes, for the only remnant of bygone days is Lola, and she is almost deaf. And so they grow mute, little by little; the hinges loosen from the rotted wood; the pier breaks apart quietly, piece by piece; soon a cat will have to step carefully on the brittle boards. Now and then one can hear soft little sighs in the silence when another handful of reddish-brown dust falls from the roof beams. Only the sea remains unchanged, rising and sinking under the docks, incessantly, day and night. And nothing happens. Only time—time seems to whisper contentedly whenever another chip falls from the worn yellow posts. The drying racks lie tipped over on the rocky surface, broken, and there are deep scars in the long proud rows. Dead. The place doesn't breathe any more."

Lady Sophie blushed and stopped abruptly. "Well, well, I guess I got carried away just as you did, Richard. What I really wanted to say was simply that the place is going to ruin, and that's indeed the plain truth. Only the smells remain—the odor of guano and fish oil, the delicate fragrant scent of foodstuffs in old drawers in the little storeroom whose door has a double lock. The aroma of spices—pepper and thyme—and perhaps the smell of cheap fabric, home-spun, and the fine clean perfume of linen. Yes, smells linger in the big silent rooms in spite of years of inrushing gales from all the world.

"And the house itself! Two-storied Becksgård with eight large windows on each floor! Ah, yes, it still stands, but it is cold and drafty for old Lola, only she isn't aware of it because she doesn't hear the wind; the elements don't affect her any more. She has been forgotten by time, left behind, transformed by the same process of crumbling away that is slowly overtaking the entire place.

"The rooms are desolate. The chairs no longer invite the memory of those who occupied them; things no longer have any recollection. Perhaps also the ones who lived here were altogether too poor for their spirit to be left in the abandoned house after they themselves were gone. In all likelihood they took with them their remembrances and their shadows when they left.

"But in the days when the dark-haired Regine ran around causing ill fortune, the decadence was not yet complete, though it was well on the way. Her grandfather, Rudolf Beck, had established and developed the place. Under his superintendence it progressed surely and steadily, and there

193

was a quiet optimistic quality of moderation in the undertaking. Fishing boats came and went; nets never hung unmended on their frames; fishermen were allowed reasonable credit. He laid the groundwork for wealth without fanfare and grandiose displays, for the old man had the same philosophy as the preacher in Ecclesiastes and knew that everything has its season and there is a time to sow and a time to reap.

"Under the management of Reginald Beck, Regine's father, however, prosperity reached its culmination, and during his last years people could see a kind of tension in the busyness, an idling of operations, somewhat of a swagger in behavior as men moved about the place. Cranes and capstans creaked excessively, barrels and boxes couldn't be shifted without the whole neighborhood's hearing it, orders and commands sounded like angry barking, and in the office where one sheet of paper had sufficed before now three were required. The clerks sat doodling and 'thinking.'

"An isle has its eras just as does an empire—only that within three or four generations it completes its rise and fall which the Roman Empire took 1,200 years to accomplish."

Lady Tennyson laughed somewhat nervously, and when she toasted her listeners drops spilled over the edge of the glass and onto the stem, and as she set it down it left a blood-red ring on the tabletop. Then she went on.

2

"I visited the isle on a Sunday. The sea was placid, the air serene as if unable to offer resistance, and through the open door in the entrance hall where we sat we heard the church bells from three different parishes. They sounded like a trio, a little in need of synchronization perhaps, but if your

194

hearing is sufficiently acute the atmosphere there is so pure that you can discern the mood of the congregations by the ringing of the bells. I shall try to tell the story just as I heard it from old Lola, but if I use words other than hers and more of them be assured it results from my love of truth. For I believe it is with truth as with recollection; it isn't a plant in the soil that you can tend to make it grow tall and beautiful, rather it is like a butterfly that flits away each time you are about to catch hold of it.

"Reginald Beck." Lady Sophie laughed again quietly and closed her eyes for an instant. "The emperor of the house of Beck, on an isle in the sea—with the soul of both Nero and Marcus Aurelius. He was tall and strong; his black curly hair stayed the same the full fifty years he was allotted. His face bore the features of an eagle and the swarthy hue of the southland. In later years his eyes, once so expressively clear and steadfast, were often bleary from drinking. A thin faint scar ran from the bridge of his nose to his mustache; he had acquired it as a seventeen-year-old by spilling corrosive acid over his face. It so happened that his father had refused to let him sail in an old leaky boat; in anger he had grabbed a bottle of acid and thrown it against a wall. Later on in life his fluctuating moods always showed first in this scar. It reflected barometric pressures shading from white to deep scarlet, and when he was asleep it revealed the secret substance of his dreams. In weak, dejected moments of inward grief, the scar looked gray, shallow, and devoid of expression.

"Reginald's parents died when he was thirty, and he, who hitherto had divided his time between otter and fox hunting inland and girl hunting on the little isles along the coast, was suddenly saddled with the whole responsibility alone— as they say. Nevertheless, he did not let this burden him too heavily. He didn't join in the proud, pompous, worried

195

conversation which tradesmen are prone to engage in when discussing their affairs because he knew very well that the outcome rested with the fisherman and the clerk.

"Now at once he had been left alone with Miss Lola, and although the house had some twenty rooms they met regularly in stairways and hallways. It seemed almost as if there were a conspiracy operating in the very architecture of the place. Reginald gnashed his teeth and gasped for breath whenever they met, and immediately afterward people could hear him shooting wildly at gulls from the highest point of the isle.

"She was fifteen years older than he—efficient and ugly—and she had indeed given him a thrashing more than once when he was a child. His mother had been essentially the disciplinary authority behind the whipping, but she had developed calcification in her elbow joints early in life so she could neither embrace nor strike; therefore she sat on the edge of a straight chair as if to take her share of the suffering, looking on while the housekeeper administered the beating.

"A year later Reginald made the long voyage to Hamburg. The Beck firm did not sail only to Bergen with dried fish; it was a step ahead of the other trading establishments in having a double-masted vessel which went directly to foreign ports."

The four at the table glanced up. Mylady had stopped. She was looking toward land, and in the silence Florelius was aware of her holding her breath—as if listening for footfalls beyond the horizon.

"It is perhaps the way with houses," she continued, "that the older they get the more acute becomes their hearing. For I believe houses can hear; they develop consciousness and moods from the feet that go through the rooms. The soul of people is contagious to them; a house acquires the senses of the inhabitants and holds on to them after their short lives are over. The old house at Becksgård had almost gone to sleep under Miss Lola's shuffling feet—she always wore slippers without heels—when suddenly one morning new footfalls echoed: little, light, timid steps. These new footfalls were so breathlessly soft that even the third step of the stairs leading to the second story—generally the conscience of the house—gave out no sound in all the years she walked there.

'I am talking about Regine's mother. She was a gentle, lost creature from the Rhineland, and it is entirely unjust and absolutely unbelievable that Fate would find a subject for tragedy in a woman so delicate in every respect. At any rate, it happened that destiny sent her to visit her uncle in Hamburg in the same house which Reginald Beck visited daily. There she sat among palms and porcelain in the semi-darkness of northern Germany, a maiden born to languish and wilt in peace. Within two months she was on her way to the Arctic Ocean.

"How this union came to be is quite inconceivable. In any case, I can only imagine it must have been one of those singular sets of circumstances that defy close examination, one of those inexplicable short circuits in human nature when coincidence robs an otherwise circumspect man of the reins. No matter from what point of view one looked at it, this marriage must have seemed absurd. It must also have been a strange courtship—half unreal as if on the floor of the sea. I visualize him rushing into that dark room, half crazy with boredom, gasping for air in that greenish repository with pots of azaleas, palms reaching to the ceiling, drapes to the floor, bric-a-brac—a room where small red rosette-like eyes in the hazel-wood furniture stare at you, subdue you, without blinking. And I think he must have stumbled over a pot, a co-conspirator, reached for something, caught hold of one of the tassels hanging under heavy arm rests, and then perhaps brushed against her thigh in his hurry, and then—"

Florelius laughed and raised his glass. "Skoal, Sophie! But I think your explanation is a fake. You evidently wanted to tell us something about the circumstances of the meeting of their souls, but in that I think your imagination failed you and so you settled for this little secondary solution. I beg you not to cheat us out of the main thing with such beguiling detours."

Mylady returned his smile, her eyes sparkled, she lifted her glass and let it touch his, gently. "You're intolerable, Richard, and I demand that you don't interrupt me again. What's more, I suspect the Evil One has his own ice-cold humor with which he deceives us to prevent our seeing the horse's hoof.

"And so there she sat, Charlotte Metzer from the Rhine-land, small, frail, with slender arms and soft ash-blond hair. To the day she died she wore it in the same chaste style, parted in the middle and combed tightly into two wing shapes that revealed the shape of her head. Nor did her later spells of hysterical weeping in the least alter the appearance of her familiar-looking flaxen-pale coiffure. Moreover, it was set off most unfortunately with little thin curls at her neck and over her ears—a hair-do that I know can irritate a man no end when she who wears it has ceased to satisfy his hunger for love.

"When she died she was placed among the empty barrels in a second-story room in one of the warehouses. She lay there the four days preceding the burial, for Reginald Beck, who had ignored her presence while she was alive, could not endure sleeping under the same roof with the corpse. Those who took away her body the fourth day reported that her hair was disheveled, that it had turned dark as mold, and that her lips were twisted into a thin mocking smile. From there she was taken to the family burial ground where the dead are allowed no more than four feet of space; for the dead should not have more in a poor district. Pine trees from Målselv were planted there instead. And under the pious darkness of the evergreens she returned to the semi-darkness of the green rooms in Hamburg."

Lady Sophie hesitated. She was frowning, and Pastor Celion noted a distinct line from the pretty dimple in her chin following the definite tilt of her nose up to the wrinkle in her forehead. He regarded her profile for a while and thought, "I swear that—forgive my sin—I swear that her face is not the same on the other side."

"I have skipped along too quickly," resumed Mylady, "for she endured many a misfortune between the semi-darkness of Hamburg and the pine trees on the Beck burial plot. But since she is not the major character, I must omit most of her story.

"She was a meek and patient enigma and left behind her two puzzling bequests: a daughter and a sixteen-yard length of lacework—neither of which can unlock the secret recesses of her life.

"When Reginald Beck courted her, she had already done five inches. Yes. It was a border two inches wide, crocheted of ivory-yellow yarn. It looked conspicuously out of place, like a path in the dark, as it lay in her lap. Surely she crumpled it in fear when she gave her answer, and she took yarn and crochet hooks up to Thule with her. As soon as she arrived she found a place to sit in a little closet at the back where she continued her crocheting. When no one was watching, she measured the size of the countless windows. Perhaps she entertained the foolish notion of making a border for all the curtains in the house. A grandiose idea—an extravagance in keeping with the nature of the place.

199

Or was it a life-long exercise of penance, the self-punishment of a languishing saint?

"Now the lacework belongs to old Lola, and I saw it when I visited her. I spread it out on two tables in the closet and tried to read the scrolled design like a filigreed manuscript, a child's little letters gone astray.

"Reginald Beck had torn her away from the security of the half-darkness into the fierce Nordland light. She was as helpless as is a bat in sunlight, and when she was about to step ashore on the isle she lost her footing on the slippery step. If someone had not caught her, she would indeed have gone right to the bottom of the sea.

"She was relentlessly abandoned, left to the chance of all that befell her—her husband's passion as well as his fits of rage. But the season of darkness itself did not affect her much. Her heart knew no seasons, and nature to her was only earth and rock and water and wind. She never understood the excited, radiant gleam in people's eyes when summer came. One day when she had wandered down to the wharf, a workman knelt before her wanting to tie one of her shoe laces that had come undone; she had cried out in fright, in German, and had run to the house.

"After two years had passed, she gave birth to a daughter in the month of April. That day a flag was flown over Becksgård, and gulls circled the pole, shrieking.

"The baby had black hair and blue eyes and didn't lose her hair as is common for infants."

3

"At that time a pair of twin sisters were servants at Becksgård, two buxom girls with fiery red hair. They laughed constantly, their complexion was like the skin of rosefish, only lighter, and their foreheads bore identical patterns of freckles.

"The earliest memory Regine had of her life was of this two-headed monster with a shrub of coarse red hair leaning over her. Four blinking eyes and two greedy mouths with unsightly teeth. They smelled alike: sour milk and sun and guano. When they picked her up, they laughed so noisily that echoes resounded in a loose parchment shade on a lamp above the bed. In order to retain one tiny iota of individuality, they had agreed to part their hair on opposite sides; furthermore, they were so lucky when they began to lose their teeth in their twenties (Bless that wretched sugar candy and that delicious Russian jam!) that they lost them irregularly. The identical resemblance was terminated when decay set in; they needed only to smile for people to distinguish one from the other.

"Thus Regine was introduced early to the dualism in life, and to this we might attribute her bad habit later of looking first straight at a person and then immediately right past him. Now you gentlemen must not take me too seriously or imagine that I am offering an explanation, but I take personal delight in such little digressions and perhaps I may stumble upon some bit of meaning by this method—some shred of sense in all the meaninglessness.

"On that April morning when Regine was born, an avalanche of snow fell into the sea on the south side of the isle. The tidal wave roared like thunder along the coast, smashing two small boats, and a bailing scoop flying through the air struck the wall near where the corpse-white Mrs. Beck lay ready to deliver her child. Indeed this snow slide helped bring Regine into the world, for just before it hit, the mother had suffered a kind of cramp, and when the scoop knocked against the wall a picture of the twelve-year-old Christ in the temple fell down, and then she lost consciousness and all went well.

"Charlotte Beck never regained full command of her

201

senses after this. She might sit for long periods as if in a
trance and then abruptly jump to her feet and push furniture
around at random. It was as if delicate and unsteady objects
were attracted to her hand, and she became so unstable
and butter-fingered that she hardly dared lift the child.
And when winter set in, her second winter here, she even
began making mistakes in her crocheting. Her hook took
strange unintended turns, and irregular whirls appeared in
the pattern. The minister's wife had made this observation
when she came to call after the baptism service and asked
whether the work had been done in poor light. In reply
Mrs. Beck only smiled her pathetic smile and said it was
intended to be that way.

"Now and then the father appeared. He always came
from something or other—from an otter hunt or a sailing
trip, or from the office or the warehouses, invariably in a
hurry and with heavy steps. She was always a little startled
when the brown eagle-like head with the curly black hair
bent over her. It was an exciting foreign image, and then
she shrieked with delight when she caught hold of his ring-
finger and his index finger, one in each of her hands. His
hands smelled of fish and rust, his breath reeked of tobacco
and whiskey, and the strong odor of leather and brine
permeated everything.

"Reginald Beck was constantly busy those first years.
He evidently did not know how to live on an isle. He rushed
through life in seven-league boots. He wore down only
every third step of the stairs. And when he jerked open the
outer door, the whole house responded from every angle;
a door on the second floor flew open of its own accord, a
gasp went through the rooms, the curtains everywhere stood
out like full-blown sails. Occasionally the shutter of the
cuckoo clock in the hallway—a gift from a German business
associate—opened, but the cuckoo never came out.

"Yes, to be sure, the king of the headland at Becksgård was persistently in a hurry—but not so much so as to prevent his taking time to show his power over people and objects. And when his married life with Charlotte came to an early end, he soon derived even more satisfaction from indulging his lust for power. At first it expressed itself in relatively harmless ways. He would stand grasping the railing of the porch while his eagle eyes mirrored a commanding and contented state of mind. Or he would stroll around thumping his possessions with his walking stick: his barrels and his crates and his walls. But then it would happen, too, that this enjoyment turned inward—like blood poisoning. It found symbolic expression in the loss, in the damage kept within reasonable limits. Once on receiving a particularly good price for his cargo of fish in Bergen he deliberately smashed a rear window in one of his warehouses. Another time when he had been lucky enough to make a big herring catch in the Eidsfjord, he went down to his boat-shed in the evening and shoved one of his small boats out to sea; no one ever saw it again.

"Time passes—spring, summer, and autumn—and winter. Time sneaks around the isle making shore raids: ice floes, bursting buds, snowstorms. Heedlessly the clerk rips the pages off the calendar until he is soon. down to the bare cardboard without even once catching his breath in fear and listening for the footfalls of time on the beach at ebb tide. Nor has he felt an inner thrill over nothing at all—or over something so slight as the quacking of a mother eider duck. Days, nights, summertime—and the bloody course of the sun around the isle—God have pity on us who do not understand!"

Lady Sophie sipped her wine in silence, and in their hearts the listeners drank a toast to her for this interruption in the story. Pastor Celion's eyes had grown misty; he looked toward heaven and recalled the ceiling in his first parish, the ceiling of the church. It was painted the same familiar color as the sky, like one big, single, deep pupil. Sometimes when he had closed his eyes he had imagined that God had lifted the roof off this particular church just to hear *his* words. "I think I was very young at the time," mused Celion," very young and—" He got no farther. Mylady continued.

"But Regine is aware of the passing of time. The clock on the wall reminds her of it, as do the winds blowing in from all corners of the world, each with its own substance under the cloak: snow, rain, black clouds, the cries of birds, the smell of the sea. Besides, she sees all things there are on an isle: flowers and heather and snowdrifts, moldy hay and spiders, and the herbs growing in the shallows on the beach. The contents of the warehouses also have their seasons. Merchandise arrives, is stored for a time, and then moves. She comes to know it all, from nails to spices.

"But even yet she has not seen the other side of the isle. That first happens when she is seven.

"In the meanwhile time lay dormant in the household on Becksgård. It stayed there along with the people and the evil it had spawned, and none of them got any further. Indeed, Charlotte Beck's lacework attained a length of six yards; the first part had already yellowed more than it ought—judging by the yarn—and no one knew what she might have confided to it. She sat in the closet, always crocheting and listening for her husband's footsteps. Regine came to remember her thus, with the lacework like a meek apology between herself and the world, and with dark shadows under her expressionless eyes. She had also heard her father strike her mother for some reason or another when he came in to her at night. The house had many big empty rooms and dark halls, and Regine could find her way from cellar to attic in the blackness like a sleepwalker.

"Just the same she admired her father even after she had begun to hate him. She admired his black curls and brown eagle-like profile, the resounding steps, and the happy shouts of command on the docks. But the mother's anxiety was passed on to her, and she had to take sides in order not to be crushed to pieces between the parents. She began to listen for his footsteps. She began to despise those things in the house that echoed when he opened the outer door. Secretly she tacked the curtains to the window frames, she locked the door of the second floor, and she stuck a piece of paper under the shutter of the cuckoo clock.

"One day she confronted her mother with the request that she teach her how to crochet. They sat side by side several evenings, each with her own hook. Regine was to make some doilies that they planned to give to the women on the neighboring isles.

"But Regine never succeeded in learning. She managed to string together a sort of octagon with a hole in it; beyond that, she never again set her fingers into any piece of needlework. But during the few hours she struggled with it, however, the two women shared a sorrowful secret.

"Reginald Beck grew a little stouter each year. His eyelids got heavier and hung like an awful visor over his eyes, and his hands were fat. He was forever hunting otter and foxes —when he wasn't hunting women on the isles. Otherwise he sat mainly in the office on the dock drinking Russian rye brandy with the chief clerk."

4

"At the age of seven Regine got her first playmate: a lamb with black wool. It had shiny hoofs which Regine polished

205

with a cloth and big mustard-colored eyes, completely expressionless, and it had none of those qualities that made people so hard to understand: hate, lust, or continual fear. It simply existed, a creature without craving or curiosity—something like the wind, the sea, and the heather. And now and then as it stood motionless on a crag silhouetted against the sea, the wind ruffling its black shag, Regine would drop down and bury herself deep in the heather, gaze at the lamb, and wish nothing would change, nothing would happen, no bell would ring for dinner, and the sun would never set at night.

"There developed a kind of sublime friendship between the two, a play of harmony, a pantomime wherein they moved like two dancers in graceful play on the wharf. Regine had none of a child's awkward movements; she was slender and limber as a willow, and one could have set their steps to music as they bounded up the stairs to the loft in the granary. They snuggled together there on rainy days and stole plump kernels of Russian oats stored in bins along the walls. The whole loft was filled with the fragrant aroma. On sunny days they ran races on the mountain on the south side of the isle, and the little girl's signal calls sounded like the cries of a big, strange bird.

"One morning Regine couldn't find her lamb. First she went down to the dock to search in all the warehouses. Then she ran to the barn and called through the haymow. She went to the kitchen and asked the twins. Afterwards she climbed to the loft in the granary, but it, too, was empty. Finally she set out for the south headland.

"On returning to the dock Regine took the path around the blacksmith's shop, and there on the end wall by the sea she saw the curly black pelt stretched out like a gigantic bat, fastened with nails driven in right behind the shiny little hoofs."

Lady Sophie took a few short breaths, blinked, and emptied her glass. "This wine," she mumbled, smiling, "this is the wine my father-in-law of blessed memory brewed in his day. It is aged and fine and not the least intoxicating. He called it 'Misty Tears,' and I can understand why, for it has the effect of slow, silent grief or of the remembrance of childhood sorrow. It has a somewhat bitter sweetness that you perhaps have detected. There is somehow no intoxicant, no stimulation—only realization, the bitter realization that all sorrow and all suffering fade away in time."

As if to recapture the mood of the story, Mylady sighed deeply, and then she continued. "That day Regine went up on the mountain. In the middle of the isle at the highest point there is a shallow tarn, a round crater resembling a saucer, which might be thought an extinct volcano. In dry summers the saucer is almost empty, but in autumn when the spigots of heaven are opened it frequently overflows and sends a deluge of little rivulets down the slopes.

"Sometimes gulls fly up here as if to a holiday site when they tire of the everlasting rumblings of the sea coming in from the west. Then one can see whole flocks of them in the middle of the tarn. They float deeply and lazily as if reclining on a sofa, while the ducks that rightfully own the place take refuge along the banks.

"On reaching the plateau, Regine struck off to the west. She scratched her legs on the thorny dwarf birch until they bled, and when she got to the tarn she took off her shoes and stockings and waded near the edge to wash away the blood. Her stepping on shore frightened a big black bird. It rushed past her so she felt a draft from its wing, and it seemed to her that she had been waiting all the time for something to scare her or to strike out at her. She ran farther toward the nesting cliff, and now at last broke into loud and bitter weeping.

207

"That was likely the last time Regine cried as a child. Later, her tears turned inward, and early in life her eyes took on a hard, dry glint. Workmen on the dock soon started calling her Miss Beck, and that mode of address not only expressed respect but repressed scorn as well.

"With the sun coming directly from the south, she got up, brushed off her clothes, and walked on farther westward.

"From the top of the isle the mountain slopes down to the west coast where the two stone pillars stand. Directly to the north there is a little bay with a sandy beach, and on the inner side there is a small sparse birch grove where the ground is flat and even and where grass and ferns grow between the sand dunes. Still farther north along some cliffs is the cave I told you about.

"I deem it a blessing that there are isles," Lady Sophie continued, "and I feel that just as a person ought to learn to read and write so he ought also to live on an isle at least two years in his youth. I have in mind, of course, a small isle, one he can row all the way around easily within a day. And when people ridicule me and contend that our world is also an isle and that we ought on the contrary to build bridges and more coastal steamers, then I recognize the voice of mainland stupidity speaking. By looking at a person I know immediately whether he is from an isle. His hands tell me. He moves them reverently, as if carrying a fistful of earth laboriously conquered, and his eyes are filled with tenderness and tranquility, for he has seen that the beginning and the end are one and the same, and that man always comes back to the place from where he started."

Pastor Celion cleared his throat at this irreligious utterance; he was about to say something but changed his mind, sighed slightly, and took a drink instead.

"From the day Regine discovered this uninhabited paradise

208

on the western side of the isle, she became an inhabitant of her isle and returned regularly to this spot.

"Regine had a fever when she came home that night, and Lola ordered her to bed. She had to stay quiet for five days, and because she made no complaint both Lola and the twins feared something serious had happened to her.

"She didn't ask about the lamb; she only lay ill, speechless, with clear wide-open eyes. She stared at the broken beams in the ceiling, and when she was not asleep she lay with a thin grown-up smile on her lips, passing the hours by counting the knots in the woodwork.

"One day when her father was gone, she went down to the water, untied one of the small boats, and rowed around the isle to her new world.

"The two stone columns stand on the same base. At low tide they adjoin, and then they resemble closely a colossal tuning fork. If one stands right between them touching both with his fingertips, he can indeed feel thousands of vibrations coming to him from far and near. They repeat orchestrations from the floor of the sea, music played long ago in subterranean grottos along the coast of Mexico. The vibrato of the currents has preserved the melodies across the oceans, and now at last they ring out here outside the isle. You can hear corals breaking, ice cracking in the Arctic, the soft paddle stroke of a canoe along the Amazon, the breathing of the pearl diver, squid, shark, catfish, and an unpleasant sawing noise of an animal not yet identified.

"Regine heard all of it—life coming out of a deep green world in movement. She couldn't yet touch them both at the same time with outstretched arms, but there was a ledge on the outer side of one of the pillars, and sitting there on bright summer days she had only to turn her head and put her ear to the mountain to hear.

209

"The boat she had stolen ended its days there on the west coast. One can still see the white skeleton sticking up out of the rubbish on the beach. Regine tied it to one of her feet when she sat on the rock shelf at high tide. At ebb tide she let it stand on the plinth of the two columns. When she had to go home at dinner time, she pulled it up onto the beach in the little sandy bay and ran eastward over the mountain.

"One morning on her arrival she saw the place had changed; spring had arrived by night, and when the sun rose in the southeast it discovered full-blown leaves on the birch trees. And the birds sensed the sweet sticky perfume on the branches where they had perched in sleep.

"Here spring always comes by night. In the brief moment of dusk, a moist heavy breeze wafts over the land, and whatever is to die this winter must do so speedily. Every second is precious to death. The last that is due to happen in darkness must occur immediately. Winter vanishes, the snow crackles and sinks, thin layers of ice on shallow water are hollowed out in the night. And the swells rolling toward shore the next morning find everything new—a bold fresh coloring on the beach. Even the cave on the north side of the isle gives out a surprised echo as the water swirls into it. And the twin obelisks sing.

"Spring comes first to Regine's own paradise, but as morning wears on the whole isle is enveloped. The building at Becksgård becomes aware of it at once. Doors warp in the dampness, and either they make no sound at all or they let out new squeaks; sudden terrifying gasps come from walls that have been mute all winter. Reginald Beck grabs his gun and jumps into his boots, and Regine's mother raises her head a moment—may God forgive what we do to one another—and suddenly she weeps quietly, sitting with her hands folded in her lap.

210

"As often as she could escape from the house Regine ran over the mountain to the west side. During the course of early summer she fashioned for herself a new world out of the fleeting stuff of dreams. Its south side was protected by a nesting cliff; her winged neighbors would issue a warning if anyone approached. In the birch grove the leaves supplied a roof, and the stubby succulent grass provided a floor. The bay yielded sand and shells for building material. Regine built herself a castle; she erected temples, colonnades, and mosques of her own design; she made sacred caves and idols. When the tide flowed she lay face down in the grass, watching the world sink slowly beneath her. The land rose and sank underneath the surface; princes and princesses floated about, caught by the undertow in sunken halls, bobbed up, and sank again. When she returned the next day, there would often lie a starfish in the center of her city; Regine whisked the dead monster away and named the spot "Star Square." Then she arranged a parade of snails, and the pope—a more elaborate shellfish—pronounced his blessing.

"When cathedrals and palaces towered and ships in harbor awaited sailing orders, she lay propped on her elbows in the sand surveying her world. Dry-eyed and pensive, she played in deep silence and showed no sign of sorrow if a tower collapsed and crushed a multitude of people in its fall.

"But it was even better to sit in the cave on the north side. When the tide was out she balanced on rocks ringing the projecting mountain. There was an opening the size of a barn door into the mountain, an entrance to the isle itself. The cave was somewhat larger than the parlor at Becksgård. The floor slanted upward a distance, but from the middle of the cave it dropped down toward the bottom, and there, deep within, it formed a well that never ran dry. When sunlight shone in late at night one could see sparkling whirl-

211

pools made by fish swimming around seeking a route of escape.

"Thus I have seen her before me: sitting hunched over on a piece of board at the highest point in the cave, her chin between her knees, her dark eyes fixed on the movement of the sea toward land. A slender young goddess in a grotto, in reality originally intended as a sacrifice to the gods of the sea but later accepted into their company. And behind her the dark well where haddock and catfish glide round and round along the rim.

"And the sounds! In all that happened to her later, she must always and forever have heard those sounds—the seething erosion of the sand whenever the tide recedes and then the quietness in the brief interval when nothing happens until it rises again and fills the shells and the little snail tunnels in the sand. Perhaps it will eventually become almost impossible for one to live simply who has shared the secrets of the isle. I think it may be impossible to act, for the noise of crumbling sand destroys will power when you most need it. You have gotten a sound and a rhythm within you, the beat of the sea against land, which is the breath of time against yourself, and when later you undertake a task that rhythm will whisper, 'In vain, in vain,' and it will poison your every pleasure; an isle has a long-lasting influence on a person.

"But the best of all was to row out to the stone pillars and sit on the narrow ledge of dreams and let her eyes peer down into the clear green water and to stare herself blind at the horizon there where the earth rounds off."

5

"Regine darts across the mountain, back and forth between two worlds. In due time she wore a distinct path, a narrow lightning-swift path between dreams and reality.

"One day a rowboat stops nearby. Regine glances up, disturbed. She obliterates a cathedral and a town hall with her right foot and stands up. It is Olaf, the son of the fisherman on Utøy. Regine recognizes him at sight. Utøy counts only for as much as a button in Reginald Beck's vest. Olaf's father is allowed to borrow it for a hundred pounds of fish each year.

"Now he is pulling in the oars, fastening the spool, and letting out his line. His blond hair gleams, as if it has just been washed, cut short like a stubble field, and shines silvery in the sunlight.

"Regine has misgivings. She is not certain how far the right of ownership extends and takes refuge behind a birch trunk to think it through.

"But the young man in the boat is on a subsistence mission. Greater things than boundaries in the sea are at stake. Surely the Beck realm reaches no farther than the shelf in the sea. Doesn't his father pay rent in the form of full-grown cod? And doesn't the sea flow back and forth of its own accord? Suppose the southwest wind carried an oat seed from the wretched test plot at Becksgård across to Utøy so oats began to sprout in the mountain crevices out there, would the nabob have any right to make a fuss about that?

"Regine's mind is accustomed only to dreaming, and hiding behind the birch tree she finds no law to rely on. Finally she goes down to the beach, sits on a log and pokes holes in the sand with a little stick.

"That brat of a boy out there is hauling in a haddock as big as the bailing scoop. He mutters in disgust and spits in its eye; with that he seizes the oars and rows a few strokes nearer. The line goes overboard again; the fish line whistles loud and shrill in the sunny summer air. He winds and releases, winds and releases; water splashes around the spool. It looks bad! Damned bad!

213

"Regine sits still, without turning. She has poked eighteen holes in the sand and is in the act of filling them up again. Is that an indication that the princess's patience is at an end? This smacks of irritation.

"Young Olaf Utøy's face is tense with business sense. He nods in rhythm with the gear. 'No! Not as much as a filthy roach! That devil of a Beck has perhaps bought the whole sea! What one can't get with money! Better move again.' He reels in, swings his boat around, and rows toward the stone pillars. There he drops anchor and throws out his line.

"God help us if he isn't trying to begin making a living right here beside the columns!"

Lady Sophie stopped talking a moment. Pastor Celion looked at her, puzzled. He didn't feel it was easy for her to be lost for words; on the contrary, he had the impression she was somewhat too garrulous at times. He thought she would do well to read the Book of Judges. And Richard? Was the light too bright for him?

Lady Tennyson continued.

"And Regine fills up one hole after another. Then she sets about to dig eighteen others. Will not God strike down a madman?

"Out there the fish line whines; in here the sand crumbles; but not a word will be spoken. Isn't there enough silly talk in the world?

"Just then someone calls out from the isle; the voice young and resonant, clear and strong, as if seasoned a long time and matured by the sea.

"Regine raises her head and listens in astonishment.

" 'The Devil!' shouts Olaf. He pulls in his line with decisive jerks and rows homeward.

"The very next day he's back again. Regine notices he has smeared red lead on his line. He spits and calls on the devil.

214

Occasionally he casts a glance toward the beach, each time with the same pretense of surprise at seeing someone sitting there. Regine scoops up a pile of sand but doesn't build anything, doesn't let herself be fooled, doesn't expose a kingdom to a twirp with red lead on his line.

"The boy lets the line out and tugs, his fish line tangles, he puts one foot on the gunwale, and he curses. But gradually he realizes all this is to no avail and sits hunched over on the thwart.

"At last he has matured and mellowed. 'May I come in where you are?' he asks as he looks up from his gear.

"Regine compresses her lips and shakes her head violently.

"The day wears on, and again Regine hears the distant deep-toned voice out across the water. A thrill of joy goes through her, she looks out at the boy, and she answers something incoherent between a yes and a no—nye, knowing at once she is about to capitulate. She had almost surrendered her kingdom, and she must not let that happen.—

"The following day with no more ado he rows all the way in to the sandy beach, climbs out of the boat, and gives her a piece of sugar candy and a necklace with a brass heart on it.

"Regine accepts and remains standing. Somewhere deep within a disapproving voice is speaking; she hears it all the time while he is pulling his boat on shore, but it is too late. She has already clasped the bribe in her hand.

"Life's own little moment has come to Becksø. The gods have caught the scent of a plot. An idea set in motion, and all the powers are happy and busy. Now they assemble and conjure up intrigue; ties will be made—and broken. They drop whatever they have in hand and abandon all thoughts of a ship in distress in the Mediterranean, for now they have something to grasp onto in an isle in Thule. Youth—the sun—

215

and a sparkling sea—come, you who hunger for destinies
of men.—

"Olaf is no artist at building castles in the sand. He confines himself mostly to flat substantial things, land and the
sea and such things as God has already done a better job
of creating. Regine frowns at his hands and speaks as little
as possible. Obviously she is not enjoying this, but he has
now bought his right of use.

" 'Your father doesn't own the isle you live on,' she says
with cold disdain.

" 'My father is usually out on the sea. He has no need to
own an isle.'

"A man's world! A man's thoughts!

"Instantly Regine retreats into her own world. She erects
a tower of sand around a stick and makes a vent at the
top nearest the roof. She makes various shapes, she bends
over gracefully like a dancer, and her hands meet as they
form a bowl around the sand.

"Days will come when a southwester surprises them, and
then if the tide is out, it may happen she will give the lad
permission to sit on high ground inside the cave—on the
condition that he keeps still. Does he perhaps chatter in
church? This is a church. The rain is hushing them to be
quiet. Isn't he aware that the minister lisps? Or maybe out
there on the skerry they don't go to church?

"Every so often when she cuts him down completely, he
gets into his boat, rows out to sea, and throws his line overboard without so much as one solitary word. She can just
sit there. He has his own concerns. His gear makes no fool
of him. He's angry, heaves the anchor, and settles himself
securely way down at the far end of the world. 'Stocking-
feet!' he screams loudly and clearly. Regine turns up her
nose at the remark. But one day she appears in white silk

hose; she shows him they reach far up. Olaf doesn't think much of it, and it occurs to him that Rosa, the only animal at Utøy, gave birth to a long-legged calf last spring.—He has his moments of triumph now and then.

"The sunny days of summer pass. Regine acquires a beautiful tan as if tinted with a brush. Olaf gets pinker every day, his skin wrinkles and wants to escape from his exposed face, and freckles spawn in a place near the bridge of his nose. Regine commands him to sit still while she leans over him and counts the new ones that have appeared since yesterday. He feels her cool warmth and catches the scent of sea and sand. But afterwards she makes fun of his freckles. Again he escapes to the sea and throws out his line. Life is frustrating. Those freckles, which are indeed nothing but a little sun shower, are the source of both happiness and misery.

"Sometimes Regine calls him in and takes him with her up to the sharp rock on the slope. She bids him lie down and focus his eyes on a point right between the two stone pillars and he will be able to see the world's end.

"He stays there a long time and takes a careful measurement of eternity, looking first with one eye and then the other—then with both wide open. 'No, nothing!'

"Regine leaves him and goes down to the beach; she hums a tune to herself without seeing him at all.

"She crushes him daily and then builds him up anew. It is wonderful to live and wield the scepter."

6

"Old Lola showed me a picture of Regine at the time she left home to enroll in a girls' school in Trondhjem—a tall, slender lass with short-cut raven-black hair, curls as if whirled by a spring breeze in frolic and fashioned with style and finesse around her head. A long thin neck that

217

stretched forward just a little, big deep-blue eyes, heavy masculine eyebrows in high curved arches. Reginald Beck had stamped his likeness on her. Her nose was slightly aquiline, and perhaps the space between nose and mouth, the space that really designs a face, a trifle too short. She had a small mouth and a weak chin, characteristics which would indeed have been accentuated had she lived to be old enough. Perhaps there is an advantage in dying young, for I think the appearance we carry with us into death will prevail through all eternity, and surely it will be distressing to see one's own face ugly and wasted for so long a time.

"Her parents were clearly reflected in her, and her father's features dominated the upper part of her face just as when a second story of an old house projects slightly out above the lower. Later, as she matured, her own willfulness served to level off that obvious difference. Therefore in her youth she would have been the very image of Charlotte Metzer the first few hours at a masked ball, but as the evening wore on and masks were removed, an ardent suitor would indeed have been startled at seeing Reginald Beck before him— if he put his hand over her mouth to prevent her from crying out.

"Thus we can see how crucial situations in a young girl's life expose one or another legacy within her, all depending on how far she has progressed in life's dramatic masquerade."

Lady Sophie reddened somewhat. "I trust the gentlemen will forgive this little digression. I was speaking of Regine's appearance. She had long slender arms and legs, her wrists were thin, and her hands evidenced a nervous composure— a dangerous indifference that might harbor both rage and strong desire.

"Then one autumn day Regine leaves. Wearing a crisp new dress and welted boots of soft leather, she is sailing away in one of her father's boats from out the bay. A flickering white light lines the heavens, and there are only favorable reports from the south—from the same direction we are headed now."

Mylady laughed quietly. "Are we following in her wake right now? That narrow path of light in the sea that refuses to close? What do you think, Eberhardt?"

The merchant's eyes searched a while. "I'm not sure, Sophie. The sea here is reputed to cover all tracks. But I understand this Regine must have been in league with greater powers. She must have had in her a spoonful of ghost's blood. It's said that a lumpfish once bit off a bogie's toe, and ever since then it has nibbled at iron. Perhaps she ate lumpfish and developed a taste for witchcraft. I shouldn't be surprised to learn that she was clever at school also without exerting much effort."

Lady Sophie raised her glass and sipped her wine, letting her hand rest for a moment on the merchant's arm. Pastor Celion noticed. He stared at the glittering wake and re-membered with sadness his first twinge of unbelief. "And when they came to the Red Sea, God caused the waters to separate and a path opened—"

"Every autumn Regine is in the boat and watches the isle shrink until no more of it remains than a grain of sand on the horizon. Her father stands right between the wide double doors of the warehouse, waving. As soon as he has waved once, he goes into the office.

"He is no longer the kingpin. Commerce has found a shorter route closer to the mainland, but there is still much going on at Becksgård. In June the Russian barges never fail to arrive with their cargo of barley, strong aromatic tea, fragrant unground oats for meal.

"When Captain Nikolai anchors in the bay, Reginald Beck recaptures his youth, and the two tycoons can be heard drinking toasts to one another into the early morning hours. The next day they continue their revelry in the cabin of the Russian boat. The wife is never invited on board though Captain Nikolai, a man of the world, extends his most cordial greetings and presents a gift of his finest tea glasses. Much profanity is exchanged in both world languages, Russian as well as Vesterålen Norwegian, and often on summer nights Reginald Beck's swift little sailboat darts into the channel with the two friends on board. There they sit at the bulkhead, arms around one another's shoulders, both holding onto the rudder, while the wife at Becksgård, pale and wan, watches at the window. They visit every isle, all the little gray-green emeralds within Reginald Beck's domain. In the midnight sun the view is bright and exciting, and the two lords miss nothing of the beauty and joy. On board they have a keg of Russian rye brandy and a salt-cured ham; on shore widows go about looking at the almanac. Yes, it is a night in June—with a glowing sun and a time of forgetfulness.

"Regine waves with her other hand, her left, to where her mother is standing at the upstairs window. The lacework, her Ariadne's thread, hangs to the floor behind her. With a linen handkerchief so stiffly starched it does not ruffle in the wind, she beckons to her black-haired daughter whom she really never understands any more than she does God's purpose with whale oil and stockfish, wind and weather, daylight and darkness. Two tears form, one in each eye as befits good breeding, and for one short moment her little mouth quivers noticeably.

"Regine is aware of it though she sees only the white outline of a person, and suddenly from within wells up violently love, tenderness, hate.

"At last the isle becomes so tiny you can flick it aside

with one finger. A point projects between you and Becksø, and then it is winter again.

"But in the interim there has also been a summer. The day after coming home, Regine races across the mountain. Nothing has changed; the stone pillars sing when she puts her ear to them, new families come to the nesting-cliff every day, the sea reaches up to the flood mark.

"Regine heaves a deep sigh; she is home. In a little while Olaf comes. She is frightened at seeing he has grown up—she realizes it—soon he will be as tall as she and his hair no longer shines like silver in the sun. Olaf has been the steward of her kingdom while she has been in the south learning to know the real world, and she observes traces of his having been here recently.

"But every summer they must discover one another anew. He approaches quietly in his boat and throws out his line, mumbles something to himself, and pretends he has never been here before. Regine sits on her log digging holes in the sand.

"At last he rests his foot on the gunwale, spits, and remarks angrily that this has been a hard winter. Poor fishing. A rotten catch. Regine nods at hearing these words. She heard the same in Trondhjem. For that matter she has been to the cathedral every Sunday. But one Thursday it happened she went to the top of the steeple and dropped a one-crown piece to the ground.

"Whether she recovered it?

"No, a child had come along and run off with it.

"Whether she had reported him?

"Reported a child? For taking one crown? No, but she had dropped another crown because she hadn't heard the sound of the first one properly. And she didn't recover that one either, for it rolled under the stairs and down into the basement of the cathedral where the kings lie in their sarcophagi.

"Olaf doesn't dare ask the meaning of the word 'sarcophagi,' but he remembers it as evidence of Regine's brilliance and wisdom.

"Whether it was high?

"Well, she had recited the entire Lord's Prayer while the coin was on its way down—at any rate as far as 'Thy will be done on earth as it is in Heaven.'

"Regine laughs, a loud and overbearing laugh. She is in her element. No one can touch her. Nothing is a lie.

"One day, however, everything has changed. Olaf is a fool and a bungler. She destroys his clumsy structures and runs away from him; she wants him to chase her. Olaf obeys unwillingly, and though she is a hare and he a tortoise, she lets herself be caught. Yes, she even stops leaning against a birch trunk, panting, and when he comes she kisses his mouth, breaks into peals of laughter, and streaks off across the mountain homeward.

"The next day she takes a little more time. She is unusually friendly, compliments him on his luck at fishing, and recounts what she has seen and learned about real life in the city.

"But then presently she jumps to her feet and tempts the tortoise. She teases him a long time, darting in and out among the birches—aware of her power.

"And he, a tortoise that catches roaches, does he suspect anything? He has, moreover, begun to get a little angry; he no longer lets himself be commanded to do whatever she wants.

"But as he approaches her, she falls down on her back, smiling up at him, draws him toward her, and kisses him three times.

"Something is happening. Regine stops and holds her breath. There's something in the air—a different something—as if a strange unfamiliar season had been thrust upon them right in the middle of a summer's day.

"At this time they engaged a new clerk at Becksgård—Martin from a neighboring isle. He was a few years older than Regine, a tall blond young man with beautiful legible handwriting.

"Regine began frequenting the office. At first she would take a seat on the wood box near the stove and study brochures of merchandise from foreign lands."

7

"In the afternoons while Lola took her naps, I would stroll around on the isle. I would walk about in Regine's world and think of her, and if I have previously reported something which Lola could not possibly have known, it must be attributed to my being carried away by the atmosphere of the place—a dangerous threat to what we call the plain truth, which again is scarcely half of it. You stand here on your miniscule kernel of reality; eternity and dreams, which for the sake of brevity I call the sea, rushes at you. Who can say he is secure? And I felt the two worlds must have collided for Regine. That's why things went wrong.

"On my return I caught the aroma of strong coffee coming from the open door. We sat in the entrance hall drinking it while Lola continued her story. I can still taste the bitter flavor of home-roasted Guatemalan coffee; it makes the tongue shrink so one can't talk too much. I shall try to confine myself to old Lola's account.

"Regine and Olaf used to meet in a cleft on the north side of the isle. Not that Lola, that old woman, spied on them, but she did feel herself the one person closest to Regine—and the isle is so small.

"It was Regine's idea for the two to meet there. She had turned sixteen one day in April; that summer she denied her friend access to her childhood realm. If he wanted to see her he would have to show up at the cleft precisely at midnight.

"And on June nights when perfect stillness prevailed at Vesterålen, a thin dark-haired girl slipped out of the back door at Becksgård and disappeared northward into the birch woods. Simultaneously, a boat set out from the shore of Utøy.

"For Regine the first love affair was a game, a continuation of her childhood play, only with something new and disturbing added. She sensed within her the rules of the game, just as a musically talented child feels melody. And when she stole away to that nocturnal rendezvous, she had imagined ahead of time all that was to take place. Olaf, to whom she secretly assigned new and more romantic names, would pull the boat to shore very quietly behind him and would approach the cleft with a pale up-turned face. Then he wouldn't say a word, only clasp her hand and with two fingers stroke her arm until he reached her neck. Then he would carefully push aside the band of her dress and kiss the hollow by the collarbone and then her mouth. He would slowly guide her to the farther depths of the chasm where lush grass grew, but then she would smile softly and warmly, run her fingers through his long black hair and whisper: someone is sitting in the sunlight watching us. And he would instantly understand and love her even more ardently. Thereupon they would saunter back and forth along the shore assuring each other of their mutual devotion.

"Regine created for herself many versions of this game, but Olaf of Utøy fell through each time. She fancied him decked out in innumerable disguises, but he didn't measure

224

up to any of them. Sooner or later the picture shattered, and there he stood in his run-down shoes without laces and tied with twine, in his blue work clothes with patches on the knees; and his eyes were neither deep-set nor strikingly mischievous but rather expressionless like the eyes of a dead codfish. It is true he had grown as tall as she and his hair had darkened, but it was by no means dark enough, and moreover it was still bristly and clipped short at the back and around his ears. Indeed he didn't say much, but his reserve was dull and without charm.

"One time Regine determined he would come disguised as his true self: a prince in blue work clothes with patches on the knees. That evening she stood waiting in the cleft with her eyes shut and her fists clenched as if to squeeze reality to its utmost. But when she opened her eyes—Heaven help—there he came in his Sunday homespun, worse than ever. She permitted him to kiss her, a wet and hasty kiss, but her throat went taut with disappointment. He was as clumsy as usual. 'Shall we set out for coalfish?' he mumbled. 'They're biting like mad north by the point.'

"Coalfish! Cod! Flounder! Lord! Did he think he was doing her a great favor by suggesting he try for coalfish in homespun?

"Just once she drew him toward her violently and passionately and pressed her lips to his in a long kiss.

"The following day when she was sure of being alone, Regine crossed to the west side. She rowed out to the stone pillars—there to meet another blighted hope. This summer the obelisks had lost their clear resounding tone. She went to the cave at ebb tide, but the sea had no secrets to share with her. The sandy beach was flat and colorless, the water sluggish and dull with gray scum in the bay. The sea rose and fell only as if from an old tedious habit.

"Regine went back, walked into the office, and gave her

225

attention to Martin. Would he help her get a kilogram of wheat flour? She had a mind to bake something. Regine in the lead, they ascended the two stairs. There was an oppressive cloying atmosphere in the granary loft; the windows were covered with dust, and in the half-darkness the sacks and bins turned into a strange and dangerous landscape.

"That summer Regine felt like a guest whenever she went to the sandy beach; things denied her their intimacy and she wandered like a homeless waif on the isle.

"Becksgård was beginning to be grown over; shrubs and yellow dock hugged the walls of buildings. Moisture was cracking the stonework; now and then a falling roof tile broke the silence. Rails tumbled out of the fences and stuck fast in the tall grass. Sometimes Regine's father would pass by to inspect and he jerked them up, only to find them white with worms and mold, and would look with indifference at the fermenting life without giving much thought to anything. He leaned the crosspiece up against the gap and went down to the office.

"Business declined. Reginald Beck started selling out— first his boats and fish nets and later his land. It became increasingly difficult to get people to stay at his place. 'In three years you can rent the house as a fisherman's shanty,' said those who delighted in the decline. And some of them wondered why Martin, that ambitious young clerk, continued to stay on at Becksø. He had made himself more and more indispensable and when people questioned him as to why he didn't take the little boat and clear out—for certainly anyone could see that Becksgård was in a sinking state—he only smiled enigmatically and said it was pleasant to sail on as long as possible. But, of course, there were always some who were sharp-sighted enough to maintain that he wanted to appear gallant and mysterious by being a part of the final crash. 'Nonsense!' they exclaimed sneeringly. 'Some people will try to make perfection out of a thing— no matter what!'

"This winter for the first time in the history of the isle the bay froze over, and every cargo boat that arrived had to drop anchor on the west, on the inner side of the two stone pillars where it was quite deep close to shore. Then they had to load the merchandise on horses to transport it over the mountain. Regine's path.

"This was also Regine's final winter at school. One Sunday in January as she was leaving the cathedral, a young man stopped her to ask her whether he might guide her up into the steeple. Regine's eyes follow the tower to its very top, and the thought comes to her that one time she dropped a crown through the air at this same place. She recalls it suddenly, an incident out of the long-ago, a scene from her childhood.

"Or perhaps she feels dizzy? Should they rather go to a cafe?

"Regine shifts her glance from the steeple to the young man; he smiles broadly, his white teeth glistening. Dizzy! Regine laughs gaily. Indeed! Delightfully dizzy! But she would be ever so happy to go to a cafe.—

"Throughout the winter the dark handsome couple were constantly seen together. They were among the first to go skiing just for the fun of it. Twice a week they could be seen in a sleigh dashing off along the shore. At morning worship they seated themselves on one of the benches at the back so people had to turn around to look at them. The plainer girls, or the girls not quite so pretty, maintained that Regine preferred to sit there. She was so shy.

"Their handsome appearance and discreet behavior were

immediately interpreted as a kind of mutual pledge of faith, more or less like an engagement. It was understood that it would have been improper for either one of them to bind himself to someone less clever and less attractive. The more highly cultured people in the town, putting their heads together and smiling benignly on the two, talked about the refinement of the species.

"Regine enjoyed her triumph but did not make it evident. Her coiffure, once designed by a whirlwind at Becksø, came to be admired and copied. The daughters of the town tried to stretch their heads forward in order to attain that demure gazelle-like grace that Regine had developed by listening to the sea and to eternity on an isle in Thule.

"To be sure, letters came twice from Lola. Her mother was ill and asked for her repeatedly. Her father often paced back and forth on the dock at night. Strangers came to examine the siding of the buildings. Regine used the letters as bookmarks, changed her dress, and gazed at her long slender legs in the mirror.

"One evening in March a caravan of four sleighs sets out along the shore. Regine and her friend are at the rear. When they are outside of the town, there is no need for them to take the lead, and as a special privilege he can hold her hand above the bearskin coverlet.

"They come to a narrow road that turns inland from the shore. As they are rounding the corner, a piece of paper blows across the road and lands for a moment in front of the very eyes of one of the horses. The horse rears and neighs in fright and then jerks around and takes off in a gallop onto the narrow side road. The young man hangs onto the reins tightly, pulls back with a jolt, and shouts a silly city swear word into the air. The horse bites at the

228

bridle and with one quick tug throws the driver against the front rest. Then he bolts off inland.

"Regine, who has been sitting safely drowsing, now wakes up and feels a sweet kind of fear when the horse rears up, but immediately the scare changes into obsession, delight, exhilaration. The sleigh bells ring out like jingling crystal in the frosty air, the sleigh lurches, and the driver strikes out frantically. Regine jumps to her feet, snatches the reins, and gives the horse a lash with the whip. Before her she sees reality as it is: a dreadfully narrow roadway and swaying trees. They race at breakneck speed—then a swift trot. The Devil! With all her might Regine thrusts the reins at the distorted face that lies against the framework in front of her, covered with its own blood.

"Regine is standing on the seat, her coat flapping; she is singing. Reality whirls all around her—down slopes, through farmsteads where terrified faces look out of doorways, up hills, over fields, through woods, straight across the mountains of Norway, in biting wind. This is living life to the hilt.

"When the horse comes to a halt, bubbles of froth blow all around them. They find themselves on a lonely road bordered by dense forests, in a land that is sound asleep. Regine climbs out and mops foam and sweat off the horse. She buries her face in the wet black mane, it mingles with her own hair, and she stands a long time listening to the wild throbbing in the animal's throat. They seem—she and the horse—to have stemmed from the same long-legged dark-hued breed.

" 'Were you frightened?' she queries sweetly and settles down under the cover.

" 'I? Was I frightened? What do you think!' He is in a rage. 'You'll find out how frightened I was!' And with one jerk he pulls her down beneath him in the bottom of the sleigh. Regine looks up into his twisted face; she is laughing.

'I'll show you how frightened I was!' Again he is screaming in anger as he presses his mouth to hers and rips open her clothing.

"Regine lies on the floor of the sleigh, still laughing. She catches a glimpse of the sky beyond his face. She sways in dizzying waves, rises and falls; again she is at home on the sandy beach, yielding herself to the soothing rhythm of sea against land, and she still smiles in a swaying dream as she feels his hands upon her.

"Suddenly they aren't moving any more. She sinks, falls, awakens, and lies half-dressed on the bottom of a sleigh on a strange roadway. She is uncomfortable; she feels a gnawing pain in her back; and she is aware of the strong smell of leather and of sweat that for a moment recalls a thought of fear and of delight. Bewildered, she feels his burning breath against her face; suddenly he coughs a dry strained cough and lays his head against her breast to muffle the sound.

"With a quick twist Regine turns on her side, jabbing her elbow into his face. 'No! Get away!' she cries loudly and sharply. She pushes him off, and she creeps out onto the road, trembling. Without so much as a backward glance, she runs—trying to arrange her dress in order as she goes.

"Shortly he turns the horse in her direction and comes in pursuit. Regine keeps to the middle of the road so that he cannot pass. In this way they go for a half mile, but then Regine is forced to step aside for someone they meet. She has to go into the ditch, and there she breaks off a long alder branch.

" 'Do you intend to walk home?' he asks by way of testing her when they are alone again. Regine doesn't answer. She goes over to the sleigh. He looks at her skeptically and draws back a little. At that instant she lifts the branch and strikes with all her might. The horse lunges forward violently

230

and, scared completely out of its senses, takes off with its lone passenger.

"Regine wades through the snow toward the town; evening is closing in on her. She hurries along, unmindful of her weariness, conscious only of deep disappointment. But along with the disappointment there is a kind of painful freedom. She has learned something; she cannot say exactly what, but a curtain has been torn away; she senses she has gained a joyless sort of strength. After trudging two hours she sees the lights of the town and the majestic structure of the cathedral dominating the horizon toward the east.

"Regine remained weather-bound in Rørvik forty-eight hours. She reached home an hour after her mother's funeral and was barely able to watch the last spadefuls of earth being strewn on the coffin. She had seen the flag at half-mast from out in the harbor, and it remained hanging that way until the following morning because the house was so filled with people and the clergyman that Reginald forgot to hoist it to the top after the interment.

"Regine went directly from the harbor to the burial ground—old Lola with her. It was at noon-time on a day in early May; a damp spring breeze lighted the sky. Gulls flew in wide circles above the sound as if sketching isles in the air with their perpetual revolutions.

"I can remember from when I was a child," Lady Sophie interrupted herself. "I can remember that in my excitement I thought I saw pathways in the air behind them—zigzagging gray pathways. Through the years these circles have become something more than mere rings drawn in the fabric of memories. They have become the subject of thought, or the symbol if you prefer, of the closed world of our minds, our imprisonment in the labyrinths of our hearts and brains.

231

"Well, well, there in the cemetery stood the spruce trees from Målselv. They had grown melancholy through the years, tall and stiff—like old men dressed in mourning who stand in a group and mumble—much too obviously out of place in the flood of light out here.

"Two men in shirt sleeves and black vests were just then packing down the sod to cover the grave, but when the women approached they picked up their jackets and left. Lola, too, left promptly, but as she turned to shut the little gate, she saw Regine on her knees beside the grave. The old woman delayed a moment. When she was about to leave, Regine rose up, and the old housekeeper was amazed to see the blending of deep sorrow and derisive resolution in her face.

"Charlotte Beck's death was not preceded by great displays or portents on either land or sea. I have thought to myself that the occasion of her death must have been like that of standing on a high point of the isle and watching a solitary bird silently disappear into the mist on the water. She didn't complain about her pain, her affliction was chaste and unworldly, and her spotless lace-trimmed sheets bore no trace of her. There was not a wrinkle in her pillow after they had taken her away. But the two workmen who carried her down from the loft gave a different account—and perhaps they reported only what they saw—though some people thought they had taken a drink before the funeral.

"Moreover, Lola made a remark, and it shocked me that the quiet old woman, herself with one foot in the grave would say it: 'If only she had been blessed with wickedness!'

"The minister was lost for words at the table. He surveyed the room self-consciously as if noting the absence of grief. Death seemed somehow to be accepted too easily. There was an atmosphere of deception, of something missing, and

232

in their own minds those present attributed the fault to the one just buried.

"Regine sat by the door—and was aware of it.

"That summer Becksø underwent a sort of feverish renascence. The isle exhibited that mysterious singular beauty that prefaces a sharp decline. In the month of June boats appeared in the bay, barrels rattled on the dock, cranes whined. One day Captain Nikolai sailed up the sound, his black beard in full view a long way off, and one could hear him bellow his greeting to Regine's father who waved from the dock.

"Reginald Beck prospered anew, feasts were held, nights and days had no end, the sun circled the isle without dipping down into the sea.

"It was indeed annoying to be plagued with an unaccountable odor drifting in from the west. They suspected a dead whale was rotting on one of the islets and sent a boat out, but on the sea there was no odor. Hence they simply concluded that much takes place which no one can explain."

8

"Regine visited the grave daily. Most of the time she wandered around with a surreptitious smile, and it seemed as if along with that smile she had inherited something invisible from her mother.

"But one evening she joined the others, drank a little wine, and entered into conversation with her father and the skippers. The next day Regine went onboard the Russian boat, and that evening she and her father sailed back and forth in the bay visiting the vessels tied up there.

"Within just two days Regine had assumed the role of hostess at Becksgård, and Reginald Beck suddenly awoke to the realization that he had a grown-up daughter. That shocked him so much he had to retreat and go off by himself to reflect on what had become of all those years. He felt time had played tricks on him and paced the dock an entire afternoon, in a quandary. When evening came, however, he had finished this whole mystifying world order; he gazed in wonder at his beautiful daughter and called in his friends from the bay.

"One evening Olaf rowed in. He docked and went to the kitchen with a catch of sea trout. Regine was standing in the entryway. She noticed he had grown half a head taller than she.

"Would she like his fish? He had been lucky with a seine-full just beyond a certain crevice on the north part of the isle.

"Regine gave him a cold stare. Did he make a practice of seining fish in other people's inlets? In any case such was not the custom here. Moreover, this household wasn't receptive to donations.

"Regine glared at him and let him flounder. He didn't handle it very well—this son of a fisherman—even though he had begun to turn dark where he used to have only down and bristles.

"Gradually Olaf's face reddened. It takes time to comprehend such a quick-witted city girl. He made a half-turn toward the door; the bundle of fish sank down with the rest of him.

"'You're messing up the floor with your fish.'

"Regine moved a couple of steps closer to him. Then she smiled quickly and graciously. 'We don't need your fish now,' she whispered. 'Perhaps some other time. But if you'll come to the gorge at eleven, we can talk about it.'

"Olaf took the sea-trout back with him to the boat, and as soon as he was out of sight behind the point he threw them into the sea. For some reason or another he remembered the time when Regine wanted him to see the world's end by sighting along a sharp stone.

"From that day on Regine adopted a hardened kind of gaiety and began to play a new and dangerous game. It made her feel deliciously dizzy—just as on the day she had dropped a crown piece from the steeple of the cathedral.

"Old Lola broke her story at this point. She had to have more coffee, and her expression told me she was straining for an explanation."

Lady Sophie drank a toast and settled back in her chair with a sigh—as if suddenly exhausted. "Why does a person act as he does? I have told all this about Regine's surroundings because I think they had a part in making her what she was. But suppose our behavior is only the fruit of a moment's impulse, entirely apart from all else? And what if all our impulses are separate from one another?—the flight of a butterfly, beautiful and without purpose?

"That night Regine hid behind a knoll to watch Olaf row in. But when he pulled his boat into the shallows, she ran back to Becksgård and sat in the swing beside the garden pavilion.

"Half an hour later the boy comes sneaking up through the woods. Regine starts to swing upward in a giddy arc between two rowan trees, but presently she slows down to a more careful, more thoughtful, motion. She hums and lets her light summer dress blow up over her legs. At last she discovers the young man behind the fence. She stops—startled and blushing. 'Heavens! How you frightened me, Olaf!'

" 'Weren't we going to meet?' he asks.

" 'Yes,' she answers, surprised, 'at twelve.'

" 'You said at eleven.'

235

"'Did I say eleven? Oh, I guess I did. But you know I was thinking twelve all the time because it was at twelve we used to meet before, wasn't it? I was thinking of that, you know.'

"'Shall we go there now?'

"'Aren't we all right here?' Regine draws her feet up under her in an effort to set the swing in motion again only with the help of her body. 'We would be glad to have your sea-trout,' she adds, and then she suddenly jumps down and goes over to the fence. 'How nice you look, Olaf! Did you go home to change clothes?' She bends forward quickly and kisses him. 'You may place your nets wherever you want to,' she whispers, 'but now I have to go. We're having visitors, and they insist that I be there.'

"No, Regine was not lying—not in her world. And people really did come to what Captain Nikolai called the Becksgård Midnight Mass.

"Early the following morning while the guests were still asleep, recovering from the night's drinking bout, Regine went down to the office. Martin sat there with the ledger; he entered a consignment of empty barrels. Furthermore, these barrels were quickly stowed away, for there was nothing to put into them.

"Regine leans across the table and fixes her dark eyes on him. 'The granary roof has sprung a leak. Shall we go up and cover the bins?'

"That summer turned out to be unusually warm, and in the blue-white nights before Midsummer's Day Regine could be seen crossing back and forth over the isle. She divided her twenty-four hours evenly between her two loves. She knew the secret places of the isle and she knew the inhabitants' whereabouts at all times. But she didn't take

236

old Lola into account, old Lola who was a visionary and who didn't need to run around to know what was happening.

"Regine bestowed kisses on them with equally playful tenderness and didn't allow one to go farther than the other. She lived in constant turmoil; she had to go through the various scenes by herself. There was no breach in her adeptness, and she prevailed over them both with that infallible method flirtatious women have always used: she alternated warmth and coldness. She knew the exact breaking point instinctively, and her greatest delight was to come close to it."

With a smile, Mylady turned toward Celion. "Haven't you, Pastor, sometimes felt the possibility of damnation as a source of profound joy, and hasn't the awareness of this possibility cast a romantic glow on even the minutest of the transitory circumstances that surround us?"

"Why especially me, Mylady?" Celion answered. "Do you think that I from my position have a better view of the possibility of damnation than your friends here have? I know the nature of God only from the Scriptures, and if all the beauty we see about us is a reflection of His being, then I cannot make myself believe in damnation. And anyway I venture to say that in my limited experience I am also acquainted with winter storms and misfortunes—even if I am too poor a sailor to study His wrath at close range. But if I believed only in the possibility of damnation, then I would judge my work a delusion."

Celion glanced up but no one spoke, and his contribution to the discussion got lost in the silence that followed. Now they all have the same thoughts in common, he thought to himself.

Lady Sophie continued. "Or, for instance, watch a glass-blower at work: how he plays with the tension of the glass, how carefully he attends to the heating and the cooling,

237

and how he creates an object of pure ever-lasting beauty by taking advantage of the exact second of the melting point of the glass."

Lady Tennyson drank a toast, and as she set her glass down there was a sharp crackle and a chip flew out of the stem. It lay sparkling like a diamond. All four stared at it a moment. Pastor Celion smiled.

Mylady laughed softly. "Be careful not to triumph too soon, Pastor. I'm not in the habit of smashing glasses, but as a child I liked to bite glass. You ought to try that, Pastor. It wards off—"

She picked up the chip of glass and held it against the sun. "Everything reminds me of something," she said, smiling. "Simple incidents can put a person in mind of precious memories. Well, Pastor, perhaps there are inadequate pictures for revealing Regine's world, but I maintain she was not unfaithful—not to begin with. At first she brought things about—as one must do always who is a prisoner in his own dream world. But neither do I deny that she had other motives. Every day Regine went to the grave with fresh flowers.

"One night Reginald Beck was walking alone around the house. The last boats had left Becksø. He had recently been visited by some bank directors, men whom he remembered only vaguely from a drinking party came to present papers bearing his signature. Other faces which he had once humbled with excessive beneficence now appeared out of oblivion. Didn't the master of Becksgård remember them? He had indeed loaned them a hundred crowns once, and those crowns had enabled them to set themselves up in business. Now they would like to buy a couple of nets, for he really was going to sell—wasn't he? Didn't he have to sell?

"Though he refused to admit it even to himself, Reginald Beck knew the business was no longer his.

"When he came through the garden, he caught sight of Olaf behind a tree. He stood still, eyeing the young man, and all at once he felt a deep sense of despondency that slowly gave way to rage. Here stood one who had nothing to lose, stood there challenging him with his youth, stood there most likely to catch a glimpse of his daughter. Regine —now the only one—

"Reginald took one step forward, lifted his walking stick, and struck. He fought; he defended himself against everything that could drive him away: youth, life, desire.

"Olaf withstood the blows. He turned white, he didn't move, he stood there accepting the blows his father had accepted all those years.

" 'What are you skulking around for?' shrieked the proprietor, lifting his stick once more. The boy's silence was more powerful than screaming scorn; Reginald struck him several times and didn't come to his senses until he saw blood trickling. Then he discarded his stick and walked off without a word.

"Reginald Beck's spirits sank lower and lower as he went on. In the midst of defeat he felt a sinister kind of peace— the final certainty that his power was gone.

"Regine had witnessed the scene from her window. Olaf's bruised face evoked a new unfamiliar feeling of excitement, an emotion she couldn't rightly fit into place.

"She slipped a coat over her night-gown, dampened a towel, and hurried down. When she got there, he was gone."

9

"The thirtieth day of July of that year was very sultry even in the early morning, and by noon haze had settled down and the sun took on a pale, sickly glow.

239

"Reginald Beck and Martin had left at midnght, each in his own boat. Becksø was now a port of call for nothing more than sea birds and driftwood. Merchandise had to be procured from a new trading center that had sprung up near the inner channel.

"Later in the afternoon it was as if a porthole were opened to the oppressive air and a warm salty breeze wafted in over Becksø. Old Lola grew uneasy when she noticed it.

"As she sat there in the front parlor relating the story, her hands and face told me that all sorts of weather had dwelt within her—by that I mean a little more than only sunshine and rain. Now she no longer pays any attention to external changes, but at that time the very first waft of a breeze could tell her a great deal.

"By eight o'clock darkness had settled over the sea, a strong steady wind blowing across the isle was clearing the air, and rain was falling heavily. When there was no sail to be seen within a half hour, Lola went to the graveyard.

"Regine sat on a bench by her mother's grave, her hair slicked smooth by the rain, and the water streamed down her face so no one could tell whether she was crying or not.

" 'Your father and Martin have not come back,' said Lola. Regine raised her head, but her eyes were still focused on the little wooden cross which Reginald Beck had made for the mother's memorial and on which the years of her birth and death had been carved with a knife. 'Yes—and so what of it?' she replied indifferently.

" 'They should have been here by three o'clock. We must sail out in search of them.'

"Regine smiled contemptuously. 'We sail in search of them? Who's a better sailor than Father!'

" 'But what of Martin?' the housekeeper shouted angrily, grabbing the girl by the shoulder and shaking her. 'Your

240

sweetheart—or perhaps Olaf is your dearest today? Don't you think I know how you are carrying on, now with the one and then with the other?'

" 'Sail!' Regine jumped to her feet. 'Sail! Sail!' she shrieked. 'Let them sail! Who ever taught Mother to sail? What have you done to her?' And she ran out of the cemetery down toward the house.

"When Lola came in, Regine was putting on her sea-boots. 'I'm going to sail,' she announced.

" 'I didn't intend that you should,' answered Lola. 'I meant you could ask Olaf. He's here now.'

" 'I know he's here,' retorted Regine with a laugh. 'I've already asked him.' "

Mylady turned to the governor. "Your lonely friend Halvor Mikkelsen had a black six-oared sailboat. That's what they had at Becksø, too, and when with the help of Lola and the twins they succeeded in launching it, Olaf took his place at the helm. He held close to shore, and when he was just opposite the cave, he veered and set his course straight north. Then they felt the full force of the southwest gale, and on looking back after a few minutes they both observed that the isle had changed into a dark unfamiliar clump of land. Farthest to the west, in front of the nesting cliff, two foamy columns rose up just where the stone pillars stood.

"In this area there are reefs not indicated on the map at that time, and even if these reefs do become visible when waves dash against them during storms, Olaf made sure he would stay clear of them by holding well to the west. Out here the swells follow their own obdurate will, and though such a violent summer squall cannot change their direction, it churns up the sea and makes it difficult to calculate.

"They headed for the northernmost point of the large isle nearest to the mainland, a point more than six miles distant.

241

" 'Do you think they've turned back?' asked Olaf.

" 'Father never turns back.' Regine compressed her lips and shook her head.

" 'But what about Martin?'

"Regine didn't answer. Suddenly she laughed aloud. 'Now we're sailing beautifully, Olaf.' She looked around, wide-eyed and eager. The clouds hung low, the rain drenched them, and drops fell on the sea like pellets of hail. Regine lifted her face to let the water beat against her; she opened her mouth and drank it. Her cheeks reddened. She glanced about boastfully and shouted, 'We would never drown, would we, Olaf? We couldn't drown, could we?'

"He looked at her quickly, and now for the first time he saw she was wearing her father's clothes: a leather jacket and a pair of men's trousers stuffed down into her boots. The proudly arched and self-satisfied eyebrows knitted into a scowl against the southwest wind.

" 'Sure as the devil we could drown,' he screamed in a rage and pitched the boat daringly into a trough between two waves. 'Luckily it isn't especially rough today, so you don't need to be afraid. I'll save both you and your father.'—

"Here in the outer channel there is a chain of little islets running north and south. One must steer on the far side in order to avoid a long flat sand bar that lies like an underwater plateau beyond the big isle. As they sailed around the most northerly of them, Olaf spied two boats cutting a path against the wind near the point to the north. 'There they are!' he yelled. 'Shall we turn around? It looks as if they're managing all right. It's because they're heavily loaded.'

"Promptly the outermost of the two boats shifted course; in an instant it had turned, running before the wind toward the boat farther in. To the two in the six-oared boat it appeared they tried to avoid colliding at the last minute;

242

the sails flapped, and they saw a figure raise himself up halfway and put out a hand as if to ward off a clash. But in the next second the prow cut through the thin layer of wood of the Nordland boat. The riggings of both splashed overboard, the boats rammed one another—the one half split and the other intact but filled with water.

"On approaching closer Regine and Olaf could see the two boats had drifted a distance apart. Regine's father was clinging to the seat; Martin was grasping an oar.

"Regine turned to Olaf; her little face had paled. 'Steer toward Father's boat first!' she cried.

"Olaf sailed on. He looked up at the sails, he looked down at the sea that was steadily sweeping over the two, and when he was a hundred yards from them shifted course and swung around toward the one grasping the oar.

"'You must get Father first!' He heard her cry but he didn't look at her, and all at once he felt the blow of her fist in his face. 'Father first, or I'll jump overboard!'

"He wet his lips. His upper lip was split open. He smiled diffidently but nevertheless contentedly to himself, for he was young and had no doubt that he would be acquitted of self-reproach. Then he jerked the rudder around, sending the boat in a wide arc directly into the wind, and so accurately did he estimate its velocity, the sea, and the weight of the boat that he stopped exactly where Martin lay.

"Then he heard her shout again and felt her fingernails like sharp claws in his face. He let go of the rudder and with one hand seized hold of Martin's shoulder while with the other he lashed out; without looking to see what was happening he was aware that she had fallen over the thwart and lay on the bottom in the middle of the boat.

"As soon as Martin was rescued, Olaf straightened the boat into the wind and steered toward the spot where he had last seen Reginald Beck. At once he caught sight of the thwart riding the crest of a wave, but no one was clinging to it, nor was there anyone to be seen on the surface of the water though he kept circling in and out a long time around the two little boats that lay with keels upturned in the sea."

10

Lady Sophie stopped. Florelius had closed his eyes, and Pastor Celion noted that his friend's mouth was twisted into the same bitter expression that comes with news of shipwreck and death during winter storms. Berg sat shading his face with his big hairy hand.

The pastor removed his glasses, breathed on them, and polished them with a big red cotton handkerchief; while he watched the others with his bare near-sighted eyes, he saw them floating away into flickering shapes—becoming unrecognizable. He listened in the darkness of the night and realized again that he was excluded from their reserve. "Who are they really," he thought suddenly, terrified. "Shall we never for one merciful moment be able to draw near one another? Do we talk together, laugh, and spend our waking hours in company only to discover in one instant of cruel insight that we know nothing about one another?"

The pastor put on his glasses again. His round boyish face bore a hurt expression like that of a child on first learning adults do not keep promises. He closed his eyes and let the soothing sound of a calm sea sweep over him. "Who are you who wants to see God?" he pondered wearily, "who are you who dares to want to know, to apprehend?" But he felt at once that this humility no longer gave peace. Deep within he felt a churning disturbance, a little whirlwind spinning in search of support.

"Are you asleep, Pastor?"

Celion glanced up, frightened. Mylady had put her hand

244

on his arm, and that startled him for he could not readily decide whether rebellion against God's plan or the touch of Sophie's hand was what generated that churning disquiet within him. "No," he lied hesitantly, "I was sitting here thinking of what became of Regine afterwards."

"Well, Lola couldn't say what really did happen to her because Regine disappeared from the isle two months later. And that came about in this way:

"One September afternoon a white seventy-foot cutter with the bright and shining name of *Silver* sailed south along the Norwegian coast. Count Reger, a young blond landowner from Skåne, was on board. With three of his friends he had spent the summer in northern waters, and now they were on their way home.

"The count, who maintained he was a descendant of the well-known Benkestokk family up here in the north, had a true passion for outdoor living and for everything related to viking life. His appearance as well as his actions showed that this inclination was more than a mere sportsman's mood. There was something steadily regenerative about him in body and spirit, something that made jaded people envious of him—though in return they agreed among themselves that the count was a little—to be frank, you understand—a little naive—you know—well—

"That he knew a great deal of geography and much about sailing they granted condescendingly, and that he was a clever businessman they, of course, attributed to the remarkable inclination which such big children are blessed with—as compensation, mind you—for—well, one doesn't say these things openly. In more sophisticated circles, people slander one another without words, you know; the insult lies in the omission. It is, on the whole, pure and simple subtlety since spoken words act as a release while silence works like poison. Call a man a downright idiot, and he will

245

never bear you a grudge. But if you say he is naive and mean something worse by it, he will bear witness against you on the day of judgment.

"That afternoon the count himself stood at the helm. A steady gentle breeze blew from the northwest, dusk was beginning to fall, rain came down softly and quietly, and in the waning light the gray of the sky blended with the melancholy complexion of the sea where they met on the horizon.

"Reger really enjoyed himself best when alone, and when he invited anyone to join him on his cruises, the offer ought actually be counted a sacrifice to the opinion commonly held that there is something suspicious about a person who seeks solitude. The fact was that he always felt uneasy because he was not self-sufficient enough in the face of solitude. For solitude demands independence, and despite his wealth and handsome appearance, he was nevertheless cramped by his environment, by public opinion. Therefore he had taken refuge behind a devilish viking bearing, which in the main became him well, and for that reason he sailed away in quest of icebergs every summer.

" 'The wind is abating,' he thought, looking toward land. 'We shall have fog—better find a place to anchor for the night.' After he had sailed toward shore for a while, a steep isle bobbed up out of the mist. 'Behind that we will stop,' he reasoned, and then he roused the helmsman and the deckhand by shouting through a funnel leading to a cabin at the front.

"When the men got on deck the fog rolled in from the sea, and Reger commanded the helmsman to keep watch at the prow while the deckhand set about to haul in the canvas.

"A few minutes later the cutter *Silver* ran aground, in calm weather, and tore a hole a yard long in its bow."

Mylady laughed softly. "A shoelace was the cause of it all. The helmsman had wanted to tie his shoelace at the same time he was keeping watch—try it, and you'll see how hard it is—and so he mistook two stone pillars to be specks in the fog. When the count came running to the stem, the schooner lay wedged between the columns as in a vise.

"The boat was in no danger, however; the tide was low when they had run up on the dry plinth of the columns, and so they depended on being freed at high tide. In the meanwhile the men got busy repairing the damage.

"When Count Reger had reassured his friends, he lowered the small light rowboat and went ashore. He wanted to climb up on the isle to get above the fog in order to see whether it reached far out.

"The count rejoiced secretly over what had happened, and though in reality it was a pitiful shipwreck, he had begun to enlarge upon it in his mind, and he hadn't reproached the steersman with one single word.

"On the beach he found the remains of a rowboat, and his boyish imagination began immediately to contemplate storms and shipwrecks and bleached bones.

"While he fumbled his way forward along the mountain in order to find a way to ascend it, all at once there came a current of air; the fog slid off the mountain like a cloak, and when he looked up he was surprised to see a young girl peering down at him from the ridge of a chasm. 'Hi!' he called, just as one would greet an acquaintance in the neighborhood, but the girl didn't answer. 'Hi!' he called again and took a few steps up toward her. 'If you're alive tell me where we are!' At that she turned around and darted across the mountain.

247

"I think," Lady Sophie went on, addressing Celion, "that two things constantly come back to us in life. The one is the incident itself; the other is our ability to react to it. Persistently we are invited by both to keep on living. That afternoon a shoelace provided the incident for Count Reger. When the girl ran away, his immediate reaction was to go in pursuit. Are you smiling, Pastor? Well, anyway it was only a passing thought; don't hesitate to use it in your sermons. But if, for example, you seize upon this as a steadily recurring theme in a musical composition, you will find that even the most insignificant story has its own rhythmical pattern.

"While Reger ran after her eastward over the mountain, he couldn't refrain from admiring her sprightly figure and the graceful leaps with which she managed to get over the rugged terrain. He saw she wore long black trousers stuffed into high boots and a leather jacket much too large for her.

"She kept a distance between them, but as they passed a little tarn on the top of the isle, he tricked her by taking the opposite way around.

"When the girl saw he had intercepted her, she stopped suddenly and stared at him, wild-eyed. 'I won't hurt you,' he stammered. 'I only want to find out where I am.'

"She ducked down with lightning speed and picked up a stone the size of a fist. 'Get away!' she shrieked. 'What do you want up here? Don't stop me!' She lifted her hand holding the stone.

"Count Reger didn't reply. He stood looking into the dark, bewildered face, and in the course of the two seconds they confronted one another, he experienced a totally new feeling, a feverish delight that can compare only with the languor and the genial enervation that comes when a south

248

breeze blows over the isle in April—torpid, heavy with sweetness and the pungent smell of earth.

"He moved a step forward and raised his hand to avert the blow. 'Don't throw it,' he whispered. 'My boat has gone aground out here.' He had caught her eye and wanted to approach nearer when she dropped the stone, slipped past him, and took off down the slope.

"He did not try to overtake her again but stayed ten paces behind, and when he watched her disappear under the porch of a big building, he went up to it and knocked at the door.—

"The two women were alone on the isle now. The twins had left; the workmen had carried off with them the tools and the nets for there was no one there to pay them wages.

"Reginald Beck was never found, but Regine had picked up a boot that floated to shore, buried it beside her mother, and nailed up a cross.

"The clerk had found employment at a trading-post farther east, and another young man who had frequented the isle had gone south.

"While Lola was telling him this, Reger looked at Regine furtively. The young woman sat curled up in a corner by the fire, staring at him resentfully, not uttering a word. Her hair was unkempt, she was dirty, her trousers were torn at the knees so he could see her bare skin underneath. After a moment she stood up without so much as a glance in their direction and slipped out along the wall.

" 'Now she'll go down to the dock,' Lola explained: 'She has been this way since the shipwreck. But she has herself to blame, for she was a shrew at the time they were rich and powerful here. She and her father were two of a kind— arrogant and pompous. Everything comes back.'

249

"Reger still remained seated a while; eventually he rose to leave. 'It's dark outside,' he remarked. 'I think I'll take a walk to the dock to look for her.' "

Lady Tennyson paused. "What about it, Celion? Do all our actions come back to us?"

"I don't know, Mylady. You mustn't ask me that, but insofar as I am beginning to understand, you have come back—if I have followed correctly. But then how did it turn out?"

Lady Sophie threw her arms above her head and laughed. "Oh, yes, indeed, the cutter *Silver* came free of its grounding at high tide, but it did not leave Becksø until three weeks later.

"They sailed in early October. The isle lay yellow and sere in the strong autumn light, bare from mountain top to beach. It looked as if it were in the process of reverting to the substance it was originally created out of before God let grass and flowers and heather spring up out of the clefts.

"Old Lola remained alone on the wharf. She waved to them with steady determined gestures as if she were fulfilling a duty. Her knuckles were big, and when she sat knitting that afternoon I could see those knuckles working like pistons in a machine under her sallow skin. She had no need of a kerchief at leave-taking, for her eyes were dry and knowing and her feelings had always been strong and unyielding. She knew what she was about and didn't give in to fleeting sweetness. Therefore her old age was calm and without a trace of regret.

"But she did not want to abandon Becksø; she had grown attached to the isle, and it would have been a painful wrench to separate them from one another.

"Out there in the cutter stood Regine waving in return.

250

She had combed her hair and put on one of her mother's dresses. Her dark eyes peered inquisitively at the figure on the wharf, but as Becksø disappeared into the sea, her whole face took on a shy, expectant tenderness. And wearing this expression Regine sailed south—into the world."

The Voyage Resumes

Lady Sophie closed her eyes and listened, and in the silence
that followed she discovered the source of the distant rumble
which had disturbed the last part of her story.

"Isn't it exactly what I felt?" she commented as she turned
to look toward land. "We have a fifth person among us,
one who is thoroughly displeased with the ending of my
story."

The three men all turned and looked eastward. The
outermost edge of the shore with its caves and clefts and
rounded knolls lay bathed in red-violet light. Now when
the sun hung low, all the features of the land were exposed: grooves in the rock from the Creator's chisel, a shel-
tering green thicket on a crag, dwellings on an isle. Behind
rose the ridges, almost black with pines; they stood huddled
together as if seeking refuge among one another. But farther inland, near the border, a thunderstorm was moving
over the barren mountain. It was visible in its entirety, as
if torn loose from a bigger storm, and at so great a distance
it distinctly resembled a clenched fist shooting out sparks
from between its knuckles as it shifted southward.

"So far away, Richard," Mylady murmured. Her eyes were misty.

"Such thunderstorms follow the mountains," observed Berg. "We aren't in any danger."

"To your health, Pastor!" Lady Sophie addressed Celion. "Are you counting the seconds?"

The pastor tucked away his watch. "I thought I'd estimate how far away it is, but you interrupted me."

"Far enough for us here. But what a beautiful sight it is! And then to know we are safe! Isn't that so, Eberhardt? Drink a toast. Your glass is full."

Celion cast a quick glance in her direction, and for one fleeting moment their eyes met. "A thunderstorm," he mused. "How strong and alive is the face of a person who admits to everything: lust, sin, guilt."

"Toast, Mylady! You are very beautiful," he said impulsively and was shocked at himself. He looked around, expecting a three-voiced outburst of laughter, but the remark elicited no response and blended with the other usual noises of that night: the gentle swishing at the prow, the flapping of gulls' wings, the creaking of ropes.

"They are thinking the same thoughts as I but are afraid to express them," he reflected, and to hide his confusion he took off his glasses and polished them.

"That was delightful to hear, Pastor." Her voice was clear and sincere. "My two friends are apparently not so sure they agree. What do you think may be the reason, Pastor?"

"That's something I can't answer, Mylady," replied Celion, who by now had regained his composure. "Perhaps they see Regine before them when there is mention of a beautiful woman, in spite of the fact that from all I can understand she was a veritable witch."

"Well, yes, she must indeed have been a witch, but after

what you have heard don't you feel she deserves only mild censure?"

"Since you state your question that way," answered Celion, "I am inclined to feel that the tale of Regine was more a speech of defense than a story. And I am willing to concede that Regine had reason to act as she did. But when Mylady made the account so long and involved, I think she ascribed to her several motives of which the young Regine herself was not aware. In other words, I think Regine was a thoughtless self-centered child who played with people's lives and that Mylady has embellished and deepened the motives in a subconscious wish to make of her a more beautiful character."

"Richard! Eberhardt!" cried Lady Sophie. "Won't you defend me! Can you sit there mute and let the pastor destroy everything I've built up?"

"Sophie." The governor looked up. "Shouldn't we let this rest? It's too painful for all of us. Celion, moreover, has no part in it."

"Listen, Richard," interrupted the pastor. "I have known you a long time, and you have never mentioned anything about this to me. But you are not going to make me out to be more stupid than I probably am. Even if I hadn't heard the three stories, I do have eyes in my head sufficiently sharp to make me suspect something. Furthermore, I have now heard you expose yourselves by turns—under the boldest of disguises. And especially since you know I have made the parable of Christ my particular area of study, you can't expect me to fail in recognizing you in the guise of Halvor Mikkelsen. I'm not going to analyze Halvor to determine whether he coincides with Florelius. For I also understand, Richard, that you have an ulterior motive relating to Halvor in that he is supposed to resemble others besides you. You have often spoken despairingly of people today in saying

254

they are so smooth that God's fist slides off them, and once you said if the Devil within us should doze off permanently, life would be intolerable. I also remember that the projecting corners showed up very early while you were a student."

Celion broke off a moment. "But then there was one other matter," he went on. "I imagine that the little isle where Olaf Utøy lived in Mylady's story must parallel closely the realm of your own childhood, and that leads me to think of something that hasn't occurred to me until now: this blossoming name of yours, Florelius, wasn't that a heavy burden for the son of a poor fisherman to carry? Or are you perhaps a prince in disguise?"

The governor smiled circumspectly as if uncovering a treasure. "Since you have found so many disguises connected with me, I can assure you the name is real enough. If it's my ancestor you're asking about," he added with gentle irony, "I can't tell you whether he stemmed from the peasantry or the upper class—in all likelihood from the peasantry if we go far enough back—you know I have never understood how to stop at the right time. All I know about the family is that with them, as is true of everything else, fortune has shifted up and down in the course of time. My great-grandfather rode high on the crest of a big wave in Norwegian industry. He dealt in lumber. My grandfather, on the contrary, carried a different and much heavier load. Therefore he bequeathed nothing more than a leaky four-oared boat and fishing gear without a line, and with those two legacies my father managed to make out on an outermost isle in the sea. In my childhood, what's more, I took great delight in watching people's reactions on discovering that someone so plebeian as a simple fisherman was hiding behind such a magnificent name. They felt they had been swindled, deceived."

255

Celion grinned. "There still is a remnant of knife-sharp bitterness in you, Richard, salt that keeps you young, but anyway thank you for the story; now I understand that when you have acted cold and unapproachable at times, it is because you were back in the boat with Regine and had to choose between the two who lay in the water—just as Halvor had to choose when he stole the sheep. There is only one thing that confuses me—"

"Don't say it, Pastor!" Lady Sophie interjected abruptly.

"Don't say it? Why not?"

"I know what you want to ask."

"And now you don't want to hear the truth."

Florelius interrupted. "It's so long ago. We won't talk about it, Celion."

Celion said, "What I want to know is: Were you aware at that time that Martin was your rival?"

Lady Sophie spoke. "I think Regine managed to keep it a secret."

"Yes, because if you had known," continued the pastor, "then you could hardly have loved her very dearly since you rescued him."

"Richard had good reasons for hating Father."

"Not with Richard's temperament. He would gladly have endured those beatings. But he would also, if not so gladly, have sacrificed his rival if he really loved her."

"There was more to it than the beatings. It was a matter of the relationship itself: master and servant, owner and tenant."

The pastor's round boyish face was stern. He adjusted his glasses. "I think, Richard, Mylady is saying that you chose to rescue Martin out of hate for another person. That is an evil thought; it makes of retribution a despicable act, which certainly it is not always. But here again we have a distortion of motive. I expect no answer from you, Richard.

But we do have Martin here, after all. Moreover, let us use real names; it simplifies matters. How about it, Berg? Was Richard aware that you were his rival?"

The merchant looked up. "That I don't know."

Celion mopped his brow. "Whew! It seems I have stirred up a tumult."

"You have a right to," replied Mylady, "since you're Richard's friend. And his pastor. Pastor Bartholin, whom you told us about, also got himself involved in unpleasant affairs —out of love for his fellow men."

Celion rejoined: "To joke ironically about love for one's fellow men is bother wasted on me. Besides, it is not my invention, but God's."

"I didn't mean to ridicule love of one's neighbor," Lady Sophie said with a smile. "But I do think when those two kinds of love clash, one must yield. Otherwise the same will happen as happened to Bartholin. And that makes me suspect, Pastor, that you perhaps knew something about Richard and me when you told the story, and that the house-keeper—Heaven help me, Pastor, you must have been malicious—that the housekeeper should be conceived to be me and so you assumed the shabby little role of Satan to warn Bartholin, that is to say Richard."

Celion laughed. "Mylady, with due respect for your sense of intrigue, I think now you're pulling in threads that are not present in the weaving. My story was completely straightforward and free of ulterior motives. If it doesn't hold up, it's for lack of native force, and in that instance well-disposed explanations are to no avail. One might be tempted to say that about stories in general. But if I now may be permitted to come back to Regine, there is yet one more thing in that tale that I don't understand: Why did Berg ram your father's boat, Mylady?"

The merchant turned around so hurriedly that his glass

tipped. His large hand with its white knuckles resting on the table at this moment looked like a desolate hilly landscape such as one sees on South Helgeland in late autumn.

"Where have you gotten that conclusion from, Pastor? You seem to be better informed than we, and yet I can't recall your presence at the shipwreck."

Lady Tennyson hesitated. She poured herself a drink; as she did so, her face became pinched and hard, and one could readily see the deep network of wrinkles spreading from the corners of her eyes. Then she began to speak.

"Eberhardt's mother was a widow. She lived on one of the little isles Father used to visit. When Eberhardt was four, he got a sister with black hair and brown eyes. But the mother died immediately after the birth of the child. The child was put away, and two years later she died—of neglect, people said. You learned of this when you prepared for confirmation, didn't you, Eberhardt?"

In silence the merchant sat with bowed head, but Pastor Celion noticed that a little white knot had formed at each corner of his mouth.

"From that day on," Mylady continued, "Eberhardt Berg had only one goal in mind, and a few years later when he came to Becksgård—as I named the place in my story— he set about systematically to accomplish his plan of revenge. Father didn't keep particularly close watch over business procedures and Eberhardt was given somewhat free rein. His goal was to drive Father into bankruptcy, and in all likelihood he would have succeeded had it not been that the depression had already started of its own accord before Eberhardt's plans were realized. Thus he was cheated out of vengeance by the depression itself, but when—"

Merchant Berg had stood up. His face was ashen; his eyes were narrowed and red from looking into the sun. "I've told you before what happened that night at sea, but I cannot

258

force you to believe me. The rudder broke, the boat was carried by the wind, and even with no more distance than there was between us, it happened before I could fetch an oar. It's true that I long wanted to get even with your father, but when I saw how the falling-off in his business was wearing him down, I thought it to be vengeance enough. I had considered moving away from Becksø—as you call it—that same summer."

Celion's smile was sardonic. "And so Richard robbed you of revenge. That was perhaps a bitter blow, especially if there was something between you and Mylady!"

Berg retorted: "According to what we've heard, Sophie had her own reasons for making fools of us."

Lady Sophie put her hand on the merchant's arm. "At the time I was sure Father's death was your doing. Now I believe what you are saying. Two weeks ago I visited your wife when you were gone, and I met your children. I got the impression you are happy together, and I do not think you bear any guilt." She laughed and raised her glass. "Skoal, Eberhardt—it was evidently you who loved the Devil's daughter. But you never loved me, Eberhardt, any more than a fencepost. I can well understand, however, that Father's death could set you free."

Celion spoke again. "Another blending of motives. Fernando's religious brooding converged with his desire for revenge and his hunger for love. Now we must make the same apply in Merchant Berg's case. Thus we can wrap one motive into the other."

For a while all on the deck were silent, and again the sounds of the surroundings intruded on the stillness; the waves lapped gently at the side of the boat, the sail flapped lazily once or twice before it fell limply against the mast, and from the shore came the cry of a lone oyster catcher.

259

The young helmsman stood motionless, his eyes riveted on a little islet in the channel toward the south.

The governor eyed Mylady stealthily. "What have I gained," he thought, dismayed, "and what have I lost by living alone—since I didn't win her? And she, has she missed anything? Indeed she is just as beautiful. More so."

Then he saw her looking at him, and the shy sweetness in her eyes disturbed him. "Where have I seen that expression before? What does it remind me of?"

"Richard," she whispered and raised her glass. "Drink a toast." "Skoal, Sophie!"

Presently she settled back in her chair and laughed secretly as if having found a joy she did not want to share with anyone. "Now I have been the Devil's daughter, Bartholin's housekeeper, and the witch Regine—but who was I relative to Halvor Mikkelsen?"

"There's a major omission in your story, Richard," she said. "Some other time I shall tell you what it is."

At this moment the pastor interrupted her. He pointed to the north. "That trail of smoke over there, isn't that the express steamer?"

"Of course!" shouted Lady Sophie. "Now they've managed to get it moving again! But we've time at least for one more drink before it catches up with us."

When the wine was poured, Lady Tennyson raised her glass. "I won't say good-bye because I have a strong premonition we shall meet again before long. Do you know who it was," she asked, turning to the merchant, "do you know who it was that outbid you when my childhood home was sold at auction a year ago? That little thin man—do you remember him? Well, he was my agent. And from autumn on you may find me at home."

Five minutes later the express steamer drew up alongside

of them, and the gangplank was lowered to the deck. A sailor came down to fetch the wicker chairs and Mylady's iron-bound chest which still contained seven full bottles.

"I'll stay on board here," announced Berg. "I have several errands and must make some side-voyages to places not on the express route."

Lady Tennyson and Pastor Celion went on board. Florelius remained standing, engaged in conversation with Merchant Berg, and as their talk seemed to be getting prolonged, Lady Sophie shouted impatiently, "Richard, now you must come! We're going on!"

The two men on the deck exchanged a handshake, and the governor embarked.

A little later they stood at the railing and waved to Berg. Dawn was breaking. The sun rose out of the sea, grew paler, and eventually took on its white corrosive daytime color again. The thunderstorm still kept moving along the mountains toward the east. Now and then there was a little flash of lightning followed a while later by a gentle rumble rolling out across the sea.

261